Casualty of Fate

Raeleigh Breaux

To Joey, my inspiration behind the name.

Prologue

I am solely focused on the woman before me, watching her every move as I bounce on the balls of my feet, at the ready in the middle of the boxing ring. I can feel sweat dripping down my skin, collecting in pools at the base of my spine. We've been at this for hours.

"There's still time to stop her you know," Niki says as she throws a left hook at my face.

"Why would I do that," I ask, dodging her blow.

Niki stands up straight, "Seriously? I don't know Torryn, maybe because AJ is the love of your life."

"She was a … *distraction.*"

AJ left me a week ago but the unwanted conversation in the ring brings back the memories of that night. It felt like only yesterday that I arrived home from my night's shift, the sun barely peeking over the horizon, casting hues of pinks and oranges across the sky.

****

I sit in my car for a moment, parked outside our apartment, staring blankly ahead. It was quiet that early in the morning, peaceful. People are just getting up and starting the day as I am ending mine.

The previous night, just before my shift had begun, AJ and I had got into a fight. Sitting there, recalling the fight in my head, I thought that maybe she had been right. It would be good to get away for awhile. Just the three of us.

I pulled a velvet square box out of my pocket. Flipping over the lid, I admired the diamond ring that sparkled inside. I had been holding onto that ring for two months, trying to find the perfect time. Being a cop made finding that perfect time impossible. And having being the first responding officer to the scene of a dead teenager only a few hours earlier had made me remember just how short life can be. Too short to waste time on finding the right time. I had to make time. I had to do this *now*.

"I can do this," I whispered to myself as I decided to just take the leap of faith.

I played out the scene on repeat in my head. During the ride home I had practiced this moment a thousand times; walking inside out apartment, dropping to one knee and asking AJ to marry me. No hesitation.

The last thing I expected was to find the place empty. I called out to AJ, receiving silence as my answer. I walked into our bedroom and read a note that simply stated, "I'm sorry."

I sat on the bed, and stared down at the ring. I fought back tears, refusing to cry.

I thought I knew where my life was headed, where this relationship was going to go. AJ had always claimed I didn't hold her as a priority, that I would always choose work over us. Well, I suppose I would no longer have to balance a personal life with my career as a cop. AJ made that choice for me.

I had spent my entire life alone before meeting AJ, learning early on not to depend on anyone but myself. As expected, AJ had become just another woman who had let me down. I should have walked away years ago when we first met.

I wiped away the first tear from my cheek, buried the pain inside, then picked up the note along with the velvet box. After placing them in the top drawer of AJ's dresser, I opened our text conversation on my phone and typed out the words, "Me too."

As I hit the send button I put her in the drawer, too

****

A searing pain pulsing through my jaw brings my focus back to the musty smelling gym and the bronze-skinned girl in front of me. I bring my gloved hand up to my face and glare at her.

"Looks like she's still a distraction," Niki taunted.

I shake my arms loose, "How is it that a rich girl from a ritzy private school is comfortable slumming it in *this place*...a smelly boxing gym?"

Niki smirked, "Nice try, but I'm not letting you change the subject."

"I came here to spar with you Nik, not to talk

about AJ. I'm over it. I'm over *her*."

"You're emotionally closed off, you always have been. But AJ changed that about you. One day you're going to regret letting her walk away," Niki responded, as she took another swing.

I ducked, swiping at her legs and Niki onto her back.

"My only regret is letting her get close in the first place," I say as I stood over her, offering my arm to pull her up.

"Pride has been the downfall of many people," the gym's janitor added as he swept trash a few feet away from us, "that's why they call it a deadly sin."

I shake my head at a laughing Niki as I help her up, "I have to go study for my detective exam."

Choices and moments. That's what life is made of. Some so big that it feels like we're going for a ride that we're too small for, to scared for, and there aren't handles for you to grip. Other times, they're so small it's hard to notice the significance. We never think about how the choices and moments can impact our whole life. We don't realize how detrimental a few tiny choices could be to our future.

-Detective Torryn Michealson

1

Now

The incessant, shrill chatter of the woman sitting across from me is interrupted by the abrupt ringing of my cellphone. Normally, I wouldn't answer my phone on a date, but it's work, and at this point, I'll take any chance I can get to end this sooner. I wouldn't even be here if it wasn't at the urging of a friend and teammate.

I glance at the woman, whose name escapes me, and apologize before answering the call. "Michaelson," I say into the receiver.

Lieutenant Timothy Harris informs me that there has been a stabbing in the alley of a nearby bookstore. Outside of demanding my presence, he didn't give me any more information, which isn't normal for him. It may have some connection to the present case I've been working on involving a string of murdered women. Regardless if that's true, duty calls.

"I'll be right there," I reply before disconnecting the call. I pull just enough money out of my wallet to cover the bill and tip. I stand and grab my jacket. "I have to go," I mutter as I make sure I still have my keys before quickly heading out of the door. I don't bother to look back at the woman at the table. She wasn't my type, anyway.

It doesn't take me long to make it from the restaurant to the crime scene, where it's already been secured with yellow tape. A crowd of nosey onlookers have already gathered as close as they can to see what's happening, despite officers telling them to back up or to go home. I step out of my car and make my way to the scene, refusing to go near the crowd that's already testing my patience.

I flash my badge at the officer responsible for allowing people to enter the crime scene. I glance around for a moment, taking in as much as I can before being given any information. I am almost immediately approached by my partner, Detective Dax Grieson. To the right sits an ambulance, which also is not normal. Typically, as homicide detectives, if we're called to the scene it would be a coroner's van instead, otherwise major crimes should have been called. I can only deduce that the reason we were called out is because tonight is Tuesday. And Tuesday has ended with a murdered woman in an ally five weeks in a row. Tonight may make six.

"Is the vic still alive?" I ask as I continue to survey the scene from just within the perimeter. I notice the position of the medics, diligently working on trying to save the victim. I glance around, noticing the closeness of the small businesses, ready to enter the narrow ally.

"Barely," he replies as we make our way towards where the medics are surrounding what I assume to be the victim of the attack.

As we inch closer, the medics begin to load the victim on the stretcher and I get a better look at the scene before me, starting with a pool of blood on the ground and the smell of iron being carried through the air by the slight, chilled, breeze of the season. Females typically have about nine pints of blood and this- the way it's spread along the concrete, how it pools in such a wide diameter- seems impossible...

"How is she—?" I begin but my eyes catch on the small frame of the body, the blood drying on the skin and clothes of the victim, the lifelessness, the limpness of the arms and legs. I've seen hundreds of crime scenes, some so burned into my mind that I still have nightmares about them, I still can recall the grotesqueness in perfect clarity, even as just an officer before I made detective. But this time is different.

I'm handed the victim's driver's license and it throws me into a spiral of emotion. I can no longer hear what my partner is saying as I stare past him, looking at the scene, the body, but no longer see anything. I open my mouth to speak, to finish my question, because it's important, but nothing happens. I must be breathing but I can't feel my chest move or the feel of the nippy autumn air filling my lungs. There is a pain crushing and twisting me from the inside out as I watch the imperceptible rise and fall of the chest of the woman being wheeled away. The woman - AJ- with blood covering her face and almost every inch of her body, who must be in unimaginable pain, who survived the attack but won't be the same after. They never are, the ones who make it, who awake in the hospital in a panic.

How could this have happened, I wonder as time seems to slow down. I had no idea that AJ was back in town. The blood pounding behind my eyes makes it impossible to hear what anyone is saying.

Please live, I think to myself, making it play on repeat, even though I know I should be focusing on the scene around me. I should be working, taking in every detail I can, collecting evidence, analyzing and connecting dots. This has to be connected to the case I'm working on. Why else would I have been called?

The sound of my partner calling my name finally pulls me out of my derailing train of thought. "Michealson, you okay?" His brows are furrowed, and I can feel him assessing me.

I clear my throat before speaking, but my voice still cracks. "Yeah, yeah, Im good."

I barely register his expression as my eyes follow AJ and, for just a brief moment, I want to accompany the medics with the victim but it can't be me. I swallow down the rising bile in my throat and wave over a uniformed officer, young and eager to follow orders from a senior officer. He jogs over to me and I direct him to the ambulance.

"Go with them, keep updated on the victim's status, and call as soon as we can interview her. Keep an ear out for any dying declarations, in case she doesn't make it" This is what I've said numerous times before, so I know I must say it, but I don't even hear myself over the sound of my own blood rushing through my veins. I only hear my thoughts say that she better make it.

I didn't have an easy life. I didn't have loving parents who adored me and supported me. I didn't have a network of friends that I could turn to in moments of crises. It's just been me, myself, and I since I was sixteen. But this? Seeing AJ almost lifeless, seeing her blood on the hard, cold, cement, knowing that the fear and pain she must have felt in that moment would always stain her, would forever change her, was devastating. It was as if I'd been thrown into a pool of icy water, weighted down with boulders chained to my ankles, desperately trying to free myself, clawing at the water, gasping for air as my lungs slowly collapse under the pressure, so cold my skin burns.

Damn that phone call! Damn this case!

I pray to a God I don't believe in to please let her live.

How did this happen?

I force myself to focus on the crime scene, then, as the ambulance pulls away and I can no longer see it when it makes a right turn at the end of the drive. It was going to be a long night and having thoughts of AJ would only make it longer.

"So, how do you want to handle this?" Dax inquired as he looks towards me, hand in his jacket pocket in his usual stance.

I breathe. Then speak. "Well, for one, we're going to need more patrols of the perimeter. I want a copy of every single witness report that we've gotten so far, and I want the crowd over there to be questioned. Someone must have seen something." I take my cellphone out of my pocket and start making notes. "No one leaves without giving their name and contact information. Anyone who refuses will become suspect or charged with obstruction of justice," I snapped in quick succession, not looking up from my phone as I continue to type furiously.

I don't usually bark like a threatened dog at a scene, I was trained better than that, I treat my team better than that. Dax doesn't say anything, though, even if he doesn't know why I'm behaving like this, he knows that there's probably a good reason. He nods silently before something catches his eye and his attention on me disappears.

"Looks like Joel's here. I'm going to go talk to him," he mentions as he makes his way to the forensic van that pulls up to the parking lot nearby. "He's not going to be happy with the medics trampling his crime scene."

I roll my eyes. His feelings about that are the very last item on my things to worry about right now. "I'm sure he'll get over it. While you're over there, I think I'm going to talk to our lead witness, see if there's anything there." I look around and spot an elderly woman still inside the perimeter that was set up earlier. "Is that her?"

Dax raises his eyebrows, "Yeah, I just told you that. That's Mrs. Parks; she owns the bookstore, said she saw someone."

I'm not able to recall any mention of the woman before and Dax just sighs, as if he knows I wasn't paying attention earlier, even if he wasn't aware of that was happening inside me. I nod once then stride away in the woman's direction.

The bookstore owner sat wrapped in a blanket held firmly around her body, face ashen, eyes too wide. Despite appearing to be a statue with how still she was, with arms folded around her distended stomach, a leaf would frighten her if it came to close. I make my way to her casually, waiting until she meets my eyes before I introduce myself.

"Hello, ma'am. I'm Detective Torryn Michealson." I wait for a response but none is given. Within seconds, she begins to visibly shake uncontrollably, her fingers wring each other, tiny jerky movements of her chest as if she can't breathe properly. I try again. "What's your name?"

This time, she answers. She meets my eyes and swallows twice before speaking. "Jos-Josephine Parks."

I show her a smile that's filled with polite etiquette and understanding. "Mrs. Parks, it's nice to meet you. I was wondering if you could tell me what happened? What did you see?"

This, apparently, was the wrong question to ask, because the woman immediately let out a screeching wail that quickly turned into gasping sobs. "I just...can't...believe...this...happened...to ...her," she manages between.

I kneel in front of her so I'm physically on her level. I place a hand on her knee and giver her a small, encouraging, squeeze. "She's on her way to the hospital and I'm sure the doctors are going to do everything they can to help her. But, right now, I need you to help me so that I can catch whoever did this. Can you do that?"

She nods, using and end of her blanket to dry her face as she chokes back another round of sobs.

"Thank you," I respond, "now, can you tell me what you saw tonight?"

She took a stuttering breath, closing her eyes tight, before sniffling and clearing her throat. "She was a sweet girl, you know, always helping me clean up after her signings."

Always. The word throws me through another loop. AJ left three years ago. How often did she return? Stop! I berate myself, tuning back into Mrs. Parks' speech.

"She's a bit of a local celebrity and it was just nice of her to help around. She'd take my trash out for me because I'm alone, now, ever since my sweet husband died and my children don't come to visit often."

I nod along, hoping that she won't start to ramble, "and she was visiting tonight?"

"Yes, she was doing a book signing and when the event was over she stayed to help me close up. She was like that, you know, always looking out for people, making sure they were alright. But that's why she was out there, Detective, she was just going to take the trash out."

It was nice to know that AJ hadn't changed, that her caring altruism never failed. "What happened when Ms. James took out the trash?"

"Well." She said as she adjusted her blanket tighter around herself, "I heard a crash but didn't think anything of it. But then she never came back inside so I went to check on her. I'm not as fast as I used to be, you know, but I tried to hurry outside. That's when I saw someone hunched over her. I yelled out, hoping that he was trying to help her but he took off. He was a skinny little thing, too, no bigger than a matchstick."

"Did you get a good look at their face?"

"It was too dark for that and he wore a hood. But I called the police and stayed outside with her until they told me to wait up here. I couldn't leave her alone, Detective, she was such a sweet girl."

"I know, and I appreciate you staying with her. You said 'he'. Are you sure the attacker was male?"

"Seemed like it to me but I couldn't see anything that far away."

"Can you remember what they were wearing or can you give me any other descriptors of the attacker?"

"Well, now that I recall, he was short too, probably about my height, definitely not as tall as you are, though. Skinny, like I said before, wore dark pants and a sweater that covered most of his face."

"Good," I interrupt, "this is really good information, thank you." This is probably the most information we've gotten about this perp, if this is connected to the others, and if this Unsub, or unknown subject, is shorter than me, that at least is something. At five foot seven, I'm the tallest female detective on the force. "Anything else you can tell me?"

A shake of her head is the only response I get before she starts to cry again.

"Mrs. Parks, do you own this bookshop?" I ask, in attempt to distract her just enough that she calms down a bit.

"Oh, yes, bought it when my children moved out."

"And you live?"

"Above the shop, I have my room and my little kitchen and everything up there."

"I see." I put away my cellphone that I was taking notes on and stand. "I appreciate your cooperation, Mrs. Parks. If you think of anything else, even if it seems silly, please call me." I hand her my card. "Call me anytime. I mean it."

She nods quietly and takes the card. I turn away, making my way from her steps, when I see Joel conducting a spiral search pattern around where AJ's body was found. He takes photographs of all possible evidence and I stop myself from shouting at him to make sure he photographs every single thing.

Recalling all the information Mrs. Parks provided, I play it over in my mind like a movie.

AJ walks out of the shop, carrying a large black bag of trash to take to the dumpster. Maybe that's where she was first attacked, I think to myself as I pull out my flashlight and shine it on the blue dumpster. There's a bit of blood spatter. I snap a few pictures.

Is this where the perp hid, on the side of the big dumpster, where it was dark? There isn't a security or flood light out here but if he walked to get to AJ, wouldn't she have heard him and called out for someone or defend herself?

I glance at the other businesses, noting that none of them have any lights on. It makes sense that there are hardly any actual witnesses to the attack itself. Other than the sparse streetlights and the businesses on either side of the road, it's too dark to make anything out clearly. Even from where I am standing, it is hard to make out the blood on the cement now that the flashing red and blue lights aren't illuminating the scene.

"What did the shop owner have to say?" Dax asked, startling me out of my train of thought, "Get a good look at the guy?"

"Said they were short and wore a hood."

He nods, just as disappointed in the lack of information as I am.

"I want to head over to the hospital once we're done here, see what we can find out about the victim's wounds," I explain, getting lost in thought, again, as I try to connect fragments of too much but too little information.

We make our way back to the mouth of the ally and I notice that there is an ATM directly across from us, "well look at that," I say to my partner as I nod my head in the direction I want him to look, "let's see if we can get video from that ATM. Maybe we'll get lucky and our perp's face will be on it."

2

Then

AJ had her duffle bag slung across her shoulder, a large caramel macchiato in one hand while the other held her cellphone to her ear. She stood in the middle of the quad, while simultaneously trying to remember which way to go while listening to her mom ramble on.

"I'm sorry I couldn't go with you, honey," her mom apologized for the third time, "I'll bring the rest of your things this weekend."

"It's okay, mom," AJ replied between sips of coffee, "You don't have to keep apologizing and yeah, this weekend would be great. "

"I know sweetheart. It's just that I haven't been able to be there for you this past year and —"

"Mom." AJ interrupted, conscious not to let her annoyance seep through her tone. She could picture the sad smile her mom was wearing, how the corners of her lips would be turned down just enough that they would wobble with the effort to try to lift them, "you gave me my space when I needed it most."

AJ did not want to get into a discussion about the past year. It would only serve to remind her of the grief she was trying to leave behind. She began searching her mind for a good enough excuse to end the call when a football hit her in the arm, spilling her coffee down the front of her shirt.

"Shit," she growled.

Her mother's voice became panicked, "What? What happened? Are you alright? AJ?"

"Nothing mom, I gotta go. I'll call you later, okay?"

Without waiting for a reply she hung up. AJ looked up from her shirt to find a boy with shoulder length brown hair running towards her.

"Sorry," the boy said, running his fingers through his sweat-matted hair. "I shouldn't have thrown the ball so far. Though in my defense, my buddy over there is a horrible receiver," he joked through his smirk.

"It's fine," AJ replied politely enough through pursed lips. She loathed boys like this, the type that think they can get away with something just because they may be charming and attractive, the type that are used to having girls melt at the sight of them.

AJ glanced down at her shirt, which now sported a huge coffee stain and frowned.

The boy offered AJ his hand, "I'm Ryder."

She looked back at Ryder, ignoring his gesture.

He lowered his hand slowly. AJ couldn't help but feel a bit better that he seemed put off by the lack of reciprocation.

"Hey, let me make this up to you. Can I buy you another cup of coffee? To replace that one?"

"Actually, if you could just point me in the direction of Clark Hall that would be apology enough," AJ responded tightly.

"Clark Hall, huh? You must be a freshman," he remarked, as if he was just now noticing the bag slung across her shoulder and the backpack on her back. "So am I," he said, as he slid his hands into his jeans pockets, "it sucks that I can't have my new car my folks bought me for graduation until next year. It'd be awesome to race around town. Have you ever been behind the wheel of a supped-up Corvette? She handles like —"

Yep, definitely that type of boy, AJ thought. She was well aware of the rules requiring freshmen to live on campus, unallowed to bring their own cars in order to save parking space for the upperclassmen who no longer live on campus. Being without her car wasn't a big deal to AJ as she had just spent a year without it already.

"Look, just tell me where the building is," AJ growled.

"Right," Ryder said, extending his arm up and pointing to the left, "It's right over there. I can walk you."

"No, thanks," AJ said, holding her palm up to dissuade any further comments. She hurried into the direction he pointed without looking back.

"See you around," his voice called out behind her, not that AJ cared.

****

A short walk later, AJ arrived at her freshmen

suite. All the dorms on campus were set up like apartments rather then the typical double room. AJ took a deep breath, taking out her key and unlocking the door before stepping inside. Through the open doorway she could see most of the layout of the suite. There was a short wall to her left, and behind the was the kitchen, presumably. The living room was ahead and had two hallways to either side of it. She assumed that's where the bedrooms would be. She walked further into the suite after taking a moment to get her key out the door.

"You must be Adelaide James?"

AJ turned toward the direction of the voice. The girl she saw sitting on a stool at the breakfast bar to her left took her breath away. Her chestnut hair fell below her shoulders, her plump and full lips looked as if they belonged in a cosmetic catalog. There was a luscious forest in her eyes, emerald green, forbidden, and enticing. The girl quirked an eyebrow when AJ stood without speaking, mouth slightly parted.

"Yeah, yes. That's me, um, AJ, actually," AJ stuttered, mesmerized.

AJ offered her hand but immediately pulled it back when the gesture was ignored.

"I'm Torryn," the girl provided, "Your room is down the hallway on the left. Door's already open, if you want to," she paused briefly to indicate AJ's attire, "change your shirt."

AJ looked down, as if she momentarily forgotten about Corvette Boy, as she had dubbed him in her head, and the large brown stain on her shirt. She grew hot and flustered, as though there suddenly wasn't enough air in the room. AJ sheepishly looked back up as Torryn ticked something off on a clipboard. AJ followed as she began walking towards the hall, but paused when she saw the girl disappear into the room next to hers.

After a moment, AJ headed inside her own room, closing the door behind her before sitting on the bed that would be hers for the next year.

"Wow," she whispered to herself, still thinking of the girl in the next room. Torryn was possibly the most beautiful girl AJ had ever seen.

AJ scanned the small room. Although it was an apartment, the bedroom was the same size of a regular dorm room. It contained a twin-sized bed with a bookshelf built into the headboard, a small dresser and a desk.

At least the closet has double doors, AJ thought to herself as she began unpacking her clothes.

Once she had unpacked the small amount of belongings from her bags and put them away, AJ booted up her laptop. She wanted to find out what was going on around campus today, even if she didn't hold any real interest in socializing just yet. Maybe she could find something to keep her occupied until orientation tomorrow, tour the campus, find her classrooms, anything that would keep her thoughts from reflecting on the past. She was here to move forward, after everything that happened.

Just as her computer screen came to life so did the screen of her phone, illuminating a text from one of her two best friends, Ava Turner.

R u here yet????

       Yeah. Clark Hall. Room 216.

  Gr8. Let's kick some welcome week ass! XD

AJ rolled her eyes at Ava's IM texting, both smiling and cringing at the thought of seeing her. It had been a little over a year since she had seen her friends. Despite dealing with a lot, too much, at the time, AJ felt bad for missing Ava's graduation when the younger girl had attended hers a year prior. Though she knew her friends would probably understand, she vowed she would make it up to them.

AJ took off her stained shirt and replaced it with a skintight, V-neck t-shirt, and threw on a jean jacket on top. She used a compact mirror from her bag to glance at her appearance, trying to smooth her disheveled blond hair back into place. She looked like a hot mess and cringed at the fact that this was her first impression to her gorgeous roommate. Once she was satisfied that she looked sufficiently more put together, AJ left her room.

AJ noticed Torryn walking into the kitchen as she exited the hallway. She stood still, momentarily distracted, and not knowing if she should initiate conversation with the other girl.

After a moment, however, AJ collected herself and walked up behind Torryn, who was grabbing a bottle of water from the fridge.

"Hey," AJ announced as she approached the girl. She noticed that Torryn stiffened at the sound of her voice from behind her, but the girl turned around coolly, unscrewing her water bottle and taking a sip with impassivity.

"Um, hey," AJ tried again, clearing her throat, "are you, y'know, doing any of the Welcome Week stuff?"

Torryn shook her head. "It's the same every year. Nothing of real interest to me."

"Wait. You're not a freshman?" inquired AJ. "I thought only freshmen were required to live on campus."

"No, I'm not. All dorm suites are required to have one upperclassman to help enforce the rules and regulations. I live here because it's my job to do so."

Before AJ had the chance to respond, there was a knock at the front door. AJ rushed to answer it. Ava stood grinning on the other side of the door.

Caught up in the arrival of her friend, AJ didn't notice that Torryn have moved into the living room. Ava, a petite dark-haired, copper-skinned girl, wrapped her arms around AJ's body and squeezed her body tightly against AJ's.

"I can't believe you're really here," said Ava, "te extrane!"

"I missed you, too!" AJ replied with a warmth in her voice, "and yeah, I'm really here."

AJ released Ava from her hug and turned back towards Torryn, who peered over curiously at this new person. She hesitated briefly before introducing the two of them. "Torryn, this is Ava. Ava, this is Torryn my suite mate and, I guess, RA or whatever they call it here."

"Hey," Ava said, waving enthusiastically at Torryn.

Torryn responded with a tight nod.

"So, we probably need to get going. Torryn, are you sure you don't want to join us?" AJ said, trying to read Torryn's expression. She was hopeful, for some reason, that Torryn would say yes.

"I'm sure," Torryn said, leaving the room quickly.

AJ and Ava looked at each other, with looks of disappointment and confusion respectively, before leaving the dorm.

3

Now

When Dax and I arrive at the hospital, Dax heads to the uniformed officer stationed in the waiting room while I walk straight to the nurse's station on muscle memory alone. My back is ramrod straight and my jaw is clenched so rigidly that it's starting to ache. The nurse behind the counter doesn't look up to acknowledge my presence.

"Excuse me," I say to her, "I need an update on Adelaide James immediately."

"Who?" Replied the nurse, as she tapped on her keyboard one finger at a time.

"The stabbing victim who was brought in a few hours ago," I say, twitching in exasperation.

The nurse looks up for the first time, annoyance and fatigue are written across her face. "Are you family, miss—" she begins.

"Detective," I quickly correct her, flashing my badge and ignoring the question.

"Detective," she corrects even as she looks at me pointedly, like my position doesn't matter to her one way or the other. "I'm sure the doctor will be out with an update as soon as he can. Until then, please remain patient." She indicates the waiting area with a practiced tone of someone who must say this all to often.

"Fine," I say through clenched teeth, as the nurse turned back to her computer screen.

"Whoa, there," Dax calls out as he approaches. "Alright, who are you and what have you done with my usually stoic partner?"

Dax is a good cop, and a good friend, so it does not surprise me that he calls me out on my most recent behavior.

"There's no point in lying to me. I know you far too well for that so spit it out."

I clench my jaw once again, close my eyes, and wish that the floor would open up and swallow me whole. My hands ball into fists at my sides as I breathe out; five, four, three, two, one. Part of me doesn't want to tell him. He already knows me better than I'd like to admit. Filling him in on something—like this— makes it too real. Especially because I can recognize that I'm in agony that it's AJ lying in pain in one of these rooms, behind one of those curtains. Or maybe she's on an operating table. Or worse, she's on a slab in the hospital morgue awaiting transport. That last thought causes my entire body to ache and tremble.

There's no reason I shouldn't tell him. Dax has always had my back, he's seen me at my worst, and he's been by my side since my first case as a homicide detective. He's my mentor and my partner, he would lay his life on the line for me, and secrets don't make friends. I take a deep, almost calming breath.

"Dax, I need to tell you...something...so I'm just going to come out and say it. The victim? Adelaide James. She's, uh, she the woman I've been in love with for the past decade."

"Shit, Torryn." Dax exclaimed, his eyes growing wide, "I'm sorry."

Dax places his hand on my shoulder. I don't respond. Instead, I scroll through the pictures of the crime scene on my tablet. I try to stay calm even though by blood boils and my teeth grind against each other. I need to get a grip. I want to — need to— feel something other than my heart breaking, again. I want to slam my fist into the ground and scream until my voice is raw, but I don't. I can't. I have to keep it together, for my own sanity, for this case, for the woman lying on that hospital bed.

I grab a cup of burnt coffee from the waiting room vending machine. It tastes just as atrocious as police station coffee. Impatiently pacing the room, I go over in my head what little data we seemed to be able to gather from the crime scene. I continue to pace the floor of the waiting room, my legs restless, and my skin crawling at the realization that this can't be a coincidence. In fact, upon further inspection, it's obvious that AJ fits the victimology of our last five stab wound victims.

"I think this is the work of our serial killer," I say, running my hands through my hair.

Dax shakes his head. "MO doesn't fit. They've never left a survivor before. Never multiple stab wounds. Plus, there isn't an X written in lipstick across her face."

Dax was a right, but there was still something about this attack that nagged at me. Something that told me there was a connection.

"She fits victimology. The timeline also fits. Attacked on a Tuesday night, exactly one week from the last victim. As for the multiple stab wounds," I shrug, "maybe the killer is deescalating, losing control."

I watch Dax's face as he looks ahead at the double doors past the nurse's station. He seemed to be pondering the idea.

"Call it a hunch," I say to him.

This attack must be connected to the serial killer; the timeline is too perfect, but there's no there apparent motive, it just seems senseless. Having something this brutal happen within the same times as an active known serial killer? Things like this don't happen, usually, for copycat killers or for random murders.

The doctor finally appears through the double doors.

"Detectives?" He questions as he approaches us.

"Michealson and Grieson," I introduce my partner and myself.

"Dr. Jenkins. I'm the trauma surgeon on call tonight," he replies as he shakes my hand. "Ms. James experienced a lot of blood loss. We had to do a transfusion and - -"

"Is she going to be okay?" I interrupt.

Dr. Jenkins removes his surgical cap in the same way cops do when we notify someone of their loved ones death. My heart stops beating for a moment.

My blood becomes heavy and my lungs constrict rapidly. Panic threatens to drown me as I sink down into the chair behind me, breath already labored. I force myself to suck in a deep breath and release as I count backwards from five.

"There is some swelling on her brain and the injuries appear to be consistent with blunt force trauma from a large, flat surface. We have her in a medically induced coma to give her body a chance to heal itself before we consider any further surgery. We don't want to risk making it worse," he explains, "and to answer your question, Detective, I don't know, yet. We're doing everything we can to keep her comfortable but, for now, we just have to wait."

Coma?

My stomach lurches violently as the waiting room feels like it is swirling around me, getting smaller with each spin. I try desperately to steady my breathing. Inhale through the nose. Exhale through the mouth. Inhale. Exhale. Nice and steady.

"We were able to collect fingernail scrapings, though, and we have her clothing bagged," the doctor continued, "an intern will sign them over to you when you're ready."

"Thanks Doctor. We'd appreciate that," Dax says.

"Can we see her?" I ask.

"I'll have a nurse escort you to ICU. Do you know of any family we can call?"

Family. Shit. How could I have forgotten?

Another wave of nausea churns my stomach as I try to imagine how her family would react to all of this. I should have called someone sooner. Her family should be here.

"I'll take care of it," I reply as I pull my cellphone out of my pocket.

I feel the light pressure of my partner's hand on my shoulder, guiding me, as I'm scrolling through my contacts. I stop scrolling as the name of my half-sister appears on the screen. My sister, whom I had only found out I had a few years ago, happens to be AJ's best friend, Niki. I wonder if she knows when AJ arrived back in town. I can't be upset that she didn't tell me; we aren't as close as she and AJ are.

I didn't notice the walk from the ER waiting room to the ICU. It wasn't until the nurse escorting us excused herself that I realized we stopped in front of AJ's room. For a moment, maybe too long a moment, I feel selfish again. I forget about making calls, about talking to anyone about this, about anything at all except the cloying struggle of whether or not to step into the room. I would have stepped inside, without hesitation, without oscillation, in any other moment, with any other victim. But this, this is different.

My body refuses to cooperate. My mind refuses to settle enough to allow myself to actually function like I know how too. I can't do this. I can't walk in there because I know that as soon as I do, I'll break. I'll crumble and my walls will come crashing down. Tiny pieces of me will smash onto the hospital floor for all to see. I'll be exposed like a live wire.

"I...*can't.*" I whisper, unable to hold back my tears.

The world becomes blurry. Dax lifts my phone from out of my hand. He places his left hand on the small of my back and urges me silently into the room, knowing that I have to despite all protestations.

The sight of AJ stops what little breath I have left.

I shake myself before I approach the bed.

There's work that needs to be done and I'm a professional. I try to remind myself of this even as I slip my right hand underneath AJ's and stoke it gently. I lean into her face and whisper into her ear, "I'm here, AJ. I'm here." I breathe.

4

Then

The quad was full with a large gathering of students, each one of them inspecting the separate activities on display. Various booths had been set up to show off all the university had to offer. AJ barely noticed any of them. Her mind was on Torryn. She wondered about the girl's sudden stiffness when Ava arrived. *Damn, she's gorgeous,* AJ thought to herself.

"Earth to AJ."

The sound of Ava's voice pulled AJ from her thoughts of Torryn's skin and starking jawline.

"Huh? Sorry, Ava. I was...lost in thought," AJ replied to her friend, her cheeks blushing.

"Well, obviously," Ava teased, rolling her eyes, "I was saying how great is was that you took a year off from school and now we're freshmen together."

The comment caused AJ to pause.

"Sorry, AJ," Ava said, turning to her friend, "I didn't mean—"

"It's fine," another ping of guilt hit AJ in the

stomach. She placed her hand on her friend's shoulder and squeezed lightly. "But can we maybe talk about something else?"

"Right," Ava agreed with a thin smile, "so what's up with your suite mate? She seems kind of intense."

"I don't know," uttered AJ. "I literally just met her."

"She's hot, though," Ava said nonchalantly, laughing as AJ's cheeks blushed an even brighter red. "Oh my God, AJ... you *like* her." emphasizing the word *like* with a quick raise of her eyebrows.

AJ quickly resumed walking, "Shut up. I don't even know her."

"That doesn't matter. You can still have the hots for her."

AJ and Ava wandered around the bustling quad. Torryn was right, there was nothing interesting going on tonight. AJ wasn't feeling the college's Welcome Week vibe, or maybe she was just to distracted. AJ stuck it out simply because of the look of wonder on Ava's face. She loved how her friend still had an innocent air about her. Ava went from booth to booth, talking excitedly with other students. AJ had seen too much gloominess in the past year to share the same emotional response that Ava did. It would take more than college activities to make her feel like her old self again. But then, when she let her mind wander, it instantly thought of Torryn. She could feel a small smile form and that was pretty damn close enough.

AJ tried to hide the look of boredom on her face as they circled the quad for the second, then third time. AJ took a few steps before she noticed Ava had stopped walking. AJ turned to Ava and shot her a quizzical look.

Ava shrugged and turned in the direction of the dorms, "Okay, now even I'm bored with this."

AJ chuckled as they walked away from the quad and down along the sidewalk leading away from the Welcome Week fair. Ava shoved handfuls for pamphlets and flyer into her bag and began chatting about the parts of her life that AJ missed out on. It wasn't that AJ didn't want to know, but it only served to remind her that she wasn't here for her family or friends, that they continued to live their lives without disruption, and that they were content when AJ couldn't be.

An obnoxious car horn blared behind them, making both girls jump and whip around to see the source. A black Mustang convertible pulled up alongside them. Top already down to reveal the driver.

"Hey!" said the dark haired girl at the wheel.

AJ and Ava called back in unison, "Niki!"

"Get in," Niki told the girls.

Ava climbed into the back seat, allowing AJ to sit in the front because Niki had known her the longest and it was an unspoken rule of theirs. AJ felt slightly envious of Niki who, being a year older and advanced enough to already be in her first year of grad school, was allowed to not only drive her car to class but also lived off campus. The feeling quickly passed, however, since she knew the three of them would mostly likely be living together next year.

Niki punched AJ playfully in the shoulder. "Hey,

stranger. Why didn't you tell me you were back?"

AJ shrugged, looking out the window to avoid eye contact, fingers fiddling with the hem of her sleeve, "I don't know. I figured I'd ease back in before reaching out to everyone. Ava's already been pretty hard to handle."

"Hey…" Ava whined from the back seat.

The three friends shared a smile and there was a moment of sad nostalgia that filled the empty spaces of the car.

"Man, it feels good to be together again," Niki said, breaking the silence.

It did feel good, AJ thought. She could almost forget about the grief the past year had brought her. Almost.

"Where are we going, anyway?" Ava asked.

"To have some real fun," Niki smirked as she pulled away from the curb and turned up the music.

The three girls sang along with the radio and enjoyed the bass of music vibrating against their bodies. It was easier for AJ to be with both of them at the same time, it hurt less and she could get away with pretending that she didn't leave them behind, that nothing had really changed for her.

Niki pulled into the parking lot of a small bar not too far from campus a few minutes later. The sign out front read, 'Epic Underground'. As the three girls walked into the bar, the bartender smiled at Niki like he was used to seeing her in here more often than other patrons. They made their way through the crowd to find a spot at the bar top to order.

"Hey, beautiful," the man called from the bar.

"Hey handsome," Niki replied, her voice light and sweet, "Vodka and Red Bull, double. Make it three, please, Tuck."

Tuck eyed AJ and Ava. AJ could pass for twenty-one. Ava on the other hand definitely could not. Even on a good day, she could barely pass for eighteen.

"Come on, Tuck, they're with me," Niki said, winking. "This place survives because of underage college kids."

"As long as *you* keep them out of trouble," Tuck countered, pointing his finger at her.

Niki saluted him as he tended to their drink order.

"Typical," Ava retorted as they headed to the only empty booth in the place.

"What?" said Niki.

"Oh, come on, Niki. You have a way of getting a guy to give you whatever you want," AJ teased.

"Yeah, girls, too," Ava said with a smile, "and you don't even have to sleep with them first."

"True," Niki smirked. "But making them think they have a chance is half the fun."

The drinks arrived then, and the three friends started to catch each other up as they sipped their beverages. For the first time in what felt like forever, AJ felt something akin to contentment as she listened to her best friends talk about their lives. Niki said she was excited to be starting grad school, despite the hard work it took to get her there.

AJ couldn't deny how hard. She was there when Niki somehow managed to balance a social life, high school and college courses. She admired her friend for having graduated high school and received her Associates degree at the same time. She was also willing to bet that while all the other kids were back at home enjoying breaks in between semesters, Niki was probably home taking online classes.

Ava talked about her senior year of high school, the dances, the exams, and how excited she was to be at college and finally reunited with her best friends.

AJ's stomach convulsed as the conversation turned to her.

"Enjoying your first day on campus?" Niki asked AJ, sipping the remains of her drink.

"I get to hang out with the two of you. What's not to love?" AJ said, with a shrug.

"Have you met the rest of your suite mates yet?" Ava asked.

"I didn't really see anybody else there besides Torryn and then you showed up, so I didn't really get a chance."

"Well," Ava paused to sip her drink, "if they look anything like Torryn you're in big trouble."

AJ lightly kicked Ava under the table.

"Ay! ¿Que demonios?," Ava whined as she bent to rub her shin.

Intrigued, Niki asked, "what's wrong with her suite mate?" Then downed the rest of her drink and signaled Tuck for another round.

"Oh, nothing," Ava said with a smirk, "she's just smoking hot. If I weren't straight I'd go after that."

"Ava, you do realize that she *is* a person and not just a piece of ass, right?" AJ snapped.

Ava turned to Niki and continued her teasing,

"AJ thinks she's hot, too."

"Can we move on, please," AJ groaned as Tuck brought over their second round of drinks, "I think I need a shot right about now."

Tuck chuckled, "I can do that."

"Yes!" Niki exclaimed, clapping her hands together. "Tito's, make it three. No, six. And keep 'em coming!"

Tuck nodded, rolling his eyes before turning away.

Niki turned back to AJ and cleared her throat. "Okay then James," She said official like, leaning on the table, looking directly at AJ, challenging her.

AJ winced, *here is it,* she thought, *straight to the jugular.* She knew she was about to get a big dose of reality when Niki called her by her last name.

"What the hell have you been doing this past year that you couldn't just pick up the phone to say 'hi' to your best friends?"

"I'm sorry," AJ replied quietly, averting her eyes yet again. She did not want to talk about it but by the gravity in Niki's voice, and the intent in her eyes, she knew she would not get off so easily, "After dad died, I just couldn't deal. I just wanted to forget about everything, so I took off with Aidan and went to Europe. Leaving was hard, but I needed space and time away, and Aidan needed me so I did what I had to do for him. I sent my mom a few postcards just so she'd know we were okay, but that was the only communication I had with anyone."

AJ paused long enough to take her first shot, completely unaware of them being placed on the table and Tuck walking away.

"I know, I messed up," AJ continued rambling. "I should have stayed in touch, I should have come home sooner," she paused. "I feel horrible for missing your graduation, Ava, but I was just so messed up when he died. If I stayed here, I wouldn't have survived it. Now that I'm back I just feel worse than before—"

"Hey, that's not—"

"It was only Aidan and me by ourselves for a year. Now I have to be without him and it hurts because I feel like I've abandoned him and just left him there with my mom, who is probably still disappointed in me—"

"You didn't—"

"And, I know this is going to be good for him later but I still feel like I should be with him. I wasn't here for you but—"

"Okay, stop it—"

"I'm here now and I'm not going anywhere. I know I have a lot to make up for." AJ shuddered out a breath, as if she hadn't been breathing the whole time she was trying to explain herself.

The girls were silent for a moment, taking in everything, and not sure of what they should say, or what they could say to make it better.

Niki spoke first. "I'm sorry. I shouldn't have said anything." She leaned in quickly and hugged AJ and soon the pair felt Ava's arms surround them as well.

"We totally understand, you were grieving. We love you." Ava said, pulling out of the hug.

Niki wiped a tear running down AJ's left cheek. "That's enough of the mushy stuff. Let's drink!"

AJ smiled, thankful that her friends cared enough to stay loyal to their friendship despite the lack of contact for so long. Ava, AJ, and Niki carried on with their drinking and laughing more and more between each one as if the time apart had just melted into insignificance, as if it had never happened. The rest of the evening passed with almost enough distraction for AJ, as memories of the last year would bleed into her thoughts and trip her in guilt. When the subject of school circled back, so did the passing thoughts of the beautiful girl AJ met earlier.

5

Now

The sound of footsteps wake me to a state of abrupt confusion. I have no idea how long I was asleep. A few minutes, an hour? I look at AJ in the bed, monitors still attached to her. The events of the evening all come rushing back. I am back there, in the alley where AJ's barely alive body had been found. Blood pooling around her body, seeping into the concrete, her life escaping her with every shallow breath that passed. Dr. Jenkins telling me AJ's in a coma.

I snap out of my daze, glance around the room and notice Dax is nowhere to be seen.

"Oh my God, AJ," came a panicked voice behind me.

I turn to see my half-sister, Niki. Behind her stood a boy of about thirteen. I stand and hug Niki, fresh tears streaming down my face. The boy watches me with an odd expression, half perplexed, half hostile.

"Torryn?" He announces.

I release Niki. "Hey, Aidan."

The teenage boy's face softened as he rushes over to me and wraps his arms around my waist in a tight hold. An overwhelming smell of synthetic spice hit my senses, causing my throat to react. I suppress the cough that threatens to gag me in order to stay in his arms a little longer. The boy's hug feels like him.

Pulling away from Aidan, I examine him. He has grown considerably from the ten-year-old boy I saw last. I hardly recognize him now that he's officially a teenager, probably already going through puberty if the small bit of acne is any indication. His blond hair sticks out from beneath a sock cap and he's wearing a black t-shirt with a skateboard and graffiti type lettering, skinny jeans that make me wonder how he can breathe, and a thick black bracelet on his left wrist. He's hardly recognizable but when I cup his cheeks with my hands I see him there, in those aqua blue eyes. Her eyes. No matter how much a person's appearance may change as they age, their eyes stay the same.

"I'm going to go out into the hall and talk to Niki real quick," I tell him. He nods, slightly before nervously embracing AJ as best he can while avoiding the wires and machinery that she is hooked up to. I can't imagine how terrifying it must be for him to see his mother like that.

I motion for Niki to follow me. Once in the hall I ask, "Do you think it's a good idea to bring him here?"

"Torryn, she's his mom. He has the right to be here."

I nod, knowing Niki is right. "But he's so young.

Don't you think it's better to…" I trail off, not really sure how to finish my thought. I want to protect Aidan from this. It's my job, to serve and protect, but more than that, he was family to me. Still is, and he shouldn't be here. He shouldn't have to see his mom in this condition, shouldn't have to worry if she's going to be okay or not.

"I know," Niki says, wrapping me in another embrace. "Who the hell did this?"

"I'm not sure, but I intend to find out."

It goes unspoken between Niki and I, but she understands I'll do whatever it takes to bring down the son of a bitch that did this to her. Even if it means I have to hunt down every lead myself.

"I called Hailey and left her a message, she's at some big medical conference…"

"Do you know where? Maybe we could try contacting the venue or the organizers to reach her."

Niki shakes her head, going through her phone for a moment before confirming that she didn't have the name of the conference or where it is located. I huff out a sigh, rolling my shoulders back as I try not to let my frustration get the best of me.

Turning our attention back to Aidan, we watch him sitting there beside her, hands clasped around hers, shaking with barely controlled sobs. I have to find whoever did this and bring them to justice, if not for AJ, then for Aidan.

"Did you know she was back?"

Niki looks at me, guilt written all over her face. "Yeah, I knew. She got back a week ago. I'm sorry I didn't say anything."

I take Niki's hand in mine and give it a little

squeeze. "Niki, she's been your best friend your whole life, much longer than I've been your sister. I never expected you to choose me over her or to stop being her friend. I only ask because that information could be useful to the case. Speaking of, I should probably get to the station," I glance towards Aidan and AJ, hesitating to leave.

Thankfully, Niki understands. "Go. Catch the bad guy. I'll call you if there are any changes and I'll let Aidan know."

Niki walks into the room and I turn away.

****

The drive to the police station allows me to clear my head and gain perspective. Driving down 380 is always a game of chance and I drew the short straw, doomed to catch all the red lights, despite it being in the middle of the night. My body no longer feels like it's wrung tight. Instead, it feels heavy. As if my muscles can no longer hold my frame, and my bones have turned to lead. My head relies on the headrest to stop it from falling towards the steering wheel.

The woman I've loved for ten years is lying in a hospital bed and there's nothing I can do except find the bastard that did this to her. I shouldn't allow myself to feel this much; it could cloud my judgment. If my superior officer finds out I'm connected to the victim, he would take me off the case without so much as a warning. There is no way in hell I'm allowing that to happen.

I call Dax. "I'm on my way to the station. Where are you?"

His voice comes through the speakers of my car,

"Well, I figured you wouldn't be home anytime soon so I took the liberty of stopping by your apartment to feed your dog."

"Thanks, Dax."

"Hey, no problem."

Silence stretched out through the car, suffocating me. I can't breathe.

"You doing okay?" He asks after a pause.

"Yeah," I lied, "I'll be fine. Go home, Dax, kiss your wife and get some sleep."

"You should get some sleep, too."

"There's too much to do," I counter.

"Anyone ever tell you you're a workaholic?"

"Occasionally."

"Why is that?"

I pause before answering, trying to figure out what exactly to say. How could I explain to him how hard it is for a woman to have both a successful career and a family? Even in today's society, there is still an absurd expectation for a woman to choose one over the other, despite being judged relentlessly either way. The career was my choice.

"You know why, Dax. I had to make it mean something. Now I'm not so sure I made the right decision."

Dax remained silent. After all we've been through together, he must know how hard that was for me to admit. Though I've seen him around the precinct and known his reputation longer, he's been my partner for three years. Mentoring me from the day I became a detective, becoming a close friend after a shoot out that ended with a dead suspect and the questioning of my abilities to do the job. His wife of twenty-three years, Shelly, often invited me over for dinner or sent Dax to work with leftovers for me. They became family, with Dax like the big brother I never had, which I guess is why he has a key to my apartment.

"Don't say that," he finally said, breaking the silence. "You're a good detective, and the best damned partner I've had the pleasure of working with in a while."

"You would know, you made me that way."

"No kid, that was all you."

I roll my eyes at the term "kid," and attempt to smile. He wasn't *that* much older than me, despite the deception of the gray hair on top of his head, he was only forty-three. But he does show a propensity to protect me like I am his own. I tell him goodnight and disconnect the call. Just like that, I'm alone again with only my unwelcome thoughts keeping me company. I glance at the time on the dash. It has been a long day and the exhaustion is starting to take its toll. I pull into the parking lot of the police station. I lean my head back against the headrest. I can't muster the strength to get out of the car.

6

Then

Drunk and clumsy, AJ stumbled through the door to her dorm after a momentary struggle of getting the key to fit in the lock. She couldn't recall how she managed to arrive back at her dorm suit, just like she couldn't manage to stay quiet if Torryn walking into the living room was any indication that her sleep was disturbed.

"AJ. What's going on? Do you have any idea what time it is?" Torryn shouted as a whisper.

AJ gazed at Torryn and dropped her phone in the process. "No idea," she said as she went to pick her phone up off the floor but instead fell over giggling.

Torryn walked over to her and tried to help her up. She handed AJ her phone. "It's three in the morning. You're going to wake up the rest of the apartment, come on," she deadpanned.

Despite the overwhelming smell of alcohol that AJ assumed to be the cause of Torryn sighing as she helped AJ to her room, which proved a challenge for both of them. AJ thought she felt Torryn tense as her hand slipped from Torryn's waist and came to rest on the girl's hip. Once they made it into AJ's room, she was carefully guided onto the bed. AJ looked up at Torryn, grabbed onto both hips, pulled her closer and smiled

"Thank you."

Torryn looked away. "Don't make a habit out of this, AJ."

"Which part?"

AJ loved hearing the sound of her name—initials?—coming from Torryn's lips. She caught herself staring at Torryn once again. Her blue eyes chased to meet green.

Shit, AJ thought to herself, *I could get lost in those eyes forever.*

She giggled at the absurdity of just how transfixed she was by Torryn. Everything about her was *perfect.* In that moment, she didn't feel the grief of losing her father, or the overwhelming guilt of abandoning Aidan. All she felt was this moment—alone—with Torryn.

"You're gorgeous," AJ blurted out before she could stop herself, alcohol inhibiting her better judgment.

Torryn stiffened at the compliment.

AJ quickly tried to recover. She hadn't meant to say that out loud. "I'm sorry—oh my God, I didn't mean it—I mean, yes, bu—I'm so embarrassed."

"It's fine," Torryn said gruffly.

AJ squirmed a bit, avoiding Torryn as best she could with the other girl still hovering.

"I should go. Can I get you anything first?"

Torryn asked quietly.

AJ shook her head, "Nope, no, no, I'm good, so good. I'm great."

AJ wondered what the girl was looking for when she caught Torryn scanning around the room. She hadn't yet had the chance to add any personality to the room. She hoped Torryn didn't find it odd that the room was so bare. *Well, I've been here less than twenty-four hours,* she thought to herself, smiling again when Torryn turned her attention back on AJ.

"I'll be right back," Torryn announced.

A moment later, Torryn returned—AJ hadn't noticed she left—with a small trashcan and blanket. *It must be from her room,* AJ considered as Torryn placed the blanket on the bed and the can on the floor next to AJ's bed then began removing AJ's shoes.

AJ chuckled, "Trying to get me naked already?"

Torryn froze, hand resting uneasy on AJ's shoe.

Oh, shit, AJ immediately realized she had gone too far, again. She placed her hand on Torryn's, which twitched slightly on contact.

"I did it again. I'm sorry—I was only joking. Promise."

Torryn took a deep breath and continued to remove the shoe. "There, lay down."

AJ did as she was told. As soon as her back fell upon the mattress, she closed her eyes and felt Torryn brush a strand of hair out of her face as she drifted to sleep.

****

The next morning AJ woke up to the atrocious feeling of her heart pounding within her skull. Her lips and throat felt like sandpaper scrubbed raw. She leaned over and vomited into the trashcan without retching.

I didn't know I had a trashcan, she thought, lifting her head up from the receptacle. *Oh, right, Torryn.*

AJ sat up in her bed and noticed a bottle of water and two Advil on her desk. An index card leaned against the bottle of water, the words "DRINK ME," written on it in neat, elegant handwriting.

She cursed herself for drinking too much the night before. She felt queasy and couldn't remember much. What she did remember, however, was looking into Torryn's eyes and a vague sense of Torryn's fingers stroking her cheek as she slept. That part was most likely her imagination but the thought made her smile nonetheless.

AJ stumbled over to the desk and drank enough water to down the pills in one shot, then went about finding something to wear. She settled on a pair of blue skinny jeans and a blue hoodie. She heard a faint chatter coming from the living room. Using the reflection of herself in her cellphone screen, AJ rearranged her matted hair to make herself at least somewhat presentable.

Before she left the room she grabbed the bag out of the trash can so her room wouldn't start to smell as bad as her insides felt. Bag in hand, AJ darted out of her room and past the blurred faces in the living room. Outside the dorm building she threw the bag in the dumpster and ran back upstairs.

When AJ re-entered the apartment, Torryn was sitting as the breakfast bar, reading a novel. AJ turned her attention to the living room where she saw two males with their backs towards her. They were engrossed in a game console hooked up to a flat screen. AJ had completely forgotten that this was a co-ed suit.

When AJ turned her attention back to Torryn, the other girl had one eyebrow raised, peering over her novel. If AJ's stomach wasn't already rolling with nausea, it'd be rolling with arousal at the image.

"You okay?" Torryn called out to AJ, a hint of concern in her voice.

"Yeah, sorry, I just really needed to take that out," AJ said.

A tight smile crept on Torryn's face as she moved to stand up. She gestured for AJ to take the stool she just vacated. When AJ obliged, Torryn walked around to the kitchen.

"Here," Torryn said from across the counter, handing AJ a glass of orange juice, "Drink this. You look pale."

AJ blushed and murmured a small thank you, at which Torryn smirked and took a sip from her coffee.

AJ turned at the sound of her name being called. The voice sounded vaguely familiar.

"AJ? Oh, man, I didn't expect to be sharing a suite with you," a male stood up from the couch and began to approach AJ.

AJ was drawing a blank. She thought she recognized him, but couldn't place him until he spoke again.

"Ryder? We met yesterday. I'm uh, the guy who hit you with the football...you spilled your coffee...?"

Corvette Boy! *How could I have forgotten?*

"Right," AJ said, "the one who ruined my favorite shirt."

The other boy stood up and shoved Ryder's shoulder and laughed at him, "Rightly done, mate," said the red-haired boy, who then introduced himself as Liam.

"Nice ...to meet you," AJ croaked looking at Liam and trying to power through the nausea of her hangover.

"Well, I hate to run off like this after just meeting, but Ryder and I have to get to practice," Liam said pulling Ryder along as he left the room.

The atmosphere of the room changed. There was a tension that appeared the moment the girls were alone. Both girl's breath hitched, their skin grown increasingly hotter.

Torryn was the first to break the silence, "How are you feeling?"

"Like I've been run over by a Mack truck."

"That's probably to be expected. Given how...lose...lipped...you were last night."

AJ's cheeks went up in flames. "Thank you for, uh, taking care of me by the way."

"Like I said, don't make it a habit."

AJ's phone buzzed. Disappointment spread across her face as she read the message.

"Everything okay?"

It was a moment before AJ responded, texting back a reply. "Yeah," she sighed. "My mom was supposed to bring me some things this weekend but something came up and she has to work."

"I see. Well, I don't have anything to do today," Torryn offered.

AJ ran her hair behind her ear, unsure why Torryn mentioned her lack of plans but she decided she would take it as an invitation. "Well, since we both have nothing to do, shall we do nothing together?" She asked as she started walking towards the couch. "We could watch a movie?"

When Torryn didn't respond, AJ glanced back to see that she was followed into the living room. AJ rolled her eyes when Torryn sat on the opposite end of the couch. *Not a perfect position, but we'll work on it,* AJ thought, feeling that she couldn't resist the increasing pull of attraction she felt. If this was how AJ was going to spend her freshman year then she might just survive it after all.

7

Now

A rapping on my car window jolts me awake. For a brief moment I'm disoriented as I try to locate my bearings and get my heart rate under control. My right hand instinctively jumps to my holstered gun, but relaxes just as quickly when I notice that it's Dax outside my car.

He holds up two cups of coffee while offering me his best lop-sided grin. I glare daggers at him through the window. He barely has time to step back enough to avoid getting hit by the door as I hastily open it.

"So, you do sleep," he teased.

"Funny," I snap, taking one of the proffered cups from his hand. Without another word, I turn to walk towards the station.

"Hey, Torryn. Hold up a second, will ya?"

I turn back to him with a raised eyebrow. It's the same impatient look I used to give AJ when she would take forever to get ready for anything.

Dax nods at the car. "I want to talk to you before we go in," he says seriously.

I take a deep breath and walk back to the car to stand up against the hood. I silently stare at him with practiced neutrality, knowing where this is headed.

"We should consider taking you off this case," he says looking me dead in the eyes. He's never been one to beat around the bush, it's something I've always appreciated about him, but it still manages to rub me the wrong way.

"And, why would *we* do that?"

"Come on, Torryn. You *know* the victim. That makes this case personal for you."

"Every case is personal to me, Dax. It's my job; I take it very personally."

"I know that, but I'm just trying to look out for you," he said. "This could be a big case for you. It could make or break you and you're just starting out. You need to remain unbiased, in every case, and this might be too much."

"I appreciate the concern, Dax, but I am perfectly capable of performing my duties and responsibilities as a detective," I reprimand, but remain unconvinced myself. "I'm not handing this case over to anyone else. Like you said, it's a big one and it's *my* case."

Dax studies me and I bristle at the assumption that I'm too young a detective to work this. I maintain eye contact, refusing to back down from this, as I've done so many times before. I knew I shouldn't get defensive. He's just trying to look out for me. It's as infuriating just as much as it is kind.

Just as he knows me, I know his silence means that he was weighting his duty as my senior officer and his loyalty as my partner. I just need to nudge him a little more in the right direction.

"My knowledge of the victim may prove beneficial to working out motive and timeline," I say with a sigh, still unsure if I sound believable. "Last night was a bit of a shock, it caught me off guard, but I'm fine now. My relationship with Ms. James was a long time ago, I'm over her." I continue, not sure if I'm trying to convince Dax or myself. "I can handle working this case. I'm also the best damned detective on the squad- new or not, you said so yourself."

"I'm not doubting that, "Dax replied. "We'll stay on it for now, but if I see any disregard for proper protocol or procedure because of who she is, I will notify Lieutenant Harris and get us pulled off this case. I need you to know that."

That's fair, I think. I nod and release a breath I didn't realize I was holding, "understood."

We walk into the building together. Once in the bullpen of the homicide division, we immediately commence work on the case. While my mind occasionally flashed to thoughts of AJ lying in a hospital bed, I remind myself to stay focused, concentrate. My career and integrity as a police officer are now on the line. I can't afford to screw this up. Dax was right, this case could make me. Or break me.

My phone rings and the name of our best forensic tech, Joel, flashes on the screen a second before I answer, "Joel, you're on speaker."

"Good news, we may actually have some DNA," says Joel. "I analyzed the fingernail scrapings we received from the hospital. Skin cells were present that didn't match the victim's DNA. An educated guess is that the victim scratched her attacker. I'll run the analysis through CODIS. It may take a while but I'll keep you posted."

"Thanks, Joel," I say and hang up. CODIS is the Combined DNA Index System used by law enforcement agencies across the nation. If the perp's DNA is on file anywhere, it'll be there.

"If this is the same killer, we may have just gotten one hell of a break." I say to Dax as I swipe away the remains of my scrawled, unreadable handwriting on the whiteboard and start over. I place a photo of AJ, supplied in the case file, right next to the five victims that weren't so lucky. I draw a big question mark along with the word 'connection.'

"What do we know?" I pose the question aloud, more to start a new train of thought than for the lack of any leads or evidence.

My cell phone rings before my partner has a chance to open his mouth and I glare at the caller ID. I don't recognize the number. "This is Detective Michealson."

Dax and I make eye contact as I'm listening to the other end.

"My partner and I can be there in thirty minutes," I reply quickly, hanging up with a simple 'see you, soon.'

"What's up?" Dax questions, already gathering his things.

"That was Mrs. Parks," I say, "She's got something for us."

****

As promised, thirty minutes later Dax and I were standing at the counter of the small bookshop, Pages Between. It was the kind of place AJ would feel at home in. I pick up a copy of AJ's latest book, *The Killer Inside,* and turn it over. AJ's smiling face looks up at me from the back cover. *Looks like she's been very busy the past three years,* I force down a sense of pride that threatens to blindside me.

"It's a great read," Mrs. Parks says as she approaches up. "AJ is very talented. She always comes here during a book release—to help me boost business. I can't believe this happened to her. She's a sweet girl."

"She's...special," I say to her.

"That she is, dear. I have your list ready."

She hands over a notepad and a disk to Dax.

"I stayed up all night putting this together for you. It took some time to even figure it all out, dears, I'm not as young as I used to be." She indicted the thin notepad. "In it are all the names of pre-orders for the book, and customers that came in yesterday and paid with card. There were a lot of people who paid with cash and I tried to find as many receipts as I could but I don't know how much help it'll be."

She hands us a stack of receipts with a rubber band around them and then draws our attention above the door. "That's the only security camera I have and you're lucky it decided to work. I had my grandson help me put the footage on a that disk."

"We appreciate it," I tell her, genuinely surprised and grateful. "Thank you."

"Anything I can do to help you catch the person who did this. She always ends her book tours here. This one was her Homecoming Tour."

So, AJ was planning on staying for good?

"Do you remember anything else from last night?" Dax asked.

"I'm sorry, but not a thing, dear."

Despite protests from Mrs. Parks, who kindly invited me to take a copy of AJ's book without payment, I purchase a copy of *The Killer Inside* before Dax and I walk out of the store.

I catch Dax's sideways glance at the book, "You never know, a clue might be inside," I say to him.

He shrugs, I assume unconvinced but he doesn't say anything.

"Since we're here, might as well do a little role-play," Dax suggests.

I nod, knowing that we can't get a report on the details of the attack because the victim is still currently in a coma, and follow him into the ally to the side of the shop. I stop at the dumpster.

"Based on the photos of the scene the suspect most likely hid here," I offer.

Dax crouches beside the dumpster, scrunching his nose at the smell, as I head to the side door. "Why can't these guys ever pick somewhere nice and clean?"

I snort, trying to hold back my amusement. "According to the witness' statement, Ms. James threw out some trash," I call out from the door. I retrace AJ's likely steps towards the dumpster. "If her attacker approached while she was facing the dumpster, she would have seen them, so—."

"They must have waited until she headed back."

I follow his lead and turn back towards the door. His arms lock around my neck and I fight the instinct to defend myself, even if I'm used to acting these things out with him.

"They grab her from behind," Dax says as he pokes his finger into my side, "and stab."

I shake my head, tapping his arm for him to release me. "AJ is five-foot-six. If our suspect is shorter than her then this position wouldn't work. Preliminary reports indicated no bruising around the neck so I don't think they went for a choke-hold."

"Fair point," Dax said, resuming his place on the side of the dumpster, "but the first attack was definitely here."

"Agreed," I say, recalling the blood smear I noticed last night, "what if she was grabbed by the waist from behind and the attacker tried to drag her back? It wouldn't explain the blood smear." If she had been trying to get away, and I can't think as to why she wouldn't, then there wouldn't be blood on the dumpster itself, given that she was attacked when she started walking away.

We resume our positions and Dax once again attacks me, this time wrapping his arm around my waist and making a stabbing motion. "If the attacker is smaller than the victim then they most likely didn't have the strength to hold her after the initial stab without falling over, so, dragging her. Or maybe just trying to get her back behind the dumpster and away from the open."

I tap his arms again and we agree to switch positions. This time I'm the one grabbing him from behind and trying to steady my footing as it does, in fact, prove difficult to hold onto him and to keep us from falling at the same time. I jerk backward and he follows the motion, arms flailing to keep balanced. We almost fall into the dumpster and it's then that we stop, convinced ourselves that this is what happened without the usual reports that we'd have by now.

"The victim falling against the dumpster is probably the sound that attracted the attention of Mrs. Parks to come outside," I explain as I slow my breathing. Playing out the scene took a bit of work, so it must have been even more exhausting to actually have committed the crime, but adrenaline can make a person do extraordinary things.

"They both stumbled into the dumpster," Dax said nodding, "and Ms. James takes the moment when the perp is down to try to get away."

"If they're wearing a hoodie there's not much exposed skin, so when the attacker ended up over her after grabbing her a second time and pulling her down," I explain as I lay on the ground and motion for Dax to crouch over me. "Neck or face," I reach towards him, curving my fingers and running my nails gently against his skin, "I bet that's where she scratched him."

Dax nods in agreement as he leans back a bit. "She manages to get away enough to walk three-feet while the suspect is recovering from the defense."

I squirm out from under him and quickly rise to my feet, as he continues his train of thought.

"The victim is most likely a little disoriented from hitting her head so she's not moving fast, giving the perp the chance to catch up to her to continue the attack."

Dax turns around and reaches for my legs, pulling on my pants to drag me down, which would be the third for the victim. I fall with practiced ease, and Dax crawls on top of me, poking his fingers hard into my thigh, hip and rib cage on his way to straddle my back, in the same areas as AJ. "This is probably when they were interrupted by Mrs. Parks. He got spooked and ran off, most likely in that direction, away from the center of town," Dax points to the right of the store, where there was hardly any light.

"Sounds like a working theory," I add as I try to get up. "Uh, Dax?"

"Yeah?"

"Get off of me." I grumble as I buck underneath him.

"Oh, sorry!"

I roll my eyes, quickly standing up and dusting off my clothes and hands. "Let's just get back to the station. We need to look at the CD and see if the CCTV footage from the ATM came in, yet."

8

Then

AJ sat at the breakfast bar, typing studiously away on her laptop. A plate of three stacked pancakes sat ignored to the side. She cringed at the document before her and envisioned angrily placing it over the trash icon. Placing her elbow on the countertop with her chin in her hand, she resigned to starting the project over. She just didn't know where to begin.

AJ glanced up as Torryn entered the kitchen, sporting her soccer uniform. "I made extra pancakes," AJ offered the other girl.

"Thanks, but I don't really eat pancakes," Torryn replied, glancing at the plate next to AJ's laptop.

AJ watched as Torryn poured herself a large mug of coffee and added caramel macchiato flavored creamer before taking a sip.

"You don't do sugar, either, I see." AJ commented with an incredulous look on her face.

"No. The creamer is sweet enough to not need it."

AJ looked back at her computer screen and muttered something indiscernible to herself, as Torryn paced around the small kitchen collecting various pans and utensils. She watched as Torryn whisked eggs and poured them into a frying pan, before moving on to chopping tomatoes. She tried desperately not to stare at the girl's small but precise movements in fascination. Realizing that she probably looked like a creep, she tried to force her attention back to her laptop.

AJ chewed on her bottom lip, trying to contain her nerves, when she'd catch Torryn stealing rare glances at her as she worked. Torryn seemed so focused on what she was doing after a moment, that it made AJ smile to herself. The sweet and savory aroma of sautéed mushrooms, chopped tomatoes, and minced garlic quickly filled the apartment. AJ's mouth watered.

With a sigh, her appetite now noticeable and her mind distracted, AJ closed her laptop just as Torryn was finishing up the omelet. She decided she would take advantage of this moment.

"You can have a seat, you know," AJ offered once Torryn plated her creation and rinsed off the pan.

Torryn flashed a rare, quick smile. She sat next to AJ, cut a piece of omelet with her fork, and took a small delicate, bite.

"That smells amazing. Who taught you how to cook?"

AJ was met with tense silence, Torryn immediately going still, not even swallowing the eggs she already chewed.

"Uh, what time is the game?" AJ asked, clearing her throat and pretending the moment didn't exist.

"Two o'clock," Torryn hesitated, speaking only

after she swallowed her food and took another bite.

AJ pushed aside her laptop and pulled her almost forgotten plate of pancakes in front of her. She cut up the stack and took a large bite. *How could anyone not eat pancakes,* the thought ran through her mind. It made since, though, the more AJ thought about it. Torryn was obviously an athlete, and although it's not uncommon for athletes to eat healthier than the average person, they still needed carbs, and pancakes were the best form of carbs, in AJ's humble opinion. Still, more for her, she surmised.

"You can come...if you want," Torryn said.

AJ coughed, almost chocking on her food in her mouth, face burning at both the embarrassment and the immediate inappropriate thought she had.

Torryn quickly handed AJ her mug of coffee. AJ grabbed it and gulped down a large mouthful.

"What?" AJ asked, desperate to regain composure.

"To the game," Torryn replied. "You can come, if you want."

"Right," AJ mumbled, "yeah, maybe."

"I mean, only if you want to, of course."

AJ glanced at Torryn. "No, it's fine. I'll go.."

Just then, before anything else could be said or done, their door banged open, and in walked their two suitemates. AJ watched in fascination at how Torryn immediately stiffened, back straightening out, and shoulders squaring off, her face a model picture of composure, without any struggle or hesitation.

Perfect timing, AJ thought grumpily.

"Hey, ladies," Ryder said out loud.

"I should go," Torryn mumbled as she grabbed the plate.

"Leave it," AJ offered, "I'll take care of it."

"Thank you," Torryn said as she grabbed her gym bag instead and headed out the door.

"Man, why is that girl so weird?" Ryder commented as soon as the door was closed.

AJ remained silent as she rinsed both plates, lost in thought. She wanted to go to the game, but knew she wouldn't actually go unless her friends were there with her. Maybe she could convince Niki to host a last minute victory party at her off-campus apartment if Torryn's team won? *Maybe then,* thought AJ, *I could actually get somewhere with her.*

****

AJ watched the object of her desires run up and down the field, and though, she knew nothing of soccer, she enjoyed watching Torryn play the sport. AJ admired the combination of determination and elegance she displayed on the field. She had assumed Torryn incapable of being a team player, as she wasn't very social, but she was killing it. The entire scene- twenty-two girls running around- was distracting. AJ barely heard the conversation going on around her. Niki had taken AJ's suggestion of an after party seriously and, in true Niki fashion, had quickly set to work to organize it. AJ glanced over at Niki. She hadn't noticed that Liam and Ryder had joined them.

"It could be a double victory party, then," Niki

said in response to Liam bragging about the boy's team winning their game earlier in the day.

Even though Liam was two years younger than Niki, the two very quickly became a pair. She sometimes regretted introducing her friends to her suitemates. It wasn't because she didn't like Liam and Niki together. She thought they were adorable. It was because where Liam was, Ryder was sure to be, as well. Somehow, and AJ wasn't quite sure how it was possible, he became more annoying the longer she knew him.

AJ turned her attention back to the field. She watched as Torryn scored the winning goal with only a few seconds left on the clock. The crowd cheered uproariously, people immediately jumping to their feet, clapping wildly. AJ smile at the overwhelming sense of pride she felt, even if it was misplaced. She hardly knew the girl, she kept thinking over and over. *Don't get ahead of yourself,* had become her new mantra lately.

Without a word to her friends she darted down from the bleachers, and made her way through the crowd to the field.

"Good goal," AJ called out to Torryn over the sound of the team cheering their win.

Torryn turned away from her teammates and jogged over. "You made it."

"I did. Congratulations! You're very good at kicking the ball." AJ internally cringed at how stupid that sounded.

Torryn laughed out loud. "Thanks"

AJ froze, at the sound that escaped from Torryn. She had never actually heard Torryn laugh before now. She thought it was the best sound she heard all day and her mind raced to try to find a way to make her do it again. They stood staring at each other. AJ shifted her weight from one foot to the other, unsure what to say next, or what to do with her hands. She didn't want to look at Torryn, too embarrassed, but her eyes kept straying to the other girl, anyway, as if there was going to be some sort of opening - -

"Congratulations on your win!"

AJ blinked and realized Ava had made her way down to the field, as well. The rest of the group was not far behind

"Thank you," Torryn replied coolly.

AJ could admit to herself that she admired how this girl could go from carefree to defensive and serious so quickly. When Niki arrived and Torryn's gaze shifted to her AJ realized that the two of them hadn't actually met, yet.

"Niki, this is Torryn. Torryn, this is my friend, Niki," AJ said introducing the pair.

"Ah, so *you're* the famous Torryn," Niki said, shooting her a mischievous smile.

"Nice to meet you," Torryn said before shooting a dark glare at AJ. "I should go change."

"Sure, sure," Niki replied as though Torryn had spoken to her. "We're having a victory party at my place tonight. You should come…with AJ."

AJ looked at the ground and pleaded with it to open up and swallow her whole.

"I'll think about it," Torryn said firmly, still looking at AJ, then she jogged her way back to her team. Once Torryn was out of sight AJ playfully shoved her friend, "Jerk," she mumbled to Niki.

9

Now

At the station, Dax and I split up tasks. He sets to work running the list of bookstore patrons Mrs. Parks was able to provide through our database of recorded criminals as well as through the FBI's Violent Criminal Apprehension Program, or ViCAP, while I watch the video.

The camera above the door has a decent range, showing the counter and chairs set up on one side of the store. Bookshelves block view of where AJ would be signing copies of her book, which I am thankful for.

For most of the video, things are proceeding normally. Patrons coming and going, stopping at shelves, looking at novels or magazines, getting in line to make purchases, sitting in chairs to wait for the signing event to start. There's decently over a hundred people filtering in and out of the camera's view. Just as I begin to wonder if we're going to see anything worthwhile, someone enters the bookstore with a dark hoodie on. Which isn't suspicious in itself, but their body language is too stiff, too controlled, too purposeful compared to everyone else around them. They're careful to avoid looking up as they move into a position where they can see AJ and still be able to stay out of her sight.

The suspect may have done reconnaissance at the store earlier to learn the location of where the camera was. I quickly jot down any and all observations. The figure was short and slim, matching what little description Mrs. Parks gave in her witness statement last night. When other patrons started to line up at AJ's book-signing table, with books in hand, the suspect backs up and leaves the store. That movement by itself is suspect, as most people would just turn around to leave.

"Look," I say to Dax, who leans toward me to look at my computer. "They waited all that time and then just left," I explain as I back up the video and play it again from the time the person entered the store to the time they left.

"Why wouldn't they want to get closer to the intended victim?"

I shrug, " I don't know. They obviously knew where the camera was. Kept their face hidden." I knew it would be a long shot seeing this person's face. That didn't keep the disappointment from creeping in. "Where are we on getting the video from the ATM across the street?"

"Just waiting on the warrant."

I nod and pull out my phone to send a quick text to A.D.A Julian Kovak asking for an update and telling him we need it pronto.

"We'll catch...whoever it is," Dax says, sensing my disappointment.

"Yeah, how many more people have to die before we do?"

That was the worst part of the job, waiting for more victims. Our UNSUB - unidentified subject - has already killed five women and possibly attacked another who remains in critical condition. How many more will fall at their hands?

"Why would they stand there that whole time and not get a book signed," I wondered aloud again.

"Maybe the changed their mind," Dax replied.

"Or maybe they didn't want to be recognized."

"Meaning our victim would probably know the perp."

It was possible, but if that were the case, what was the connection between AJ and our five other victims?

"Michealson. Grieson. Get in here." A deep voice boomed from behind us.

We turn in unison to see Lieutenant Harris standing in the doorway of his office. When we enter I notice a man leaning against the polished oak desk, arms folded across his chest.

"I called in some reinforcements on your case. The Dallas FBI field office sent over their best agent to offer assistance."

I keep my face calm, though I'm clenching my jaw. *Way to show the faith Lieu,* I think to myself. This guy looks like a pompous ass, with his black hair swooping down one side and dressed to impress in an expensive-looking suit.

He stuck out his hand.

"Special Agent Caspian Drake," he said as firmly as his handshake.

With as much composure I can muster, I return his handshake. "Detective Torryn Michealson. This is my partner, Detective Dax Grieson."

"I hear you have yourselves one smart UNSUB. No evidence left behind at the scene of the crime, other than a signature," he commented, shaking Dax's hand.

"Marks an X on the victims' face with lipstick." Dax offers. "We're confident that we'll catch them soon. They got sloppy. The last victim may have fought back. She's...*survived.*"

I winced at the idea that AJ only lived because her attacker was sloppy.

"I say we take a look at what we've got, start building a profile to narrow down the suspect pool."

We? Who does this guy think he is? I am not going to give up my case to the FBI. I worked too hard on this for the FBI to swoop in and take credit for my collar if - when- I solve the case.

I give Drake my best calm and collected go-to-hell look.

"Detective Grieson will show you to the conference room," Lieutenant Harris says to the agent. "Detective Michaelson, a word?"

Dax leads Drake to the conference room that currently housed our large white board as I stay behind.

"Sir?" I say as I stand to attention, head straight and arms behind my back.

"I don't need to remind you how big this case is for the city...and for you."

"No, sir."

"Good. You moved up the ranks fast. I can't take

that away from you. But if you want that to continue, you'll have to play nice. Agent Drake's expertise- and experience- is invaluable. I suggest you listen carefully to it. We can't have a serial killer on the loose for any longer."

"Understood."

I leave the room to join Dax and Agent Drake in the conference room where they are studying the photos and theories that are written on the murder board.

"This last victim's attack is much more violent than the rest," says Agent Drake. "What makes you think they're connected?"

"Timing for one," I reply confidently. I avoid looking at the bruised face of victim number six pinned on the wall. "All the victims were murdered precisely one week apart. Victim number six fits that timeline... as well as the physical description of the other five victims."

"But..." Agent Drake quizzed. "Where's the signature? If there's not a stronger link and the victim is alive this attack is a major crimes case, not homicide. What's the angle you're trying to work here?"

"Her attacker was interrupted by Mrs. Parks, the owner of the bookshop," I state. "Why don't you get caught up on the case," I say handing him the case tablet. "Dax and I have a lead to follow up on. We'll be back and then we can discuss connections."

Once we're alone in the car I let my frustration out. "We're perfectly capable to solving his case, Dax," I exclaim. "But...Harris...brings in the FBI to take over."

"To consult," placates Dax. "It's one agent, Torryn. If Lieu wanted he could bring in a whole team of the FBI. But he isn't, He has faith in you. All you have to do is...*play nice*."

"Play nice? Seriously, who does this Drake guy think he is? And how are you okay with this?"

"I'm not happy about it but Harris is our commanding officer. And, we could use the help we because you're right, this is the biggest case of *our* careers. There's been at least five victims, possibly six now. We have to solve this...and quick. I know there's a lot of beef between cops and FBI but I don't think they'd send only one agent if they intended to take this case away."

I shoot Dax a fixed stare.

Dax returns the look. "You have a bright future ahead of you, Torryn, but you're not going to get very far if you can't cooperate with other law enforcement agencies."

"Yes dad," I tease, struggling to regain my composure.

10

Then

AJ couldn't help herself as she leaned against Torryn's doorway, dressed in her favorite pair of blue jeans, a red tank top and form-fitting leather jacket. AJ's arms were crossed in front of her in a way that accentuated her cleavage. She could feel the connection, the chemistry between Torryn and herself, but Torryn was so reserved that AJ felt afraid to push too hard at first. Reserved problems required bolder solutions and luckily thanks to the drinks she had after the game with her friends, she was feeling more confident than usual, she decided that maybe she'd try a different approach to getting Torryn's attention.

AJ smiled, feeling emboldened once she notices Torryn's terrible, yet obvious, attempts at trying not to stare. There was a heavy draw to Torryn that AJ still hadn't figured out, but the most frustrating thing was that Torryn didn't even seem to be trying to seduce her in any way, like she wasn't aware of the magnetism she exuded.

Maybe she's just not into girls, AJ thought to herself before speaking aloud to the brunette standing before her.

"Are you seriously not going to come?" AJ pouted.

Torryn visibly swallowed. "I don't do crowds. Or parties. Or any of the probably illegal activities that will undoubtedly occur at such college parties."

"How about fun? Do you do fun?"

"I—"

AJ jutted out her bottom lip, drawing her brows together, which made Torryn pause.

"—I know how to have fun, yes."

AJ smiled like the Cheshire Cat. "Good, so do I. So, let's go have fun together."

Without giving the girl time to react, AJ grabbed her wrist and pulled her from the room when she was within reach...*Victory at last,* AJ thought, as they made their way out the building and outside.

AJ didn't let go of Torryn's wrist until they were a safe distance from the dorms. She was thankful Niki's apartment was within walking distance of the campus. She enjoyed the cool autumn breeze as they walked together in silence. With each step they took, her previous confidence dwindled rapidly as she couldn't find anything to talk about. She really didn't know much about Torryn, so she didn't know which topics were safe, as she'd witness Torryn balk at various conversation starters previously. She was pretty sure that family was one of those things that were off limits, though AJ didn't understand why. Regardless, she wanted tonight to be about showing Torryn that she could be trusted and fun, someone she could enjoy spending time with on a more regular basis.

She led Torryn through Niki's apartment once they arrived. AJ scanned the densely packed room, quickly finding a path to the fire escape that would lead them to the rooftop. They passed a group of students hovering above boys playing video games as AJ led Torryn to her friends.

AJ turned to look at Torryn only to realize they had become separated by a disturbingly drunk male blocking her path, leaning into her personal space and slurring out disgusting remarks on how good she looked.

She rolled her eyes and walked around the guy to grab a hold of Torryn's hand, lacing their fingers together. "Hi," AJ said, perhaps too cheerfully. "There you are, babe." AJ smiled as she leaned in close and whispered in Torryn's ear to go along with it.

AJ then kissed Torryn's cheek and giggled at the blush that slowly crept across it. Turning to the boy, who sported an odd combination of excitement and disappointment on his face, "Thank you for keeping her company, but we have somewhere to be now."

Keeping her hold on Torryn's hand, they left the boy alone in the crowd. AJ led Torryn across the apartment and out onto the fire escape, where she finally let go of Torryn's hand. She didn't miss the fact that her hand felt cold by the sudden lack of contact.

"Oh, my God, that was epic," cried AJ. "Did you see his face? He didn't know what to do! We're definitely going to star in his dreams tonight."

AJ indicated the ladder next to her, "the rest of the party is up here. Come on." But when she started to climb, she noticed that Torryn wasn't following.

"Something wrong?" She asked from a few places on the ladder, turning around slightly to see Torryn with hands resting lightly on her hips.

Torryn took a deep breath and arched an eyebrow. AJ waited for a few more seconds before she started up the ladder again.

"It's just, while, I appreciate your intention and enthusiasm to act in those situations, I didn't need you to do that. You didn't have to kiss me or pretend that you're my girlfriend."

AJ stopped climbing as she reached the top and looked back down at Torryn with confusion and hurt in her gaze. She was only trying to help and now she'd messed up. "The guy was drunk and hitting on you, which you obviously didn't want him to even be near you so I was just trying to help."

"I understand that, but I could have handled it fine without you jumping in," Torryn snapped.

AJ didn't understand. Where was the harm in stepping in? She would have done the same thing for any of her friends—and in fact, has had to do it a few times before. Was Torryn more upset at the kiss and the false pretense? Or was she genuinely annoyed that AJ stepped in? Was she suppose to just stand back and wait? And what if it escalated to touching? Alcohol and reasoning don't mix well together.

Without much reason, even though AJ was taken aback by Torryn's tone, she felt anger start to bubble. It wasn't enough to boil over, more like a low simmer, but she knew this would bother her if she thought more about it. She shook her shoulders and let it go.

"Fine, I'm sorry," AJ eventually said. Now, she wasn't sure if Torryn would stay or not. This was the first time there was *actual* tension between them, and AJ was sure that if she pressed enough, it would have turned into an argument.

She didn't look down as she climbed over the ledge onto the rooftop. She stood there for a moment, waiting and looking for her friends, but refusing to see if Torryn followed when she heard the sounds of footsteps on the rickety ladder and then smelled Torryn's perfume, she glanced at the taller girl.

"It's fine," Torryn mumbled as she slipped her hands in her pockets.

AJ nodded and began leading the way to her friends, who were gathered around a makeshift bar.

"Something to drink?" AJ asked Torryn.

Torryn eyed the bar with obvious suspicion that only made AJ roll her eyes in return.

"You are aware that underage drinking falls under one of those illegal activities I mentioned before?"

"Good thing you're twenty-one, then."

"Yes, but you are not."

AJ stifled a chuckle that she quickly covered up as a cough.

"AJ!" Niki screamed when Torryn and AJ approached her at the bar. "Finally! I'm glad you two made it."

Niki folded AJ into a tight hug, squeezing the breath out of her. "Let me get you a drink," Niki said to them both as she released AJ and turned to the bar. She plucked two beers from the cooler, twisted off the caps and handed them over.

"Congratulations, again, on the big win." Niki said to Torryn, before winking at AJ. "Enjoy your party. I'm going to go mingle with the rest of my guests. I'll catch up with you later."

AJ chuckled as her best friend twirled away. "I think she might already be a little hammered."

Torryn shrugged, sipping her beer and fidgeting. As she went for another sip someone bumped into her, causing a small amount of the beer to spill on her chin and top of her shirt.

"Excuse you," Torryn muttered.

AJ couldn't help the smile that bloomed. "Uh," she pointed to Torryn's chin, "you have a little—" she waived her hand and Torryn made a move to wipe her face, "no, lower, here, let me—" and without thinking, AJ ran her thumb over the loose droplet of beer, wiping it away from Torryn's chin.

It wasn't until after she wiped her thumb off on her pants that she realized how close they were now, and how very little Torryn was breathing. Her own heart stopped beating as their eyes met—Torryn's saucer-wide and unblinking, and AJ's dilated and wanting.

When Torryn averted her eyes as she cleared her throat, AJ stepped back, shuffling her feet and looking anywhere but at Torryn.

"Do you play?" Torryn asked after a moment.

"Play?" AJ looked back, hopeful that it was a euphemism of sorts.

"Billiards."

AJ and Torryn turned to a weathered game table near the far wall.

"Never tried," AJ said with a slight shrug.

Torryn grinned and walked towards the table, picking up two cues on route. Handing AJ a pool cue, she explained the logistics of the game.

AJ watched as Torryn racked up the balls in the shape of a triangle. Her gaze remaining locked on Torryn's body and the way her jeans fit, firmly shaping her toned ass. AJ couldn't help but hope that what she felt between them was, indeed, chemistry. Between the events of earlier and the lack of progress, she wasn't all too sure now if her advances would be welcomed. That didn't stop her from openly staring at the girl, not even blushing when Torryn caught her. She took a sip of beer.

"You can go first," Torryn said.

AJ shifted her gaze between the table and Torryn, unsure of how to start the game, but unwilling to actually admit that she'd been too distracted to pay much attention.

"Here, I'll help you," Torryn offered as she moved to stand behind AJ. "Hold it like this."

She positioned AJ's hands on the cue after she placed her beer on the edge of the table, fingers of their left hands intertwined. "Bend over the table," Torryn whispered in her ear, as if this were a response and call to AJ's earlier flirting.

AJ swallowed, perspiration building up on her palms, forcing her to grip the cue tighter in order to avoid giving herself away, but then loosening it when Torryn told her to. She could feel Torryn's body pressed just barely against her own, how the heat radiated off her body and warmed AJ's back. There were small huffs of breath at the edge of her ear as Torryn explained how to aim and how to hold the cue. AJ thought she smelled of sunflowers and crisp cotton, like fresh laundry on a summer day, which oddly reminded her of home. Torryn's hands were softer than AJ would have thought for someone so active and athletic.

If Torryn moved, just enough, if she turned her head, AJ could press her lips to Torryn's, taste her, run her tongue over-

"I think you can handle it from here."

AJ felt a surge of disappointment when Torryn took a step back, and embarrassment that she couldn't really recall what Torryn has just said to her.

AJ took her first shot after a moment of reeling herself back in. Now, although she would like it to be, would not be the best time to try to kiss Torryn. She didn't make any of the balls in the pockets, but she felt a little better at the fact that she actually did hit the cue ball with enough force for it to knock into the others and separate them. When she turned around, she couldn't help but notice that Torryn was picking at her nails, as if she were just as nervous as AJ.

They didn't speak for a few more turns, Torryn landing balls left and right, and AJ missing most of her shots. The silence grew thicker each minute, so thick AJ thought she could cut it with a knife.

"So what's your major?" Torryn blurted out with a bit more force than necessary, as though the silence was smothering her the way it was with AJ.

AJ turned to look at Torryn, who had her lips scrunched up as if she didn't actually mean to ask the question. "English Lit. You?"

"Criminology."

This peeked AJ's interest, "Oh, that's really cool. Like, a Lawyer?"

"No, cop."

That explains a lot, AJ thought to herself. "Woman in a uniform, very hot."

Torryn didn't respond to the comment, but rather called corner pocket and the eight ball sailed into it. "Game over."

"Yeah," AJ said, "I'll um, I'll be right back. Will you be okay for a bit?"

"I'll be fine," Torryn assured her.

AJ made her way back down to Niki's apartment. It took several minutes to get through the line for the bathroom, where she splashed some cold water on her face. *Well, you wanted her to react to you,* AJ thought while trying to control the hormones surging throughout her body like an electric aftermath of being struck by lightning.

When she returned to the rooftop she went to the bar before going to search for Torryn. She leaned over the countertop and grabbed two more beers, hers forgotten and she wasn't sure about Torryn's. She then scanned the crowd and spotted Ava coming towards her.

"Hey. Where's Torryn?" Ava asked.

AJ nodded her head towards the silhouette of a girl leaning over the railing, looking into the night. She hadn't seen her before, but somehow when Ava asked, she knew exactly where Torryn was.

"Having a good time?"

"Yeah," AJ replied, "Not sure if she is though."

"Hmm, I don't recognize that look on you."

AJ turned to face Ava, "What look?" She questioned defensively.

"Mi amor, the love-sick puppy look. You're completely into this girl, aren't you?"

AJ opened her mouth to deny it, but she couldn't. Ava was right, of course. They had only known each other for a few weeks, and had hardly spent much time together, but there was just something about Torryn that AJ adored. There was also something else about her that AJ couldn't work out, but she lived for puzzles. Torryn had been standoffish, even awkward at times. Though, when it was just the two of them in the room, Torryn seemed to relax a little. AJ hardly knew anything about her other than the fact that somehow she was falling for Torryn, feeling as if she were drifting off to sleep, aware but unable to stop it.

"You shouldn't leave a pretty girl like that alone," says Ava. "You never know who might whisk her away."

AJ playfully shoved her friend, "yeah, yeah. I'm going."

"Good luck Romeo," Ava called out behind her.

She rolled her eyes and walked towards Torryn.

AJ slid up next to her, and leaned against the railing. "You there?" AJ asked, as she handed Torryn a beer.

Torryn smiled and looked at AJ, "Yeah, unless it's possible to be in two places at once."

"Well, just stand over a state line," AJ teased.

"Does that work for cities, too?"

AJ couldn't tell if Torryn was teasing or being serious as the girl's face gave absolutely nothing away. "You're not having fun, are you?"

"It's not that, it's just, I don't —"

"Well, I was going to suggest leaving—" AJ interrupted, trying to make it easier for Torryn.

Torryn eyed AJ. "I don't want to make you leave."

AJ leaned into her, their arms touching. "It's okay, I'm not really feeling it anymore, anyway." Torryn didn't have to know she was lying to benefit her.

They finished their beers quickly before searching for Niki and Ava. Niki whined about how early it was and that they should stick around. AJ then pointed out that the sun would be rising in a few short hours and some of them have class in the morning. They left to the sound of mocking boos and jeers.

In the parking lot of Niki's apartment building, a group of drunken guys brushed passed them. The boys were loud and slurring their words as they playfully shoved each other. AJ and Torryn watched them pile into a car and drive off.

AJ stopped walking. Her chest began to hurt as her heart fluttered, breath becoming labored with the pressure that began to build beneath her rib cage. She squatted down, feeling dizzy, as the world began to spin around her.

Torryn knelt in front of her and placed a strong hand on AJ's shoulder to steady her. "AJ, what's wrong?"

AJ's breaths were fast and shallow. She opened her mouth but couldn't speak. Sweat beaded on her forehead as she trembled, looking at the concrete below her feet.

"AJ look at me, focus on me," Torryn demanded, placing her other hand on AJ's knee before tilting AJ's head up by her chin,

Looking into Torryn's eyes, AJ tried to focus on her breathing. Tears ran down her cheeks. Torryn wrapped her in a firm, unyielding hug as one hand smoothed down her hair.

"Take me home," AJ whispered, almost inaudibly, still struggling to control her breathing.

****

Torryn walked AJ to her room and sat her on the bed.

"I'll be right back," Torryn whispered just before she left the room.

When Torryn returned she held a wet washcloth, which she pressed to the back of AJ's neck as she knelt before her. AJ bent over, allowing the gesture, and put her face in her hands.

"What happened back there?" Torryn asked.

"Panic attack," AJ responded too matter-of-factly, as if she's had to explain this before. It wasn't as if she thought Torryn didn't know *what* happened, but it was a precursor to the explanation of *why* it happened. AJ felt she owed it to Torryn to do so, especially since the other girl was taking the time to make sure she was alright. "It's kind of a recent development but I, um, get them sometimes. Usually when I get too scared, or stressed, or overwhelmed—or."

"What are you afraid of?" Torryn pressed when AJ stopped talking.

AJ shook her head. "I don't know. I guess when I saw those drunk frat boys get in the car it reminded me of my dad. He, um, the day of my graduation he was killed by a drunk driver. He left work early to see me walk across the stage," the words tumbled out in a rush, no breaths between. AJ could feel her palms start to sweat again but she couldn't stop now that she had started.

"I know this is really silly to think, but it feels like if I hadn't been graduating that day, then he wouldn't have left early and he wouldn't have been at the intersection at that time and he wouldn't have gotten hit. If it hadn't been for my graduation he would have been at work still."

"Hey," Torryn said, looking into AJ's eyes, "You know it's not your fault, what happened to your dad, right?"

"Yeah, I *know* that, but it doesn't *feel* that way. He was my *dad* and I *lost* him."

"I'm sorry you had to go through that."

AJ looked up at Torryn and couldn't help but act on the urge to touch her. She brought her hand to rest lightly on the girl's arm, fingers drifting over bare skin. "Thank you, y'know, for help me. A lot."

Torryn smiled.

AJ slid her hand from Torryn's arm to gently place it against the girl's neck, thumb coming to rest just on the tender spot underneath her ear. She felt Torryn's muscles tense as she did this. She leaned her forehead against Torryn's and hoped she didn't scare her off. AJ wanted to close the distance between them, to finally kiss her, but it could end badly. Their noses brushed together when Torryn pulled back.

"Why don't you lay down," Torryn said, "we can watch a movie until you fall asleep."

AJ watched as Torryn grabbed her laptop from her desk and powered it on. AJ didn't so much as lay down as she did lean against the wall, leaving enough room for Torryn to join her if she chose to. AJ tried to keep the eye roll and disappointment to herself, though, when she noticed that Torryn positioned herself on the floor, her back against the bed, laptop propped on her knees in such a way that it was easy for AJ to see. *How thoughtful,* she thought rueful, as she reached above her head and to the right to switch off the overhead light.

As the movie played a few moments later, AJ didn't even care what they were watching—most likely something streaming on Netflix—as she paid more attention to Torryn's face than anything. She loved the way Torryn's lips turned up at the goofy scenes an how she looked so serious during every other part. She just wished she could get Torryn to relax enough to smile like that all the time and decided that would be her mission.

She tried to keep her eyes open, because she knew when she awoke that Torryn would be gone. She blinked heavily, her eyes beginning to shift in and out of focus. Exhaustion swept over her in a instant, catching her off guard, and she let it, despite her attempts to just, stay, awake.

11

Now

I park in the hospital's parking lot and shake off the chill that runs across my back. I always hated going into hospitals, even before AJ was attacked, stemming from my days as a beat cop—never knowing if our victims would make it or not, if they had family waiting for them, scared for them, or if they were alone with no one so much as thinking about them—but now it just served as a reminder that AJ, like so many others, may not make it.

Dax and I make our way silently up the the ICU floor. When we approach the nurses' station, I ask for an update on AJ and flash my badge.

"No changes so far, detectives," the nurse responds softly.

I thank her and we make our way to AJ's room. Niki is standing outside the room talking quietly into her phone when we approached. We offer each other warm smiles. I pause at the threshold to the room, wondering if I can go in or not.

Leaning against the doorway, I watch Aidan sitting next to his mother, reading from a book and holding her hand.

He glances up and grins at me.

I leave Dax standing in the doorway and cross the room to Aidan. "How's she doing?"

"I just want her to wake up," he shrugs.

"Me, too."

"You catch the bastard that did this to her yet?"

"Hey! Language," I automatically reprimand without thinking. AJ wouldn't have liked Aidan cursing in that way. The occasional 'damn' was fine, but never anything derogatory.

He looks away and apologized, and I can't help but let out a tiny laugh.

"But did you?" He urges

I shake my head. "Not yet."

"Then, why are you here instead of out there looking for him!" He shouts, the question echoing in the small space.

"What's going on here?" I turn at the sound of Niki's voice, pressing with a simple look for her not to intervene.

"Aidan, the whole precinct is working really hard to find the person did this. We even have the FBI helping out."

Aidan's shoulder slump forward as he holds his head in his hands. "This...just...sucks," comes the muffled reply. I have to hold back from wrapping him in my arms like I used to when he was upset.

Stay professional, I berate myself. Again.

I point with my thumb to Dax. "This is my partner. We wanted to ask you some questions, maybe you could help us?"

He nods, sniffling, and straightens up.

I look at Niki. "We're going to take Aidan down to the cafeteria, get him some food. Maybe some ice cream."

She puts her hand on Aidan's shoulder when he walks past her. "I just talked to your grandma and she's on the first flight home. She'll be here in the morning."

"Okay, thanks, Aunt Niki."

Dax, Aidan, and I make our way towards the cafeteria, through the hospital's maze of corridors. No one speaks until Dax brings Aidan a plate of beige food and a bottle of water. We find an isolated table in the corner, away from enough ears to speak freely.

We start off easy, asking simple questions—*How often do you travel with your mom on a tour? How many does she do? Haw many books has she published? How long do her tours last?*—just to get an idea of a timetable and locations, breaking the ice.

The next set of questions are always designed to make people think, to really look at everyone as a suspect. It sometimes lends itself to false leads, but, ultimately, the more personal details we can get, the better. "Aidan, can you think of anyone who would have wanted to hurt your mom?"

His words came out garbled as he talked around a mouth full of food, "No. Everyone loved her."

"What about her readers?" Dax chimed in. "Did your mom have any obsessed or creepy fans?"

"She's gotten a lot of fan mail lately. But I don't really know what they write to her."

"Does she keep all of the mail?" I ask.

"She usually puts it all in a box until she has the chance to read it. After that she usually throws it away. She used to keep them all, though, but there are too much now."

Dax looks at me. "We should probably go through it, see if we find anything threatening."

"Do you think that would be okay?" I ask Aidan.

"Yeah. I guess. You can come over to the house after school tomorrow."

"Deal. What about in her *personal* life?"

"You mean like her friends?"

I pause, trying to articulate my thoughts. We have to rule out friends. There's also another part to my question that I'm not sure I want to know the answer to, but the detective in me needs to know, so I explain. "Yes, friends, or anyone you mom knows romantically? Typically, its those that are closest to us that—"

"Are you asking if my mom is seeing anyone?" He squints his eyes at me, as if it's a silly question, as if I should know the answer.

I nod.

"No, she's not dating anyone. I don't think she got over you breaking her heart," Aidan says with enough venom that would cause me to look at him as a suspect if he were anyone else.

The answer brings me both pain and relief. Did I ruin any chance of happiness for her? And, Jesus, how egotistical is that to think?

I choose not to linger on that right now.

"Have you seen anyone strange or suspicious hanging out around your home, or your mom, lately? Notice anyone following her, or anything happen out of the ordinary?" Asks Dax.

"Like a stalker?"

"Perhaps. It's not unlikely. Someone would have to have been aware of where she was going to be, at the very least."

"No. We only moved back to the States a week ago, she was finishing her book tour here," he said, his foot tapping nervously on the linoleum floor.

I pulled out a still-photo from the tape, the image of the hooded figure slightly blurry due to it being zoomed in. "Does this remind you of anyone?"

Aidan's brows furrow as he looks at the figure. "No. Well, I mean, it doesn't look like anyone *I* know, but—I don't know? Maybe. I mean I can't see their face so I don't—"

"Thank you, Aidan," I say to further assuage Aidan's agitation. "You've been a big help." I grab the photo off the table and Dax and I move to stand.

****

Dax and I arrive back at the station. Agent Drake is in the conference room, legs propped obnoxiously on top of the table. I'm instantly peeved. If it were anyone else that actually worked here, it wouldn't have been as annoying. I have too many other things to worry about, so I don't have the time or energy to deal with him right now.

During the ride from the hospital, a thought had occurred to me. I told Aidan that we always look at the romantic partner first. I may be AJ's last but I am certainly not the only. In fact, there is one for sure that I know of, I just need to find out his name.

I start searching through past case file on my computer. I type in AJ's given names and find what I'm looking for. A mug shot flashes up on my screen.

"Well, hello to you, too" Agent Drake quips as he stands and starts to move towards me.

"Sorry," I mutter as I catch Dax's eyes.

"Well, anyway, I'm caught up on your case now, and I think we have enough to build a solid profile."

"That's great." I say distractedly.

"Who's that?" He asks as he stands behind me, looking over my shoulder at the picture of Derek Williams.

It's a stretch but we have to start somewhere. "This is a person of interest," I tell Drake and Dax as I pull out my phone and make a call.

The line rings only twice before it's answered with a brief greeting of name and department.

"Joel, where are we with the DNA analysis?"

His teeny voice comes through the speaker. "You know how long that takes, Tor."

"Yeah, I know, but expedite it?"

"Not without Captain's approval."

"Fine. What about possible fingerprints?"

"Well, most of the ones found at the scene belong to the victim."

"And the others?"

"Could be anyone who took their trash out to that dumpster. We have partial of known homeless, the shop owner, whatever her name is—"

"Yeah, got it." I pinch the bridge of my nose. "How soon can you get a match with specific in the system?"

"Depends on the servers. Usually it takes an hour or two. Got someone in mind?"

"Yeah, run the partials against Derek, D-E-R-E-K, Williams, W-I-L-L-I-A-M-S. Date of birth, March fifteen eighty-six. He's a convicted sex offender so he has a file."

"Okay, got it."

"And, Joel?"

"Yeah, Tor?"

"Call me back, will ya?"

"Sure, sure." He disconnects the call and I slip my phone back into my pocket.

It was now late in the evening, but there was still time to pay Mr. Williams a visit. I stand up and start to walk out of the room. Halfway to the door I turn and look back at the two men still standing by my desk, obviously lost, "Coming?"

In the elevator down to the parking lot, I offer a rundown of Derek Williams, a man with a criminal record and Aidan's biological father. "He has a history of minor sexual assault charges, only one stuck. Thirteen years ago he was found guilty of the statutory rape of the then fifteen -year-old Adelaide James for which he served eight of his sentenced ten years in prison, released on parole for good behavior.

****

In the car we discuss strategy and decide that we'd come at him hard. Given his history we'd probably get a better reaction if I, a woman, was hostile towards him in questioning. Dax would play good cop and Drake would observe Williams' body language. A part of me detested the Good Cop, Bad Cop trope, but it was effective with certain types of people.

With Agent Drake behind me, examining my every move and motive, I have to keep it together more than ever. I take a calming breath and knock on the door.

When the tan-skinned man with dirty blond hair opens the door, Dax and I flash our badges. Agent Drake hangs back as planned.

"Derek Williams?" I ask.

"Yeah?"

"Detective Torryn Michealson, PHPD. This is my partner, Detective Dax Grieson, and Special Agent Caspian Drake with the FBI."

"Okay?" He doesn't move further way from the door, but does close it slightly, as if to shield the living room.

"We're investigating a string of homicides in the area. May we come in?" Dax asks

"Look, you're barking up the wrong tree here, man. There's no reason for you to be on my doorstep."

Before Dax can answer, I interrupt, growing impatient already. "One of the victims is a Ms. Adelaide James. Still think we don't have a reason to be here?"

"What?" The guy's face pinches in what I can only assume to be a mix of confusion and anger, maybe just a bit of hesitation. "That's a name I haven't heard in thirteen years."

"You don't seem that shaken by the news." I say.

"Lady. That girl is the reason I spent eight years of my life in prison," he said defensively while stepping away from the door, letting it remain open for us to come in.

Anger bubbles at the surface at the comment. *Of course, there's always someone else to blame for your actions.* I subtly pick at my ring finger with my thumb as I walked past.

"Have a seat," Williams says, waving towards the couch. We remain standing while he takes a seat in the recliner opposite.

"That's pretty rich to blame a girl of fifteen for your poor choices," I blurt out, unable to hold back.

He jumps off the seat, his hands waving wildly as he yells. "We me at a *college* party! How the hell was I supposed to know she was only fifteen? She looked older, so, yeah, I fuckin' blame her."

"Seems like you're holding on to a lot of anger," Dax points out.

He folds his hands together, lacing his fingers, and gives us each a bitter smile. Something dark gleaming in his eyes.

"Detective," he replies slowly, as if he's trying to make sure he doesn't lash out, again. "I am a registered sex offender for the rest of my life because I had consensual sex with a girl I thought was of college age. I am limited in everything I do and where I can live. Of course, I have some anger."

"Angry enough to kill? You saw how far she's come, that you didn't ruin her life like you did yours and it made you furious. You wanted to destroy her life because you don't have one. Is that it? Did you try to kill her Mr. Williams?"

"Now, hold on just a minute, lady," he snapped as he put is palms in front of him. "I haven't done anything to anybody. Why would I? I'm trying to get my life together."

I didn't lay off. He needed to sweat, to feel the pressure. "Oh, the angry revenge not motive enough for you, Mr. Williams? Maybe you wanted the boy? She wouldn't let you see your son so you decided to kill her and take your claim to him? Is that your idea of payback? Take her life and her son away from her?"

Williams' face turned red, sweat beading on his receding hairline. "I don't want anything to do with the kid! If I did, don't you think I would have reached out by now?"

"*Did* you try to reach out to her, Mr. Williams?" Dax asks. "We'd understand if you did. If I had a kid out there somewhere I'd want to try to make contact with the mother. I'd want to get to know my son."

"I think it's time for you to leave," Williams implores, folding his arms across his chest. The three of us share a look, then make our way to the door.

Dax turned back after opening the front door, "Oh, one more thing Mr. Williams. Where were you Tuesday night at say eight o'clock?"

"I was working."

"Don't think about leaving town, Mr. Williams."

"Wouldn't dream of it," he spits right before he slams the door in our faces.

"Well, that was fun," Dax said as we made our way back to the car.

"You have no idea," I say.

"He never answered the question." Agent Drake spoke up, scratching his chin.

Drake was so quiet I had almost forgotten he was there. "Which question?"

"If he tried to get in touch with her when got out. Given his reaction, I'm willing to bet he did try."

We get into my car.

"If he did, he probably didn't want to incriminate himself. Reaching out to her would most likely have been a violation of his parole," I replied.

"The guy's a creep but I don't think he's our creep," Dax suggests.

"My gut tells me you're right," Drake said.

12

Then

AJ tried focusing on the textbooks and notes in front of her. Finals were next week and all she could think about was the girl in the next room as the sounds of classical music wafted through the walls. The serious girl who only very briefly lets her guard down. The girl that took care of her a few weeks ago when she had a panic attack, who listened as she spoke about her father being killed by an drunk driver. The girl who makes AJ's skin tingle at the mere sight of her. She often found herself smiling at the way Torryn's eyes changed shades of green depending on her mood and was pleasantly surprised when she realized she had started to be able to distinguish the changes in her roommate's odd moods.

But, it was more than just the physical attraction that pulled at her, Torryn made her feel safe. Even with the distance between them over the last few weeks, which AJ found stranger than usual, she genuinely enjoyed being near Torryn. Although, today she found Torryn's choice of study music slightly annoying. AJ understood that classical music is supposed to be relaxing, but it isn't having that effect on her at the moment.

In attempt to drown out her thoughts, she put her headphones on, chose her '90s best pop' playlist and turned the music up. It was her temporary cure for the thoughts that took over her mind, and she hoped it would allow her to focus as she tapped her foot anxiously on the floor.

AJ didn't hear the knock on her door when, in frustration, she threw her note book at the wall before she realized it was now open and Torryn stood in the doorway. A hint of a smile flushed across Torryn's lips, which only intensified the feeling of horror AJ felt at being caught throwing a college student's equivalent of a toddler's tantrum.

Torryn quickly apologized, "it just opened when I knocked. I, um. I was about to leave, sorry for intruding."

"No, I'm sorry. I uh- -" words failed AJ as Torryn stepped just inside the room, her stomach twisted with mortification. She opened her mouth in attempt to continue speaking, but no sounds came out.

"Looks like you're studying too hard. Your friends are here," Torryn offered in explanation of the intrusion.

"Why?" AJ said curiously, momentarily forgetting that she made plans. It wasn't until she watched a look of confusion dance across Torryn's face that it all came back. "Oh! Right! Uh, thanks."

AJ looked at Torryn in the doorway for a moment, taking in her slightly disheveled and tired appearance, which somehow made the tiny scar across her eyebrow more prominent. AJ couldn't recall seeing Torryn look so stressed before. She shuffled her feet, beginning to mutter under her breath about people not texting or calling before showing up as she turned to grab her jacket.

"Uh, we won't—I mean— you didn't see that," AJ rushed out as she passed Torryn, who stood silently in the hallway. A small, amused smile graced the girl's lips and caught AJ off guard.

"Excuse me," she breathed as she closed the door and stepped into Torryn's personal space. A brief moment, too brief, really, passed where they shared the same air and AJ couldn't even breathe it in for fear of further embarrassing herself. It passed just as quickly as it had happened as soon as Torryn stepped back enough to let AJ by.

"You're awfully red," Ava pointed out once AJ entered the living room.

The sound of a door closing made it clear the Torryn wouldn't be making her way towards them and AJ instantly regretted everything she had done today.

"Miss tall, dark, and moody get you all hot and bothered?" Niki teased.

AJ didn't deny the accusation. She only muttered a sharp *shut up* in response.

Niki smirked. "AJ, I love you, but you have been pinning over that girl for weeks. If you don't do something about it, I'm going to have to do it for you."

"Jesus fu—shush! What if she heard you?" AJ

replied in one massive breath, stumbling over her words.

"Well, someone has to tell the girl that you're completely in love with her."

AJ groaned. *Lust, definitely. Love? Highly unlikely. Right?* AJ thought to herself. She barely knew Torryn and, so far, what she did know was still wrapped up like a mystery. She couldn't be in love with someone she hardly knew. Could she?

"Hey, Torryn," shouted Niki down the hallway, voice echoing in the tiny space and bringing AJ out of her thoughts, "Would you like to join us for a night out?"

AJ threw her head into her hands. She hadn't mentioned to her friends that she felt that Torryn had seemed to have been avoiding her ever since Niki's party, which she had hoped was due to finals coming up.

Torryn's voice echoes down the hallway, impressive considering that AJ could have sworn the door was still closed since she hadn't heard it open. "No, thank you! I need to study for finals."

"No big deal!" Niki shrugs, a mischievous look speeding across her face, "But you know what is a big deal? AJ's birthday. We're going out this weekend celebrating before everyone heads home for winter break. You should come with."

A door opens and Torryn soon enters the living room. AJ catches Torryn's eyes and didn't really know what the other girl was waiting for.

Ava clears her throat.

"Right, yes, you should definitely come," AJ announces a little to enthusiastically.

"I think I can fit that into my schedule," Torryn says, before she disappears back down the hall. Her bedroom door snaps shut.

"There," Niki tells AJ, "I made it easy for you."

AJ glared at Niki.

"So, can we go now?" Ava asked, always playing referee between AJ and Niki as if they were siblings and she were the middle rather than AJ.

"Why don't we stay in?" Niki offered. "Get some pizza, drink some beer...wait for the rest of your suitemates to come home."

"We can't have alcohol in the dorms," AJ replied.

"Since when have we followed the rules? Is your girlfriend going to rat us out?"

"She's not my girlfriend," AJ muttered glancing toward the hallway. "Fine. Let's stay in."

Niki strode out of the dorm with a triumphant expression on her face. She returned thirty minutes later carrying two twelve-packs of cold beer.

"Hey, look who I ran into," Niki said as she walked into the apartment, holding the door for Liam who was carrying three very large pizza boxes in his arms.

"We having a party then?" Asked Liam.

She placed the beer on the breakfast bar, then turned and kissed Liam on the cheek as he did the same with the pizza. Ryder walked in behind them, carrying two more twelve-packs, which he placed next to the others.

"Should be enough!" Ryder said to no one in particular.

AJ and Ava stood from their seats on the couch to join the others in the kitchen, where Ava took over handing out plates and pizza.

"Go take this one to Torryn," Ava instructed as she passed a plate to AJ.

AJ smiled at her friend's thoughtfulness and walked down the hallway, holding the pizza.

"Come in," replied Torryn's voice to AJ knocking on her bedroom door.

Opening the door, AJ saw Torryn sitting cross-legged on her bed, wearing flannel pajamas and a black tank top. Open laptop and books sprawled out in front of her.

"Sorry to interrupt," begins AJ in a hushed whisper as she tried to avoid looking at the cleavage that peeked through the top of the tank. " I just came to offer you food," AJ said holding out the plate of pizza. "Though, in hindsight, you probably don't eat this kind of stuff anyway."

A large, and very real, smile spread across Torryn's face. It even reached her eyes. AJ had never seen this particular smile before. She liked it.

"I thought you were going out?"

"Yeah, but then we decided to just stay in, hang out. We'll keep it down so you can study. The offer still stands for you to join me — us, join *us.*"

Torryn snorted through her nose, "Thank you for the pizza," she said as she held out a hand to take the proffered plate.

AJ immediately moved further into the room, a little surprised that Torryn would accept. "No problem. Enjoy your studying."

Torryn nodded, and , as silence filled the room, AJ turned and left, smiling to herself as she made her way back to her friends. Everyone was already gathered in the living room, holding plates of pizza in their laps as they nursed beers. AJ took an empty spot next to Niki who handed her a plate and a beer that was already open. Conversation floated around on what to do in between bits about school, finals, and for some, their jobs.

Just as AJ had settled into the flow of conversation with the group, Torryn came out of her room, still in her pajamas and wearing a hoodie over her tank top.

AJ followed Torryn's eyes around the room and inwardly groaned, knowing that the beers would be the source of the problem for the RA. "AJ a word?"

AJ handed her beer to Niki and followed Torryn down the hall.

"You know the university's policy on drinking in the dorms," Torryn told AJ with a fixed stare.

"Yeah, I know, we're just having a few beers. We're being responsible."

"We could get into serious trouble, I could lose my scholarship and my job."

"Not if we don't get caught," AJ said.

"You do realize I'm studying to be in law enforcement, right? I can't allow this to go on, it's against the rules and you're under age."

"First off," AJ said frustrated, "I was still nineteen a few weeks ago when you were drinking with me at Niki's party. Secondly, I promise we won't get out of hand. Please, just let us blow off some steam. We've all be working really hard this semester and we need this. Especially you. You're always so tense, and you hardly ever come out of your room anymore."

Without thinking, AJ grabbed Torryn's hand, and stepped closer to her, their faces only inches apart. AJ couldn't read Torryn's troubled expression as she looked down at their hands and AJ couldn't figure out what she was going to say next.

"I'm sorry, we'll go." AJ began to turn away, dropping Torryn's hand.

"Wait," Torryn sighed, "Stay. But no one drives home if they've been drinking. Got it?"

AJ pursed her lips, grabbed Torryn's wrist and pulled her towards the living room. "Come on, you've been studying for hours."

Niki was the first to speak up when AJ and Torryn emerged into the living room. "So, are we all in trouble?"

AJ looked at the group then at Torryn, who had simply rolled her eyes. She chuckled, then announced, "Of course not. Carry on."

The pair sat next to each other on the floor. Niki handed Torryn a beer, winking as she did so.

"So, what did we decide on?" AJ asked the group.

13

Now

Agent Drake was the first to speak as we pulled into the parking lot of the station, "I was able to create a geographical profile, and a decent one of our person of interest, too."

I turn around to face him, studying his body language and hoping that he didn't purposely allow us to waste time with Derek Williams.

"Hopefully it proves helpful. If we don't catch this killer soon I'm going to—"I stop myself from finishing that sentence.

"We will," Dax said, placing his hand on my shoulder.

I turn to face my partner. "Preferably before Tuesday when we find ourselves standing over another victim."

"Well, let's get on with it then." Agent Drake said as he got out of the car.

Dax and I follow. We make our way to the conference room, where Drake unravels a map of Parker Heights, population 116,000.

"I put this together a little earlier, just to help visualize everything," Drake says as he points to various colored markings on different locations.

Pointing to the red marks, Drake continues to explain, "These circles are where the victims were found. Using criminal geographical targeting I've determined that this area," he said tracing his finger along an irregular shaped circle drawn in blue, "is the most probable area for the killer to either live or work."

I study the map. It was still a large-sized area. If this geographical profiling actually works it could help us narrow down the suspect pool. Of course, we have to have a suspect pool to start with. I notice right away that Derek Williams' home was on the edge of the blue area. *So not entirely a waste of time.*

Drake continues, "Keep in mind profiling isn't an exact science but it's a good start. Our killer probably came from a dysfunctional home life, most likely abused or a witness to abuse. Though it's not unheard of, serial killers typically don't cross-racial lines so our perp is probably white male, given that the victims are white women.

There were no hesitation marks on your first victim so I'd guess this wasn't their first kill. I ran your signature through the FBI database, but it came back with no match of any known persons of interest. My guess is that the perp started with animals before moving on to women based on the precision and knowledge something like this takes."

I consider Drake's words, soaking them in. He wasn't wrong. According to the M.E. report, the victims all had one fatal stab wound that went through the great arteries and on to the left atrium. The victims hemorrhaged and died within a few minutes. It had to take profound knowledge to hit that same spot each time. The M.E. also determined, based on the direction of the bruising around the victim's neck, our killer is left-handed. This information was the one thing that caused any doubt that AJ's attack was even related to the others. Drake was still going over the profile, so I put those thoughts away to turn my attention back to what he was saying.

"Lack of evidence left behind indicates an organized killer, so we're probably looking for someone in their late twenties to mid thirties. Though age is one of the hardest things to predict. It has to take incredible strength to stab a knife through the chest cavity enough to puncture the heart. They don't seem keen on torture given how quickly the victims would have bled out, so their motive is unlikely to be related to a God complex or any personal gain, sexual or otherwise.

Considering the only commonality between your victims is their physical appearance, it wouldn't surprise me if our killer wanted to rid the world of blond haired, blue-eyed women. We figure out why, we figure who your killer is. The last attack, though, assuming it's the same person that committed the others, is troublesome for two reasons. Either they are deescalating, which could lead to a much higher body count, and quickly, or your last victim was the intended victim all along. Their endgame, so to speak."

He paused to look over the pictures that are still

hanging on the board. "Either way, she," he pointed to AJ's photo, "was a personal attack. But the only way to know that is if we catch the kill, or—"

"Or wait to see if we get another victim," I finish.

"Bingo."

"If Ms. James was the intended victim then delving into her life is going to be our best bet in finding the killer," Dax speaks up for the first time since entering the station. "We've already interviewed her thirteen-year-old son."

"Could he be a possible suspect?" Drake asks.

"There is no way in hell that boy hurt his mom, or anyone else for that matter," I react immediately. *Way to keep if cool,* I chastise myself.

Drake holds his hands out in front of himself, "It was a logical question, detective. According to the statement from the bookshop owner and the video, we're looking for someone much smaller than the average adult male. A teenage boy would fit that description, though not the probable age."

I knew Drake was right, but to hear the question reminded me of just how close to home this case was. We have to look at all angles, all suspects, I know. In a case with no leads and very little evidence everyone is a suspect. It was truly a completely logical question. Unlike Agent Drake though, I know Aidan. I know he'd never be able to hurt a soul, especially his own mother.

Do not get yourself kicked off this case. I breathe. "It wouldn't hurt to have Joel run the DNA for a mitochondrial match to rule him out. I'm meeting up with Aidan James tomorrow, actually, to search through his mother's fan mail. Maybe that will produce some leads."

"I'll go with you," Drake offered, "If you don't mind."

"Sure, but I'm driving."

Drake opened his mouth but before he could respond, Dax put up a hand, halting any protest. "Don't even argue, my friend," Dax advises. "She *always* drives."

"One more thing," Drake said, "If our prep is on a mission and Ms. James is the endgame, they catch wind that she's alive, they'll try again. Let's have a uniformed officer posted outside her room at all times."

We agree that a security detail would be a good idea. The three of use went to Lieutenant Harris' office to request a twenty-four hour detail on AJ. Once approved, we set about finding a uniformed officer to agree to work some over-time tonight until we could get a scheduled assignment out during tomorrow's debriefing. We catch up with officer Lipscomb, a young officer who was eager to prove himself, and roped him into taking the first shift. With that settled, Dax went home to his wife and kids, while I debated on going home or going to the hospital. I decided home would be the safest choice.

In the parking lot of the station, Agent Drake calls out to me and I try my hardest not to roll my eyes. I just want this day, this case, to be over.

He calls out again as he jogs up beside me. "Detective Michealson. Can I speak with you a moment"

I nod even as I open my car door, reach over and

start my engine.

"I think we got off to a bad start. I'm only here to help, not take over your case."

"Don't take it personally," I shrug.

"So, you're like this with everyone?"

"Pretty much."

He looks at me, then, and I can't help feeling like I'm in trouble, like I'm sitting in the principal's office or in detention. I slip my hands in my pockets just to have something to do.

"A good detective knows when to set her pride aside and accept help. Don't let you get the best of you. There's a lot I could teach you.'

I don't respond.

"Well, have a good night, Detective Michealson."

He turns and begins to walk away before I have the chance to respond. I slip into my driver's seat and slam the door closed.

I shouldn't let his words get to me. *If only he knew what the case means to me,* I thought. But, perhaps, he had a point. I shouldn't even be on this case. My connection to the sixth victim, despite it being years ago, makes me an ethical and professional liability. If there's a trial, they could use that against me, against the evidence, and twist it to fit their needs. I've got to control this. I've got to focus.

I check the time. I realize that visiting hours at the hospital wouldn't be over for another hour or so and as I put the car in drive my destination changes.

14

Then

Liam suggested a game of 'Never Have I ever.' AJ groaned as everyone agreed. She always ended up completely smashed by the end of this game. With only two people in the room that really knew her, she hoped that it wouldn't get so bad this time. So long as her friends didn't gang up on her, she might have a chance of making it out alive. The game was a good —albeit sneaky—way to get to know other people, though, and AJ was curious to know how Torryn would react to the game.

Torryn leaned over and whispered in AJ's ear, "What's 'Never Have I Ever'?"

AJ shivered as Torryn's breath ghosted over her ear. She whispered back, "It's a drinking game. You say something that you've never done and anyone who has done it has to drink. The object is to get everyone else drunk before yourself."

Torryn nodded in response.

"I'll start," AJ offered. The game would move in a clockwise rotation, giving Torryn the chance to go last and see how it's played. "I'll make this one easy. Never have I ever…had a sibling."

Ava, Ryder, and Liam drink.

Ava was next, "Never have I ever…been arrested."

Ryder was the only one to drink.

"Aye, mate, you've got to tell us the story on that," Liam said.

"Not much to tell. Got into a fight with my sister's ex-boyfriend. Hurt him enough so that he'd leave her alone."

Liam narrowed his eyes. "What did he do?"

AJ could only imagine what the boyfriend did. By Ryder's expression, it clearly wasn't good and at the thought of it, AJ's blood simultaneously ran cold and boiled over.

"He was an asshole, man, but we didn't know about everything until she showed up one day at our parents' house," he started to explain, but swallowed before continuing, "with fresh bruises and a huge cut on her arm."

AJ breathed slowly, trying to stave off the rising bile in her throat.

"Hey, you don't have to talk about—"Liam tried to interrupt.

"He got what he deserved and I don't regret doing it." Ryder finished firmly and it seemed to solidify something for Liam, because he only nodded, obviously impressed.

Everyone was silent for a moment, not knowing what to say or how to continue the game now that the atmosphere was heavy with the knowledge of what Ryder, and his sister, had been through.

"Well," Torryn piped in and AJ swirled her head

to look at her, "I think you did the right thing. Abuse victims have a hard time being believed, and an even harder time going through the system to prevent anything from happening to them. You protected your family."

AJ blinked. Wasn't Torryn going into the police force? Wouldn't she be on the side of the system?

It seemed like the others were surprised, too, if their face were anything to go by.

"Thanks," Ryder replied sincerely. He clapped his hands together, then, getting the attention of everything at once. "Alright, whose turn is it?"

"Mine," Liam replied. "Never have I ever...gone skinny dipping," he finished with a lewd wag of his eyebrows.

Ava, Niki, AJ and Ryder all took a sip of their drinks. AJ stole a glance at Torryn wondering what she was like as a teenager. *What would make her drink?*

"Never have I ever done drugs," Niki said after Liam.

"Does pot count?" Ryder asked.

"Uh, yeah, it's still a drug even if you think it's not." AJ said, rolling her eyes.

Ryder and Ava were the only two that drank.

"Never have I ever been to another country," Torryn said after a quick pause.

Liam mumble about that being unfair as he and AJ took a drink.

AJ glanced at Torryn, who kept switching her gaze between Liam and AJ. It took her a moment to realize that Torryn probably wanted more information. "Oh, I went to Europe for a bit and

Liam—"

"Was born in Liverpool, love, so this is the new country for me," he chuckled when he finished AJ's sentence.

"Alright, baby round over," Niki said when the game made its way back to AJ. "Make it a good one."

"Fine, never have I ever...had sex on my best friend's bed."

Ava laughed at the glare Niki gave AJ as both she and Ryder drank. AJ knew that Niki would have to drink because it was her who walked in on Niki having sex on her bed when she arrived home from theater rehearsal freshman year of high school.

Niki got her revenge when it came to her turn. She scanned from AJ to Torryn and back, "Never have I ever...had sex with a girl."

Both boys drank. So did AJ and Torryn. The girls shared a look as the sipped their beer. AJ smiling into the bottle as Torryn raised one eyebrow at her. She would have been mad at Niki if it weren't for a newfound confidence she felt, now that she knew for a fact that Torryn was into girls. They played a few rounds, each one getting more and more ridiculous than the last, eventually leading to everyone drinking on the last round—Never have I ever been born—before they were ready to call it a night.

The boys switched on their video game console, gearing up to pull an all-nighter with Call of Duty. AJ stood to start picking up their empty plates and bottles, throwing everything into the trash. She wasn't at all surprised, honestly, when Torryn retreated to her room quietly after awkwardly standing in the middle of the room. When AJ turned around, she saw Niki and Ava put on their jackets.

"Uh, guys," AJ said, stopping them, "you can't leave."

"Why not?" Niki asked.

"I made a deal with Torryn that I wouldn't let you leave if she let us keep the beer."

"Shit, fine," Niki replied with a roll of her eyes, whipping off her jacket in one smooth motion.

Ava stifled a yawn but accepted the information. "Okay, but where will we sleep?"

AJ looked around and saw that the boys had successfully taken over the living room so that wasn't an option. She'd probably wake up to them passed out on the couch in the morning.

"Come on," AJ said as she led them to her room. Her bed was barely big enough for two but she offered it to Ava and Niki anyway.

"What about you?" Ava asked.

"I'll just grab a blanket and hit the floor," she shrugged, "it's fine. Besides, Niki's already passing out."

True enough, when AJ indicated the direction of her bed, Niki had already claimed a good portion of the bed as her own.

With Ava distracted by the image of Niki's face smushed into her arm, one leg dangling of the edge of the bed, AJ swiftly exited the room. As AJ emerged from her room, Torryn opened the door to her own bedroom. She was no longer wearing her hoodie and pants, but sported a tight fitting tank top and boy shorts. AJ was momentarily distracted, not expecting for Torryn's sleepwear to look like that. For some reason, she thought the other would sleep in workout clothes.

"Aren't you going to bed?" Torryn inquired, looking slightly uncomfortable as she fidgeted in the doorway.

"Uh, yeah, was. Niki and Ava have my bed."

"Oh."

"Yeah, uh, would you happen to have an extra blanket I could use? Or a pillow? Anything to make the floor less uncomfortable." AJ plowed through, scratching the back of her head.

After a moment, Torryn stepped aside and motion for AJ to enter her room. When she had offered Torryn pizza earlier, she hadn't really looked around or paid much attention to anything. Now, however, she noticed that Torryn's room was a lot neater and more organized than hers would probably ever be. It made the space seem larger than it was, so maybe there was a benefit after all, to being neat. Her bed was pushed into the corner to allow more space in the center of the room, probably for her workouts, AJ decided. There wasn't much in the way of useless decorations, like posters, or pictures hanging on the wall.

Torryn opened her closet door. "I'm not sure if I have a blanket thick enough to make the floor actually comfortable."

Torryn pulled out a blanket from her closet. "The rooms are a little crowded for three. So, you can take the blanket, or you can stay here," Torryn offered as she sat on the bed, placing the blanket beside her.

AJ stopped breathing for a moment as she considered what Torryn was suggesting and wondered if she was aware of the undercurrent to her offer. She didn't recall Torryn drinking much during the game, maybe, at most, two beers. The memory, however, of her answers to the sex questions came flitting back and made her heart pound heavily against her chest.

"You can share the bed, if you want, or you can sleep on the floor. Your choice," Torryn offered again, shrugging as she settled back against the pillows.

AJ closed the bedroom door and glanced between the floor and the bed, considering the implications of both. Making a decision, she took a deep breath and climbed onto the bed. "Yeah, I'm not about to wake up tomorrow morning stiff as a board," she explained as she maneuvered her way to lay on the inside of the bed with her back against the wall, giving Torryn plenty of space on her open side. Despite hoping that maybe Torryn wasn't as reserved as she came off as, AJ sighed when Torryn turned off the lamp and lay on the edge of the bed facing away from her.

She felt awkward with the situation, as they were trying not to touch each other or cross a line AJ knew would be impossible to uncross. It was far too soon and she didn't want something being brushed off as a drunken mistake. Her mind drained by impulse and exhaustion, AJ decided to take a smaller risk. "It's a small bed, y'know, don't be afraid of getting into my personal space."

It was silent for a moment, both of them

unmoving in the face of AJ's statement, until
Torryn let out a small sigh, as if she needed to think
about the pros and cons of the situation. AJ silently
congratulated herself once Torryn scooted further
into the middle of the bed, her body heat more
noticeable now.

AJ allowed herself another risk for the night,
knowing she could blame it on the alcohol making
her loose if Torryn questions anything, as she
placed her arm around Torryn's abdomen and
pulled her backwards to close the last inch of space
between them. She rested her arm gently under
Torryn's ribcage. AJ felt Torryn clench her muscles
though she didn't offer any resistance and
eventually relaxed into the embrace enough for AJ
to smile. *It was a pretty smooth line,* she had to
admit. With her arm draped over Torryn, she could
feel the brunette relax further, breathing becoming
slower, as she fell asleep. She followed Torryn's
lead not a moment after.

****

AJ stirred as she felt Torryn slowly slip out from
her hold and sit up. She groaned as she opened one
eye and saw the digital clock on Torryn's desk read
5:30am.

"Sorry," Torryn whispered, "I tried not to wake
you."

"It's way too early," AJ mumbled sleepily as she
reached out and pulled Torryn back down beside
her.

AJ quickly opened her eyes in a slight panic as

she realized what she just did. She expected Torryn to shoot from the bed and tell her it was time to leave. Instead, Torryn just rolled to her other side and faced her.

"I was going to go for a run," Torryn said softly, whispering it as if AJ wasn't already awake.

AJ rolled her eyes. "From the pizza right?"

Torryn smiled. "Yeah, that was a lot of calories."

AJ chuckled. She hadn't seen this side of Torryn before, it was a refreshing change. Slowly, AJ moved her hand down to Torryn's hip and held her breath as Torryn closed her eyes. AJ could see the muscles in Torryn's cheeks tighten, her jaw hardening in a clench.

AJ whispered back, "but, the sun isn't even up, yet. Also, your hair is a mess."

Torryn opened her eyes, got off the bed and began running her fingers through her hair before she reached for her hairbrush that rested on the desk. "This is part of my daily routine. You can join me if you want or you can sleep in. I won't be long."

AJ considered the offer as she watched Torryn grab a pair of sweatpants and a tank from her dresser.

"Well, I won't be able to go back to sleep, now, so what the hell, might as well go for a run," AJ snarked. She could have sworn that the rapid movement of Torryn's shoulders meant she was holding back laughter at her expense.

AJ went to her own room to gather some appropriate running attire. Soon, they were both dressed and met in the living room, where, AJ predicted, the boys were passed out on the couch and floor. After the both double checked to make sure they had their phones and their keys, they left, picking out playlists to listen to as they ran around campus.

15

Now

Visiting hours were almost over by the time I arrive to the ICU section of the hospital. I explain to the doctor on duty the situation of the case. I'm told that they have weaned AJ off the medication that was keeping her in the coma but she hasn't woken up yet. The doctor allows me to set up a chair outside of AJ's room for Officer Lipscomb, who would be here as soon as he finished the dinner I advised he actually eat instead of skipping. This would give me enough time to pop in and check on AJ.

"Hey you," I whisper in the quiet room. "So, they took you off the medicine keeping you asleep. I don't know if you can hear me, but I'd really like it if you could wake up. I could really use your help with this case."

My chest begins to ache the longer I stare at her. Some basic instinct in me that still exists after all these years wants to lie beside her, wrap her in my arms. But there's still to much that happened between us, and then this brutal attack happens and

I can't allow myself to think, or function, on 'what if's. They don't exist.

I decide to focus on work, and pull my three-inch ring binder from my bag. I carefully scrutinize each section, reading over the case notes, witness statements, evidence logs, the medical examiner's reports, and reviewing crime scene photos.

Connecting to the hospital's free and painfully slow Wi-Fi, I not for the first time, begin my Google search of possible murder weapons. According to the description of the wounds it could be any number of variety of straight edged knives. This is, obviously, a dead-end.

I move on to studying the perimeter of our geographical profile. Not the most affluent side of town. Mostly old apartment buildings and small, run-down businesses.

A nurse walks into the room and I move to put away my binder and leave. She raises a hand to stop me and speaks before I have a chance to ask her anything. "I just need to change her bandages and check her vitals." She explains with sympathy, cocking her head just ever so slightly with understanding eyes.

Did my face give away that much? Or did she just know, instinctively, like mothers do about their children that lie to them?

"Just stay over there and stay quiet. You can stay for however long you need to be." She continues as I move off to the side.

As she tends to AJ, I count twelve sets of stitches sewn about her abdomen. The sight makes my own stomach itch.

"Wounds seem to be healing well, no infections. Vitals are strong," the nurse informs me, though I'm sure she doesn't have to at this point, before making her way out of the room. I resume my spot next to her bed and rest my head back against the chair, trying to keep my eyes open to continue my reading.

"Well, here's something I didn't expect to see."

The whisper of the familiar voice doesn't startle me awake, and I'm glad I have a chance to regroup. My head is resting gently against AJ's hip, though, I'm not sure when that happened, and I stay there as my eyes come to focus. It's still dark out and visiting hours obviously aren't over yet, so I haven't been out too long. When I look up, the sight of a beautiful, blonde-haired, fifty-year-old woman meets my gaze.

"Hello, Mrs. James," I whisper through a broken yawn. I smile gently at her, knowing that she probably understands better than anyone my position right now.

She leans down and hugs me tight. "Hello, Torryn."

Hailey James cups my cheeks in her hands, looking me over in much the same way I did with Aidan two days earlier. Before I can say anything she embraces me in another hug. When she releases me, I move aside so she can get closer to her daughter.

"The nurse says she's doing well, considering her current condition," I announce.

"My daughter is a fighter, she'll make it through. She always has."

I check the time on my phone; Officer Lipscomb

should already be stationed outside the door. I step back slightly and crane my head to see out the door.

"He's out there," Mrs. James informs me. "That young police officer, though everyone looks young to me these days."

"I'll be leaving soon," I say bluntly, not sure if I should continue to stay or not, if I'm allowed to now.

"Aidan tells me you'll be searching AJ's home tomorrow."

I nod. "It could generate a decent lead."

Mrs. James looks away from me and down at her daughter, a hand coming to rest on AJ's. "I always knew she'd find her way back into your life. My daughter always had a flare for the dramatics, didn't she?"

"That she does," I exhale. "I would have been happy with her just showing up on my doorstep, or maybe throwing a pebble at my window with a boom box over her head."

Mrs. James half laughs and looks back up at me. "I'll make sure to tell her to do just that when she's recovered. How have you been Torryn?"

I shrug. "I've been better."

"Hmm, that's funny. AJ said the same to me recently."

Hearing those words made the hairs on my neck stand up.

"I'm sure she's been busy. But, uh, I should get going. I'll, uh, update you on her case when I can."

Mrs. James hugs me goodbye. I leave her clutching the hands of her daughter.

I spend the drive home lost in my thoughts. My

muscles feel tight as I approach my apartment. Nothing a long run and a hot shower wouldn't fix, I think to myself as I unlock the door. The moment it's open, my black and brown German Shepherd, Atlas, is charging full-speed ahead. Atlas's massive paws rest on my shoulder as I scratch his head.

"Hey, boy, how about a run?"

A minute later Atlas was armed with his harness and leash. With ear buds in my ears, we run for what feels like hours. Running helps me focus my mind and calms my soul. At least, it usually does. Tonight, though, the music playing in my ears is unable to drown out thoughts of the case, or AJ, or of Agent Drake, whose words eat away at me the longer I think about them. It only serves to fuel my rage and push me to run harder. My companion easily keeps up.

I'm a good detective, the youngest in the precinct, there's no case I can't solve, I assure myself. I haven't failed, yet, so there's no reason to doubt myself now. If only I could figure out what we're missing. We've got mostly dead-end leads, very little physical evidence and a handful of unconvincing theories. I have a feeling that I'm missing something elemental, and if I could just figure out what, it would tear this whole case wide open.

My thoughts change gears without warning, switching from thoughts of the case to AJ lying in the hospital bed. Drake could be right, she could be our killer's endgame. If the killer finds out that AJ is alive, they could come back to finish the job. If we don't find this person soon, we may need to use her as bait.

The thought doesn't sit well with me, and not because of the way things ended between us. We both chose our paths. It churns my stomach to think of putting any victim, no matter how brutal the attack, or crime, in the path of his or her assailant. No one should have to face their attacker, especially one as violent as our suspect is, more than once. But, it might be the only way to catch our killer. The question now, however, is whether I could risk AJ's mental health and life just to catch them. Or should I keep her as far away from this as possible and hope we can find them on our own?

The logistics start making themselves known. Someone would have to be in constant contact with AJ. I wouldn't trust anyone with keeping her safe but I may not be the best one, either. We wouldn't necessarily have to be near her physically. Just close enough to jump in at the first sign of trouble. She'd have to wear a microphone, of course, that transmitted in real time along with a camera on a button or necklace, nothing to obvious. A code word or phrase she could use if she needs us to intervene sooner than planned. How would we set this up? Just follow her around once she's out of the hospital, hoping that the killer would actually want to finish the job? That's all assuming she wakes up and can't tell us who attacked her. But who knows when that would happen and how long before she's released once she does wake up. No, it needs to be sooner. If we used her as bait before she wakes up, if she wakes up, then we wouldn't have to worry too much about her mental health, only her physical safety.

Too many roads to go down tonight. I'll run the idea by Dax and Drake tomorrow if searching through her fan mail doesn't pan out a solid lead.

We finally make it home. Atlas eats and I shower as part of our normal routine. As the hot water runs down my back, I stand motionless, allowing myself to be overcome with emotion just this once. Memories invade my mind as tears stream down my face, draining away with the shower water. Seeing her like that, again, was almost too much.

I step outside the shower and wrap myself in a towel, forcing myself to not have a complete breakdown. That's not who I am, but then again AJ somehow always managed to get me out of my comfort zone. I wipe the fog off the bathroom mirror and instantly I'm back to my normal self: calm, composed, and exhausted. When I leave the bathroom, Atlas is already curled near the foot of the warm and inviting bed. I slip on a tank top and shorts before I delve beneath the blankets. I toss and turn for the better part of an hour before I can finally relax my mind and body enough to sleep.

When I wake the next morning, I'm on autopilot, pulling on a clean pair of jeans and a white button down shirt. I open my sock drawer, the same one that had been home to a note that read, simply, *I'm sorry,* and a velvet box containing a ring I could never bring myself to return. Armed with my police issued, .40 caliber, semi-automatic pistol, I grab my leather jacket and head out the door.

Agent Drake is waiting in the parking lot of the station when I arrive, leaning against his FBI issued

Chevy Suburban. He holds up three cups of steaming coffee.

"Detective Grieson said that coffee is the quickest way to get on your good side," he says to me, handing over one of the cups that has my name scrawled on the lid.

I thank him but neither confirm or deny his comment. We walk towards the station and I can't help but notice the bumper sticker on the back of his vehicle that reads 'Proud Fish Dad'.

"What's with the magnet?" I ask, then immediately regret asking as Drake's face beams with excitement.

"I absolutely love fish."

I roll my eyes and mutter, "couldn't tell."

"Judge all you want but I'm the proud owner of several tanks, some of which could be placed in the finest doctors' offices, thank you very much," he teases politely enough. I nod and he continues. "I actually do have a tank that is 160-gallons. It's a saltwater tank. Full of anemone, clownfish, tangs, seashores, and damsels."

"I've also got a 25-gallon in the bedroom, freshwater, full of platies and guppies. I have a beta fish in my bathroom and another in the kitchen."

"So, your name literally means sea dragon and you're obsessed with fish?"

This statement causes Drake to pause before bursting out in laughter. "I guess that's true. I never really thought of that before but, man, that's ironic. My parents really did a number on me, didn't they?"

"Don't they always," I mutter, I guess what they say is true: your name really does seep into your personality and this guys was living proof.

Once we enter the station, Drake immediately went from boyish and carefree to serious federal agent. It was, to say the least, disturbing to watch the change happen. More disturbing to realize that he may be a completely different person outside of work and that I might actually enjoy his company.

I spot Dax leaning on the back wall of the big conference room as we enter, the entire day shift of uniformed officers and detectives alike ready for the morning debriefing. Drake hands over a coffee to Dax as we stand beside him.

Lieutenant Harris stands in front and his deep, booming voice fills the room quickly. "Alright everyone, let's get started." The small chatter instantly dies. "As you are aware, we have our first, and hopefully last serial killer. The mayor and I agree that this case in now our top priority. Any active cases that can be given to another unit will be reassigned. Grieson, Michealson, what's the progress?"

Dax and I stand straighter as everyone's attention averts to us.

"Agent Drake has been instrumental in helping us build a profile of the suspect as well as a geographical profile," Dax says to the room, "and we'd like to request that uniformed officers make round-the-clock routine canvas of the areas we believe are most likely the next for attack or where the suspect is likely to be."

Harris nods. "We'll get on that. Make a list of everyone available and which shifts they're going to be on. You have the whole precinct at your deposal,

I don't want any cracks in this case. Detective Michealson?"

I clear my throat before speaking. "Based on the profile provided by Agent Drake, we believe that the attacker may have specifically targeted our last victim so we've also requested a protection detail for Ms. James until the killer is apprehended.

"I want a list of who's on babysitting duty, too."

I nod, pulling out the schedule I already planned out this morning as I ate breakfast.

"Any leads on who we're looking for?" Another officer asks from somewhere in the room.

"Not at this time, though we will be searching through Ms. James's home this afternoon and we're hopeful it will provide some decent leads," I provide. "I'll hand over the floor to Agent Drake so he can present you with the profile."

Drake starts with reminding the room that a profile is a guide and not an exact science, just as he did with Dax and myself the day before. As I listen to him speak, I can't help but admire the confidence he exudes in his body language. He commands respect and authority, as officers and detectives hang on his every word.

I think back to his words yesterday, about not coming to take over the case, about teaching me while we are working together. Listening to him speak to the room full of my fellow officers, I start to feel some admiration and respect for the agent. I know I'm young, though it's been a while since I've felt like it, feeling biased and still vastly inexperienced.

As the debriefing comes to an end and officers

start piling out of the conference room, I spot Joel amongst the crowd and pull him aside.

"Now can you expedite that DNA analysis?" I ask confidently, if not altogether snappish.

"I'll see what I can do. Also, none of the partial finger prints match anyone in our database," he replies, then turns his attention to Agent Drake. "Is there someone in the FBI that I can send them to? See if they match anyone in the federal database?"

Drake provided Joel with a name and number for a forensic tech that works for the FBI. "Tell 'em Drake is cashing in a favor to expedite anything related to this case that we send over."

16

Then

AJ sat on the floor of her dorm living room. Aidan sat next to her, lost in play, surround by toy police cars. His blue eyes, shaggy blond hair and happy smile were brightened by the dazzling sunlight shooting in through the small gaps in the window blinds. AJ's mom, Hailey, sat on the couch watching her daughter and grandson. The three of them shared a striking resemblance, AJ thought, as a glow of happiness spread across her face, thankful that Aidan looked more like her than—well, she had the better genes.

AJ tussled the boy's hair. "Looks like it's time for a haircut. I can't see your pretty face."

"Boy's aren't pretty," he pouted, a look of concentration on his face.

AJ and her mother both chuckled at this.

"Oh yeah," AJ said, "says who?"

"The other boys at school. Only girls can be pretty."

"Then what are boys?"

"Hamsome," the boy replied distractedly playing

with his cars.

"Handsome," AJ replied, enunciating the 'n' and the 'd', "and yes, you are very handsome."

"How are your classes going honey," her mother asked when Aidan returned his attention back to his toy cars

"They're okay," AJ said taking the red fire truck the boy handed her. "I mean, it's a little tough but I'm managing. Finals are this week."

"That's great. Is there anything you need? Do you need me to transfer money into your account?"

"I'm good for now, mom, I'll be home after finals so I'll be good until then. I'm just glad you brought Aidan to visit."

"Of course. He misses you and it is your birthday after all. Oh, that reminds me," Mrs. James said, pulling a small giftwrapped box out of her bag, "this is for you."

"I want to see," Aidan exclaimed, crawling into AJ's lap with the enthusiasm of a nosey preschooler.

AJ took the gift and opened it. She gasped, tears welling up at the sight of what was in the box. She carefully pulled a thick, silver-braided chain out, running a finger across a class ring attached to it.

"This is dad's ring," AJ said, remembering how she admired it as a child.

"Your father would have wanted you to have it. He would have been so proud of you."

"Thank you, mom," she said in a brittle voice.

"Here," her mom said, holding out her hand, "let me put it on you."

AJ handed it over, turned her back to her mom and lifted her blonde hair.

Aidan lifted his hand to touch the ring. "Pretty," he said before sliding off her lap to resume smashing his cars into each other.

"What about your life outside of class?"

The question caused AJ to blush as she thought of Torryn. She turned towards her mother.

"Uh, oh," her mother said, "I know that look. It's the same look you gave your father and me when you thought Niki was a beautiful princess, and later when you told us you lost your virginity and got pregnant. Who is it?"

AJ sighed, "Her name is Torryn. I really like her but things are um, complicated."

"What's so complicated?"

"Well, for one, she's my suite-mate and kind of the RA. And secondly," AJ stopped and gestured towards Aidan.

"Minor complications."

As if being summoned, Torryn entered the apartment, bags of groceries in her hand. She paused at the sight of the visitors before placing the bags on the breakfast bar.

AJ jumped up. "Hey. Need a hand?"

"I can manage, you have company," Torryn replied.

AJ turned her head to face her mother. "Um, mom, this is Torryn. Torryn, this is my mom, Hailey James. And this little guy is Aidan."

At the sound of his name Aidan looked up briefly, "hi, Torn."

Torryn flashed one of her rare smiles, "hello Aidan. It's very nice to meet you."

Aidan smiled at her, holding up a police car,

"Wan' to play cars?"

"No, thank you. I have lots to do," She turned her attention to AJ's mom. "It's nice to meet you too, Mrs. James."

"You as well Torryn."

When Torryn turned away, Mrs. James mouths *she's cute* to AJ, who in turn gave her mom a pointed look. A warning and a plea to not say anything.

"Are you staying for dinner?" Torryn asked as she put away groceries. "I can whip something up for everyone."

"That's very sweet of you, but we should get going; it's a bit of a drive," Hailey turned to Aidan, grabbing her bag, "Aidan, sweetie, pack up your cars."

"I don't wan'a go!" He screeched. "Please can I stay?"

AJ knelt down to look at the boy's face. "Hey, I'll see you again, soon. Okay?"

AJ's heart felt as though it was breaking into a million pieces at the sight of tears rolling down his cheeks. She wrapped her arms around her son and picked him up.

"I love you, so much," She whispered in his ear as her mom packed his toys.

"I love you," he sniffled.

"Good-bye, Torryn, it was lovely meeting you," Hailey James said as the three of them approached the door.

AJ handed Aidan to her mother, "bye, mom, thanks again."

"Happy birthday," her mom said, kissing her

cheek.

AJ closed the door and went to help Torryn with the remaining groceries.

"You don't have to," Torryn told her.

"It's okay, I want to."

Torryn pulled out a chocolate cupcake from one of the bags. "I got this for you."

AJ smiled. "Thanks. Is this an apology for being such a distant friend lately?"

"Your brother is cute," Torryn said, pointedly ignoring the question.

"Yeah," but then the words caught as AJ started to panic, chest aching as she desperately tried to control her breathing. Her earlier comment of her life being complicated slammed against her skull, the fear of how Torryn will react to the truth producing a migraine. AJ's mind raced to come up with a way to tell the girl who Aidan was without scaring her off. There wasn't any way to tell her that wouldn't make things less complicated. She decided to just come out and say it, rip it off like a band aid and suffer whatever fate awaited her, "Yeah, he is pretty darn cute. Aidan's, uh, not my brother, though. He's my son."

The look on Torryn's face crumpled, as though someone stole something from her, was heart wrenching to AJ. As she realized that she most likely just lost her chance with Torryn, a feeling of grief washed over her, but in an instant was replaced with a feeling of defensiveness. Being as young as she was, AJ was used to people looking at her with concern and pity, as if she were some hopeless case that couldn't be a proper parent. She didn't need that from Torryn and she definitely didn't need Torryn to feel sad for her.

"I was young and dumb," AJ stated, her eyes challenging and posture rigid, daring Torryn to judge her, "I don't regret the choices I made that gave him to me. I love my son and if it weren't for trying to provide him a better future I wouldn't have left him with my mom so I can be here."

Torryn put away the last of the groceries. "You should eat that while it's still fresh."

AJ completely forgot about the cupcake but shook herself before replying. "Thanks, I will."

A moment passed where AJ almost felt bad for feeling as if she had to defend herself, but she decided she wouldn't. She took a small breath and indicated they move to the living room. "Want to watch a movie until we meet up with the rest of the gang?"

"It's your birthday, we can do whatever you want."

Oh, that's dangerous, AJ thought. She could think of about a dozen things she'd like to do with and to Torryn, but she pushed those thoughts away. They didn't matter anymore, and maybe that was for the best.

****

AJ stood in front of her bedroom closet trying to decide what to wear for her birthday night out. Ava lay on the bed, already decked out in a red dress and red heels that belonged to AJ.

"Thanks again for letting me borrow these."

"Anytime," AJ responded.

"Mi amiga, why are you so stressed out over what to wear?" It's not like you. Plus, you look good in everything."

"I'm the birthday girl," giggled AJ. "I have to be the hottest girl in the bar, that's the rule."

Both girls giggled, but only briefly before AJ sighed loudly. AJ explained to Ava what happened earlier that day; how her mother had brought Aidan to the dorm to surprise AJ for her birthday, how she was delighted to see her son, but also worried that Torryn prematurely meeting Aidan may have scared Torryn off, and how Torryn had actually met Aidan and the weird conversation, or rather lack of, they had afterwards.

"I think I lost my chance with her," AJ said concerned after she was done retelling the events of the afternoon. "Nothing scares off a prospective partner faster than the baggage of being a teenage mom, especially if that person is an ambitious twenty-one-year-old woman with career goals to be a detective."

Ava got off the bed and hugged her friend. "Well, we'll just have to think of something so brilliant she won't be able to resist you."

Ava tenderly shoved AJ aside and began rummaging through AJ's closet. AJ watched as Ava examined and picked through every item of clothing twice before she settled on a black sleeveless dress.

"Perfect," Ava declared, handing the dress to AJ and turning around to give her friend some privacy.

"Last time I wore this, I got pregnant." AJ said as she slipped on the dress and looked herself over in the full length mirror hanging on the closet door, recalling the last time she wore this dress and how tightly it had clung to her then, accentuating her breasts and the curves of her body just as it did now.

"Exactly! No one can resist you when you look that hot. I'm just glad is still fits four years later."

AJ rolled her eyes and smiled at the thought of being irresistible. A hint of red spread across her cheeks as she remembered how it felt waking up in Torryn's arms. AJ decided that tonight would be the night she would tell Torryn how she felt. With Torryn having now met Aidan, AJ could no longer be a victim to her fears. For better or worse, she would tell Torryn how she felt about her.

"Niki's here," Ava announced, "should we go get your girl?"

AJ shook her head, "Torryn's at some study thing. She'll meet us there."

****

The local bar featured a live band so the atmosphere was much more vivacious than what even AJ was used to. Even with the band, though, it was still quite enough to still be able to hear her friends so it was perfect. Almost perfect. The group sat at their usual booth, with a couple of extra chairs pulled up for Liam and Ryder. AJ kept glancing at the entrance, searching for Torryn. They had been at the bar for more than an hour and Torryn still hadn't shown up. AJ felt rejected and drowned her sorrows with shots.

Ava leaned over and whispered, "Mija, don't

worry, she'll be here."

AJ gave her friend a grateful smile. "I'm ready for another round," she said, turning her attention to the whole group. She dragged Ava along to the bar.

AJ smiled as she talked to the bartender and laughed at the compliment on her dress. She had hoped that being extra friendly would take her mind off Torryn standing her up. AJ heard Ava's phone chirp so she glanced at her friend whose face was lit up by the light of her phone's screen.

"Torryn's here," Ava announced.

AJ quickly turned to look towards the booth. Her face lit up when she saw Torryn sitting there, watching her.

"And she thinks you're flirting with the cute bartender."

"What?" AJ blurted, flummoxed. "I was just—I was hoping to get a free drink!"

Ava showed AJ the text from Niki telling her that Torryn was jealous of AJ's flirting with the bartender.

"But I wasn't flirting." AJ said defensively.

"I know, but it looked that way to Torryn."

"Well, shit, what do I do now?"

"Um, I don't know. Maybe tell the girl the truth? Just walk right up to her and say, "Torryn, I'm in love with you.' She's obviously into you if she's jealous, right?

AJ glared at Ava.

The bartender, whose name now escapes her, finished filling a pitcher of beer. "There you go birthday girl. Get you anything else?"

AJ nodded to the booth. "We'll need one more glass. And can I get six shots of something, one each damn color of the rainbow."

The bartender smiles, "You got it gorgeous."

Ok, so maybe I was flirting a little, AJ thought.

"Ava, can you take the pitcher to the table and find some excuse to get Torryn on her own? Go dancing or something."

"Go get 'em, tiger," Ava growled as she walked towards the booth.

The bartender loaded a tray full of shots. AJ watched as Ava motioned Niki and the boys to join her on the dance floor. Ryder must have tried inviting Torryn along, if the fact that he was now limping as he walked to the dance floor was any indication. Knowing Ava, she probably kicked him, and AJ only shook her head and marveled at Ava's tactics. AJ headed towards the booth once she saw everyone safely on the dance floor.

"Hey," Torryn said as AJ reached the table. "Sorry I'm late. What's this?"

"Liquid courage," AJ replied, ignoring the apology and placing the shots on the table. She sat next to Torryn, slammed the red shot and pushed the orange one towards Torryn. "Care to join me?"

Together they drank the shots. AJ pinched her face as the shots burned her throat and she wondered what she was actually drinking. By the time all six shots were gone, it wasn't too long before AJ felt pretty good, her inhibitions suitably lowered.

"So, what is it that you need courage for?" Torryn asked with curiosity in her tone.

It was now or never, AJ thought.

"I wanted to tell you that I like you," AJ declared without preamble.

She itched to grab Torryn's hand, but, although part of her knew that Torryn wouldn't brush off the contact, at least until the others returned, she decided against it. Instead, she chose to lean into the other girl's space, close enough that it was hard to focus.

"I wanted to tell you that I think about you all the time," she brushed her nose against Torryn's pushing further, "about being with you," a barely there whisper against parted lips and Torryn still hadn't moved away, "and I know my life is complicated," millimeters apart, AJ could feel Torryn's lips trembling against her own, " but I really want you—"

It was this moment that the song that was playing suddenly changed and AJ's friends returned to the table in a rush, all out of breath and laughing. AJ pulled away from Torryn just enough to have their own air again, but remained sitting pressed against her, thighs touching as much as possible, shoulders knocking against each other's.

AJ accepted the shot Niki handed her, Torryn did the same, her face not giving anything away of the last few minutes.

"To AJ, happy birthday, my love. May this year bring you *everything,*" Niki shot a look to Torryn, "your heart desires."

The group downed their drinks and AJ's attention quickly returned to Torryn. She felt warm from the buzz of the alcohol and , oddly, at peace sitting next to Torryn. She knew Torryn felt the same. AJ just had to draw it out of her.

"Dance with me," she whispered to Torryn.

Torryn silently followed her.

AJ chose a spot on the dance floor in front to the band and started dancing, swaying her hips to the beat of the music. Torryn straightened her shoulders when AJ wrapped her arms around her neck. AJ had passed the point of no return.

"Say something," AJ encouraged.

Torryn slowly put her hands on AJ's hips, "I, um."

AJ waited for the rest, but apparently, it wasn't coming. She watched as different emotions played across Torryn's face. Could she have been wrong about Torryn wanting her back? Did she press too far, to soon? Did all this come off entirely the wrong way and now Torryn was feeling violated and guilty? Even in AJ's inebriation, she could tell that Torryn wasn't into this.

AJ dropped her arms as if she had been burned. "You know what, never mind. Forget I said anything."

AJ stormed off to the bar and hoped that Torryn wouldn't follow.

Luck was not on AJ's side as, precisely two minutes later, she saw Torryn approach through her peripheral.

"Hey!" Torryn shouted to AJ when she finally made her way to the bar.

AJ turned to her, a look of hurt but fierce stubbornness in her teary eyes, "What?"

"Let's talk," Torryn suggested.

"Now you want to talk?"

Torryn brushed a strand of hair behind AJ's ear, then cupped her cheek. "Yes, very much so."

AJ looked at Torryn expectantly, waiting for an explanation, because so far, nothing made sense.

"I'm sorry I made you feel," Torryn paused again. "I'm not good at, uh, expressing my feelings. There were a lot of things that happened to me that, well, I just don't—I don't do well with—but then you—"she let out a frustrated growl and ran a hand through her hair.

AJ opened her lips to speak, but Torryn held out a finger in front of her lips, not quite touching but close enough that AJ imagined licking it.

"I do care for you, AJ. You're special..to me. I..." Torryn moved her hand down to find AJ's and hesitantly laced their fingers together. She rapidly scanned the crowded bar, and then just as quickly separated their hands. "Can we talk about this later? Somewhere more private. It's—well, I don't want there to be any misunderstandings and there's a lot to talk about."

AJ nodded, too stunned to really disagree. After all, she wanted Torryn to be open with her. And if she had a past, maybe one just as complicated as AJ's, then she'd listen.

"Okay. Well, your friends are waiting for you."

17

Now

Drake and I arrive outside the front of Aidan's school. I park and get out of the car, texting Aidan that I was here. Leaning against the passenger door, it feels like old times. Except this isn't my police cruiser and Aidan isn't ten years old anymore. A few minutes later, I hear the bell ring. Another fifteen and the blond-haired teenager is out the building and down the steps.

"Listen, I need you to address me as Detective Michealson, okay? The guy in the car is with the FBI. If he finds out about our history I could get in a lot of trouble, I could get taken off this case." I say to him when he reaches the car.

He gave me a lopsided smile, "No problem, *detective.*"

I smile at him and open the back door.

"Thanks, Detective Michealson. Who's the suit?" Aidan asks nodding at Drake, sitting in the front passenger seat.

I climb into the driver's seat and glance at him through the rearview mirror, "This is Special Agent

Drake. He's with the FBI. Drake, this is Aidan James."

"How's it going, son?" Drake says, turning in his seat to shake Aidan's hand.

"Well, my mom's in a coma so I going to go with not so great," Aidan replied before telling me his address and leaning back against the seat. He places ear buds in his ears and precedes to stare out the window.

I decide it's best to remain silent for the fifteen-minute drive from Aidan's private school to his home. The more Aidan and I speak, the more likely Drake's suspicions are to be aroused that we know each other outside of the interview Dax and I did with him. Maybe he doesn't even suspect anything and maybe I'm just being paranoid. But, always better safe than sorry.

As I park outside of AJ's home, I can't help but feel impressed. By the looks of it, AJ has done well for herself. Their house was moderately sized, large windows on either side of the wooden door, donned with a golden knocker and a camera above the doorbell. Brown and beige stones littered the archway above a the door, similarly colored bricks lined the outside walls, and a single spiral column indicated a small porch to the left of the home. There was shrubbery placed neatly, and kept nicely, along the walkway leading to the front door, flowers and small bushes making it look idyllic, like something out of a Home and Garden Magazine.

It dawned on me that this was it, the dream house AJ always talked about having built for us. I smile at the memory as Drake, Aidan and I enter the foyer.

We follow Aidan through the living room. He stops in front of a closed door, "that's her office. My room is a little further down the hall. That's where I'll be when you're done."

"Thank you, Aidan."

"Oh, when you leave could you drop me off at the hospital?"

"I don't see why not," I tell him just before he disappears into his room.

"Remember," Drake says, picking up a bunch of letters from AJ's desk, "the killer is most likely local so pay attention to the postmark. There's no sense in reading letters too far out of our geographical profile."

It feels odd rummaging through my ex-girlfriend's personal fan mail. Drake and I sort through the mail, creating two piles, not bothering with any letters outside of state lines. Aidan mentioned that AJ didn't really keep the letters anymore, so it's also probable that she threw out a letter that could have led to the killer.

We've been at this for a good hour already, and still, there was nothing that screamed out *Hey, I'm the killer.* There were a few letters written by all the usual suspects – perverts, haters and super fans- but that came with the territory. A few came off as creepy, statements along the lines of having a gross desire for AJ, of inserting themselves into her novels, but all were ultimately harmless.

"This is a complete waste of time," I say to Drake after I toss out what seemed like the hundredth possible suspect but ended up being someone with a tendency for pornographic dreams for AJ's characters. "I'm going to go get Aidan. We should get back to the station."

"Yeah, I'll just straighten this mess we made."

"Thanks," I say as I walk out of AJ's office. I knock on Aidan's half-closed bedroom door.

"Come in," comes his muffled response.

I push the door open and see him sitting at his desk, writing something. I glance around the room out of habit, trained to always be aware of your surroundings, and notice dirty clothes are strewn haphazardly across the floor. Sports posters and ones of half-naked glamour models are taped to the walls. A TV and video game console face an unmade bed. I step further into the room and approach a shelf on the wall that contains Aidan's various achievements, the ones I've missed over the past few years, keeping an eye on the doorway. One in particular catches my eye.

"You still play soccer?" I say, indicating a large golden trophy.

Aidan approaches me and shrugs. "Not really. Though, I got really good when we lived in London. Mom used to say I was as good as you."

"Well, I did teach you how to play." I say fondly.

"I remember," he replies, anger creeping into his voice.

I face Aidan, trying to ascertain the root of his teenage angst. His mom is lying in a coma and sure that's enough to make anyone angry, but there's more beneath the surface.

"Aidan, your mom left me," I stop then, not knowing what else to say. I wonder if I stepped out of line telling him that. It wasn't fair of me to try to put the blame on her, not when we both bear that burden. "That wasn't fair for me to say. We both..."

"*You* didn't fight for us," Aidan states, now visibly angry.

He was right. I didn't fight for them. I didn't go after her when I found them gone, I didn't show up at the airport to stop them, or show up in London to be with them. He has every reason to be angry with me.

"I know," I reply, another glance out of the doorway. "Your mom wanted to follow her dreams and I couldn't be the one standing in her way."

"You could have come with us," he whispers.

I place a hand on his shoulder and glance briefly towards the hallway. "I couldn't for the same reasons. I always hoped that you would someday understand. We both chose our careers and we both knew it was important that we follow our own paths. Back then, I would have given almost anything to go back to being a family but I couldn't chase her around the world if she wanted to leave that badly," I sigh, trying to figure out how I could phrase this in a way that he'd understand.

"Yeah, well, she wanted you to."

"You're probably not wrong."

"What about now?" It's innocent enough, and reasonable why he'd ask. His reaction is that of any kid who wants their divorced parents to get back together.

"I don't think we could ever really go back to what we were." My response is instant, not an admission that I want nothing more than a second chance, but not an outright refusal either.

He's silent for a moment and I think that maybe he starts to understand that the feelings AJ and I shared for each other aren't there anymore.

"I care for her, still" I amend, "and for you, too, but-"

"Yeah, yeah, I know," he interrupts as he hands me a folded piece of paper, wiping his eyes with the sleeve of his uniform blazer.

I unfold it to reveal a list of names, "What's this?"

"Niki and I made a list of everyone mom knows. She said it would help you."

"Yes, it will help. Thank you."

I look up and notice Agent Drake walking up to the doorway. I panic briefly at how much of the conversation he heard. His face gives away nothing, however, and it only serves to make me question how much of the exchange he heard, if any at all.

"Ready to go see your mom?" He asks.

"Yeah," Aidan replied, grabbing his backpack.

I ask Drake to drive us back to the hospital, so that I could review the list of names Aidan gave me. We drop Aidan off and I fight the urge to go in with him to check on AJ. If her condition hasn't changed, then it wouldn't make sense for me to go, and Drake doesn't know anything. I want to keep it that way.

We exit the parking lot and it takes me a moment to understand why it feels like we're going in the wrong direction.

"What are you doing? Station's that way," I say pointing to the left.

"Sorry, I need to go to this pet store, my fish need their flakes."

"We're on duty," I point out to him as he goes through the light and turns into a shopping strip where there's a little store promoting exotic fish, aquariums, food and 150 accessories. "Wait, you're really going to make a stop here?"

He blinks at me as he opens the door. "Uh, yes," he replies, as if my question is absurd.

I shake my head, dumbfounded and exasperated.

18

Then

AJ emptied her closet into her duffle bag, ready to go home for winter break. Despite feeling excited at having an entire month with Aidan and her mom before the spring semester began, she felt equally anxious. She was leaving to go home soon and she had yet to talk to Torryn about her revelation during her party last night. If she didn't see her over the next couple of minutes, she may not be able to at all.

She powered through the migraine her hangover produced as she zipped up her bag, letting out a puff of breath. When she opened her bedroom door, she was surprised to see Torryn, fist raised as though she were just about to knock. *Speak of the devil, and she shall appear,* AJ thought comically.

"Uh, hey," AJ said, shifting her weight awkwardly, feeling uncomfortable. She could no longer deny the chemistry between them but now there was an underlying tension, sexual or maybe just due to all the drunken confessions that transpired last night.

"Hi. Are you leaving now?"

"Soon," AJ replied just as her phone chirped. She looked at the screen, "Actually, yeah. I'm leaving now."

"Oh. I guess it's not a good time to talk?"

"Walk with me," AJ offered after a moment, trying not to make it obvious that she noticed the way Torryn picked at her fingernails.

When Torryn stepped to the side AJ closed her door and made her way through the apartment. The halls were quiet and empty, as most students had already left to go home. AJ didn't want to be the first one to say anything, not quite sure what Torryn wanted to talk about. Maybe she wanted to let her down easy? Maybe she wanted to keep things discreet?

AJ couldn't help but feel a semblance of frustration at the continued silence. Torryn had yet to speak and they were almost to the parking lot. When a clearing of the throat didn't promote any conversation, she had almost given up altogether if it wasn't for Torryn suddenly holding out a hand as they approached the door, fingers grazing the handle.

"About last night, I —" Torryn took a deep breath before she continued, "I don't want you to think I don't feel the same way. I do."

This caused AJ to pause and turn toward Torryn, "you do?"

Torryn nodded, "It's just—uh, hard for me."

"Why?"

Torryn ran a hand through her hair before placing both on her hips. "Just, well, last time it didn't end so well."

AJ nodded. She didn't need any further information if Torryn wasn't willing to give it out. "Yeah, well, that's life," she supplied, shrugging her shoulders as she adjusted the strap of her bag on her shoulder.

Torryn huffed out a bemused chuckle and rolled her eyes.

AJ, already frustrated with her inability to say anything to Torryn in the previous months, her inability, now, to apparently say the right thing, and Torryn's inability to open up enough to let AJ in, turned to continue walking, pushing open the door.

"Wait--"

"Look," AJ snapped as she stepped outside, Torryn hot on her heels, and instantly regretted her tone. "I like you—"

AJ's phone chirped again. And again. Sighing, she opened her messages. "Shit, she has *no* patience. C'mon."

AJ grabbed onto Torryn's wrist and pulled her along as she made her way through the parking lot. Eventually, they stopped at Niki's car, the trunk open and waiting. The top was down and AJ could see Ava already in the back seat. She tossed her bags in the back, ignoring Niki's pointed looks, and slammed the trunk down.

"Hey, watch it—" Niki blurted but was interrupted by AJ demanding a few minutes alone with Torryn. Niki threw up her hands and climbed into the driver's seat, turning on the radio loud enough that it could have woken the dead.

Torryn remained silent and AJ was grateful for the chance to gather her thoughts together.

"Look," she started over, "I like you. A lot. And I want to see where this goes but I can't promise anything other than I'll do my best to not be like the others."

When Torryn opened her mouth to speak, AJ put a hand up. "I'm not finished."

"Uh, sure—"

"I don't know what you have going on in your past, and I don't want you to feel obligated to tell me anything right now. But if you like me, and if you want to give this a shot, you have to give me something to work with. I can't be left in the dark. Everyone has issues, Torryn, but you don't have to work through them alone if someone is willing to be with you. And you don't get to keep giving me this hot, cold routine"

There was silence for two minutes before AJ sighed loudly, "Okay, I'm done, now."

AJ noticed a small smile form on Torryn's lips as she replied, "You have a point—"

The horn sounded and made both girls jump, AJ's heart racing as she glared through the windows to Niki, who just seemed exasperated as she continued to wait for AJ to get in the car, tapping her hands impatiently on the steering wheel.

"Look, I have to go, so—"

Niki held down the horn, the loud, blaring, shrill sound making AJ cover her ear with one hand and bang on the car with the other. "Hold on!" She yelled, even though she knew Niki didn't care.

"It's okay, go—"

"But, I can't, we just—"

"I'll text you. She's been waiting on you to—"

"Yeah, she can wait a little bit longer—"

"I'll text you, it's fine. Go."

AJ sighed and groaned. "Fine, fine. I'm holding you to that text. This conversation isn't over," she joked, poking a finger at Torryn's chest. She stepped forward, pushing into Torryn's space before walking to the passenger door and climbing in. She glanced at Niki, who only gave her a roll of the eyes, before shrugging.

AJ waved 'goodbye' to Torryn as they pulled out of the parking lot.

Five minutes passed before AJ's phone chirped and she couldn't help the dopey smile that crossed her lips as her phone continued to go off. In the driver seat beside her, Niki groaned. In the back seat, Ava leaned forward and asked what was happening. AJ focused her attention on the texts that came through, some in paragraphs, some in single lines, following the way Torryn would be speaking in person.

I've been hurt a lot, in ways most people don't like to think about.

AJ wasn't sure if she should reply so she continued to read text after text.

I grew up in the foster system because my own mother didn't want me. I never knew my dad. I bounced from home to home. Some were nice but most of them were just as abusive as the families we were taken from.

AJ paused at Torryn's inclusion of herself in the statistic. A few things began to fit together like puzzle pieces and AJ began to feel more uncomfortable as the messages kept coming.

There was a family I was staying with when I was 16.
They had a daughter who was my age, Savannah.

We got involved after we figured out we had feelings for each other. Her parents caught us in her bed one afternoon.

They were strictly religious and blamed me for leading their daughter into a life of sin. Said I was an abomination.

They said I was going to go to hell.

Then they kicked me out and I didn't hear from Savannah again for a whole year.

Turns out, her parents sent her to a conversion camp.

AJ's stomach twisted. She knew of their existence, their popularity decades ago, but she didn't think anyone actually sent their kids to them anymore. Well, anyone who was a decent person, at least.

She started dating some boy. I was confused and hurt and concerned for her but she didn't want anything to do with me. Avoided me like the plague, her parents warned me to stay away from her, so I did.

She wasn't happy but there wasn't anything I could do.

She killed herself a year later.

I thought I loved her, but even if I didn't, I couldn't let myself get involved with someone like that again.

AJ didn't know what Ava and Niki were talking about. They tried getting her attention but she ignored them as she waited for another message. When non popped up, she took a breath and typed a reply.

I'm not sure what I can say to all of that.
None of that was your fault.
Her parents were obviously messed up in the head.
You couldn't have done anything to prevent any of that.

I still blame myself for what happened. That's why whatever is going on with us scares the hell out of me.

I think that's normal but you shouldn't let it hold you back.

It's difficult to be yourself when the world tells you it's wrong
That you're damned.

The world is a dangerous place for people like us.

True
But we don't have to let fear run our lives.
I'm taking a chance ... you should too.

Yeah, maybe I should.
Let me know when you get home?

Yeah, sure. And hey. Thanks for telling me all that
I'm sure it wasn't easy.

You said to give you something to work with.
We'll talk more later.

Great :)
This is going to be a long month

I think you'll live

Says you

****

AJ watched her son brush his teeth while she held her phone to her ear. She smiled when Torryn's voice came through the line.

"Hello?"

"Hey, you!" AJ said into the phone.

"AJ...it's six in the morning...what are you doing awake?"

"Apparently three year olds don't know how to sleep in. Why do you sound like you're out of breath?"

"I'm out…for a run."

AJ smiled as she pictured Torryn on her morning run, ear buds in, listening to whatever music she liked to listen to. *Maybe we could start running together more,* AJ thought. They only did it the one time but AJ enjoyed it. She'd always enjoyed running, though preferring the evening where as Torryn preferred to run first thing in the morning. AJ enjoyed her sleep too much.

"I'm all done, mommy!" Aidan yelled, bringing her out of her thoughts.

"I should probably go. I just wanted to hear your voice."

"Have fun. Bye."

****

AJ woke up to Aidan running into her room and jumping on her bed.

"Mommy! Wake up. Wake up!"

AJ groaned as she pulled Aidan down next to her. She wrapped her arms around him as she struggled to get up, "just a few more minutes."

"But mommy, it's snowing!" Aidan replied with excitement.

AJ sat up, "then I guess you better go put some warmer clothes."

"Yay!" The boy yelled as he hopped off the bed and out of the room.

Her phone buzzed on her night stand. She picked it up and smiled when she saw it was a text from Torryn.

Hey. Are you awake?

I am now.

Oh, sorry. I didn't mean to wake you.

What? No.
It wasn't your fault, Aidan had that pleasure two
minutes ago

How'd you sleep?

Fine

AJ did not want to text Torryn this morning. Not when she had been missing her so much she'd dreamt about her more and more. She decided to place a video call and felt a calming peace wash over her when Torryn's face appeared on her screen.

"Hey, you," Torryn said.

"Hey. I had to see you." AJ said into into her phone, happy when Torryn smiled in response.

"So, How'd he wake you up today?"

"By pretending I was a trampoline," AJ replied as Aidan ran back into her room. "And he apparently gets his energy from the sun."

Aidan climbed on the bed, and onto AJ's back. "Hi Torn!" He said looking over AJ's shoulder at the phone.

"Hey, Aidan. You look very warm."

"Uh huh, and guess what. It's *snowing!*"

Torryn laughed. "That's very cool."

"It's very cold."

AJ loved how the two of them responded to each other. Aidan had been a part of many of their conversations over the past couple of weeks. It didn't take long for Aidan to warm up to Torryn, who was always so sweet to him.

"So, classes start back up in a couple of weeks," AJ said to Torryn. "So, um, I was wondering if maybe you'd like to go on a date when I get back?"

AJ held her breath as she waited for Torryn's response, sure she'd say no or change the subject. They talked every day since AJ had been home, but they always seemed to avoid the topic of a future realtionship.

"Yeah, Torn! Mommy really wants a date," Aidan said into the phone, and then, quieter, "What's a date?"

"It's where two people who like each other go out and spend time together." AJ explained to her son.

"Oh, den I go on lots of dates wit you mommy," he exclaimed happily, wriggled around on top of AJ's back.

"Sure do, kiddo." AJ laughed.

"Okay," Torryn said.

"Hm?"

"I said, 'okay'."

"Okay, what?"

"I'll go on a date with you."

AJ pushed up in her excitement, jostling Aidan, who only laughed and tried to climb higher on her back, wrapping his legs over her shoulders. "Really?"

"Yes," Torryn laughed.

AJ pumped her fist in the air and high-fived her son.

"Does dis mean we can play in the snow, now?" Aidan asked, throwing around his saddened puppy eyes that AJ caved to.

"Yes, but I have to get dressed, first."

"Bye, Torn!" Aidan hollered as he clambered off AJ's shoulders and bolted out the room.

"So, looks like we're going to play in the snow. Do you have time to talk later?

"Always."

"Okay, great, I'll call you later."

"Okay. Have fun!"

"I will."

AJ disconnected the call, feeling a bit shocked. She couldn't believe that Torryn had actually agreed to go on a date with her. If she hadn't known she was awake, she would have pinched herself like she was a little girl again just to make sure she hadn't dreamt the whole thing. Smiling to herself, she hurried out of the bed, excited at the idea of going on a date with Torryn, finally, but more so that she would get to build a small snowman with her son on the first snow day of his life.

19

Now

I stand up and position myself in front of the white board in the conference room. My body aches and I am running on caffeine fumes. I study every piece of information before me.

The victims: All females between the ages of twenty-five and thirty-five. All with blonde hair and blue eyes. Similar body structure. Various occupations. The early victims were all high risk but, as is common, as the killer's confidence grew, so did the level of difficulty, the lower the risk, the victims became. Then there was AJ, whose career as an author was rapidly growing.

The MO: Identical stab wounds, and, according the Medical Examiner's report, the same weapon was most likely used on all the victims. Lipstick markings of an "X" across their faces, could mean a number of things. Crossed out of existence, 'X' marks the victim, crossing off a list. No evidence of sexual assault so that can't be the motive. The first five victims had no defensive wounds, meaning they didn't fight back. ME found a small puncture wound on their necks. Toxicology came back negative so ME's best guess is the killer used succinylcholine to paralyze them before stabbing them.

But AJ's attack was different. Almost as if the killer was rushing the assault or wanted her to have the chance to fight back; maybe they had a personal connection to AJ, maybe they lost their ability to control themselves. Or maybe, out of a misplaced sense of arrogance, the killer simply didn't care. What did that tell us? Was that a clue? Was AJ's attack even related? There are similarities, sure, but it lacked most of the MO. I only have my instincts to go on and my gut tells me its related.

He took his time. Why? I hesitate. I look over Mrs. Parks' vague description. *He was a skinny little thing, too, no bigger than a matchstick.* She mentioned 'he', a slight frame and from the rest of her statement, it doesn't appear to be that 'he' was taller than the average.

How did she know the killer as a 'he'? She didn't hear his voice. She didn't see his face, it was too dark, he wore a hood. It makes sense—statistically, most serial killers are male, but women are more than capable of committing violent acts. They're more prone to stabbing their victims, poisoning, using short-range weapons of opportunity rather than guns or heavy tools, like axes or shovels. Could our killer be a woman? Drake's profile assumed the killer was a male, but women would present their obsessions differently, they would interact with their victims differently, their reasoning would influence they motives differently.

We've been looking the wrong direction. We would need to change our entire approach.

"Shit," I curse under my breath. I poke my head out of the door frame of the conference room I took over, "Dax, get in here!"

Dax rushes over to me, spilling coffee onto his hands in the process. Agent Drake looks at me expectantly from his position at the table.

"I think we messed this up."

They share a pointed look between themselves then glance at me with with questions on their tongues, so I hold up a hand to stop them before they have a chance to ask.

"I think I'm on to something here so bear with me."

Their silence allows me a moment to try to get my thoughts together enough to speak.

"Okay. Let's pretend none of us had any training. What sex do you think the killer is?"

I glance between the two men men and wait for an answer. When none is forthcoming, I groan aloud. "It's not rhetorical."

Dax huffs out a small snort. "Profile says male. Most serial killers are."

"Right!" I raise my arms in exasperation. "Right, which is why we weren't looking for indicators of a female killer."

"Which would be? Female killers can kill in all the same way a male can—" Drake tries to interrupt.

"No sexual assault''_

"Doesn't mean anything. Women are capable of—"

Dax makes a nod of agreement with Drake but I

push through. "Yes, I know, *but* look at the sixth victim! She's not wearing lipstick!"

Both Drake and Dax look at the photograph taken at the crime scene and nod, if only to acknowledge the information I've given them. I doubt they understand where I'm going with this.

Drake asks. "I realize the lipstick 'x's are a signature, but what does the victim wearing it have to do with anything?"

"We assumed that the killer was using the lipstick of the victim to mark their face. Victims one through three all wore red lipstick the night they were murdered. Victim four was found with several lipsticks in her belongings, and five worked for a beauty supply company."

"Right," Dax agrees, crossing his arms, "But the sixth victim didn't have any of her personal belongings next to her. She was taking out the trash when she was attacked. So, the killer must have had the lipstick already."

"Exactly!" I shout, excited that maybe this is our breakthrough, the connection of dots that we weren't seeing because we had unwittingly assumed too many things in the very beginning, "Forensic analysis finally came back indicating the same tube of lipstick was used on all five of the murdered victims. How many men do you know that carry around lipstick?"

Drake smiles for a moment and I'm please to see that he's responding well, so far.

"So, if our killer is a woman—"

"Wait," Drake interrupts, "What if the killer bought the lipstick for this specific purpose? What's to say that a male can't carry lipstick around?"

I think about if for a moment. "Wouldn't it make more sense for a male to use a marker, or the knife itself? If you were to go purchase supplies for your murder kit, would you include lipstick?"

"I don't know that *I* would, but who's to say our killer wouldn't."

"A man in the cosmetics aisle of a store would be noticed, people would talk."

"I see your point," Drake concedes, an expression that looks a lot like pride taking over his face, "It does make sense. It's normal for a woman to shop for lipstick, but a man would draw at least someone's curiosity, no matter how accepting the community."

I stand a little straighter, mentally giving myself a round of applause, and continue on with my theory.

"The attack itself is still a little on the fence. Either it's personal *because* of the amount of rage involved, or the killer is getting frustrated that they aren't getting attention they think they deserve and we've done our best to keep much of this out of the news. Everyone wants to eventually get caught, they want to know that they are feared. It's hard to know for sure, but we definitely know that they got sloppy with Miss James. It still looks as if they wanted to inflict the most damage without actually going for the kill immediately—"

"Unlike the other victims, which were quick one stab kills," Dax interjects, "even though the UNSUB didn't kill the victim, he or she was still rushing the job itself. Otherwise, why would this perp have chosen such a bad spot to commit the crime?

"My point! Every other victim was in a secluded area, narrow alleys away from heavy road or foot traffic. Even though victim six was in an ally like the others, she was still more out in the open than usual. She had *just* finished a book signing so the killer risked being seen, risked being caught in the act, which they were. They didn't *care* because AJ was always the target!" I immediately notice my slip up, but in my excitement I forgot to censor myself.

"If that were the case, then wouldn't it make sense that the killer would *want* to take their time? Make it a slow and painful experience rather than a rushed butchering?" Dax suggests.

"Maybe she didn't have anywhere to take her. Maybe she didn't want to risk losing her if she tried to escape. Maybe she lost objective and acted on animalistic instincts. She's raging, sees the victim, doesn't want to lose her chance of killing her, so she jumps at the first moment she can take." I remember the security video, how the hooded figure had stood there and then walked away without so much as interacting with anyone. Just stared and left. "She couldn't have done it during the signing, she wouldn't have had enough time to do any damage. She waited long enough."

"That's a lot of supposition but you're definitely onto something, kid," Drake says, leaning back in his chair and taking some folders off the table to look through them again. "Where's the list her friend made?"

I rifle through my binder and take out a copy of

the list, passed it to Drake. He glances over it for a moment before setting it in front of Dax. "Let's look them up," he says as she stands to crack his back. "This time let's focus only on the females, look for anyone who has a history or an associate who has a history of violence."

Dax nods and leaves the conference room to go into the bullpen, Drake and I following closely behind him."

Dax gets settled in front of the computer and begins searching the names on the list that was given to use a few days ago. I oscillate back and forth, chewing on the inside of my mouth, frantically trying to calm my nerves. I can feel how close we are on this now that I've changed my thinking.

I ignore all the pointed, questioning looks that Drake shoots me from his perch on the desk top.

Another moment of silence passes and I start to think we aren't going to get anywhere with this list. That is, until Dax pipes up with, "huh, this is interesting."

I quickly move to stand behind him, leaning over his shoulder so that I can better read the monitor. "What?"

He makes a few keystrokes, the screen changing too fast for us to catch it. Dax hovers the mouse over a name. "Ava Turner lives right in the middle of our geological profile. Known associates are Isabella Turner, sister, who," he types in her name and a profile pulls up, "has a sealed Juvenile record. No known address for her." He clicks on another name. "And their father has multiple domestic violence charges that were all dropped."

I grab my jacket from the back of the chair, "I'm going to pay a visit to Ms. Turner. Dax, you stay here and try to get those records unsealed."

"Yeah, sure," he replies quickly. "Take Drake with you for backup. I'll call the DA, see what I can do."

"Text me Ava's address," I say, already halfway out the door.

I didn't look to see if Drake was behind me, too busy trying to push back memories that threatened to break my resolve. Ava and Isabella Turner. It's been a while since I've talked to Ava, three years in fact. I cut ties with her after AJ and I split. Isabella always made my skin crawl and the hair on the back of my neck stand up. I always thought of her as being heartless

I allow Agent Drake to drive. My mind reels, turning over more than a dozen thoughts per second, trying to piece my memory of Isabella together with potential motive.

Drake's voice startles me. I didn't realize it was that quiet in the car. "We're making a quick stop by my place, gotta feed the fish."

It takes me a moment to understand what he's talking about, but when I do, I can't help but seethe with anger. "What the hell!" I shout. "We finally have a sold lead and you want to *feed your fish.*"

"Well, yeah," he shrugs nonchalantly. "It won't take long."

"What in the actual hell is wrong with you?" I continue to protest. "This is definitely the wrong time to entertain your unhealthy obsession with your damn fish."

This makes him laugh, a low amused chuckle. "Possibly. But you don't know me outside the office. I do have other interest outside of fish."

"I doubt it," I sigh.

He shrugs and I enjoy the silence for a moment before I start panicking again. If Isabela is the killer, and that's still a big 'if', then Drake is no doubt going to find out about my past, especially since we're on our way to speak with her sister. *Shit,* I curse myself. *I'm going to have to tell him.* We finally have a decent lead that could lead us to closing the case and I've worked too hard to lose my career now, I've sacrificed too much to get everything thrown into my face. If I don't tell him, I risk being caught in my own web of lies. If I do tell him, then it's all been for nothing, anyway.

I groan and Drake glances over at me. "You okay?"

I take a deep breath before I speak. "I'm familiar with Isabella Turner."

"Did you work a case or just know her by name?"

I fidget in my seat, unsure of what to do with my hands. "Something like that. There was an accident a number of years ago. I'm pretty sure she was involved in a near drowning of Aidan James, our victim's son who you met, but there was no evidence."

He nods, following my story, "so you were still a beat cop and got called to the scene?"

"No. I was already there."

"It was on your route?"

I roll my eyes, hating that I have to spell it out for

him. He's FBI and he can't put this together? "No. I was already there because I was spending time with Miss James…AJ…and Aidan."

I can see the exact moment the information clicks for him. His shoulders tense as his grip tightens on the steering wheel. His jaw locks and he refuses to look anywhere but at the road directly in front of him, not even blinking or glancing out his mirrors. This is his quiet before the storm. I can feel it. There's a static like tension in the air and it's almost suffocating. I know this confession changes everything for me, for this case.

"What are you thinking?" He asks calmly, and somehow that's worse than him yelling at me.

"I haven't done anything any different than I would have if I didn't know the victim," I try to defend myself.

"What about when it's time to testify at trial? Did you consider how much the defense will eat you alive it they get wind of this?" He finally looks over at me, but only briefly. "It doesn't matter that you've done everything the same, the mere fact that you once dated the victim is enough for a defense attorney to tear this whole case down because *your* motive is no longer objective enough.

It jeopardizes your integrity, along with that of the entire department. Not to mention how extremely unethical of you to not mention this to your Lieutenant. You should have pulled yourself away from this case the *moment* you knew who the victim was. It we catch whoever is responsible, it might not matter now, because they could walk."

I sit in the passenger seat in silence as I let the

words sink in, feeling as if I'm sitting in detention at school all over again. Ashamed and guilty. However much I hate to admit it, he is right. Just my being in this case is a liability, but still I cannot bring myself to walk away from it. I stand by my decision but before I could speak my mind about it, Drake shuts off the engine and it surprises me to see that we've stopped in a driveway.

"C'mon," he demands, expecting me to follow, and I do so reluctantly. He unlocks the door, and we step over the threshold into the living room. He flicks on the light and I am immediately thrown back as I look at his modest furniture, solid color rug, and sparse decorations. He seemed to be the type to be wholly eclectic, if not just simply indiscriminate about such things.

Two huge fish tanks, taking up the majority of the far wall, stand on matching wooden dressers, the dark finish in stark contrast to the beautifully vibrant and colorful fish that were swimming lazily around the themed accessories.

"I was a cop before joining the FBI. When I first started out, I was also young and full of myself," he starts without preamble, and although I stiffen at his assumption, I don't interrupt him. "There was a call that came through the radio, a mugging victim had walked herself to the station to report the guy. They gave me his description and I followed up on it. I didn't find him that night but when I went back to the station, I saw the file they made and the name of the victim."

I watch him as he feeds his fish, hanging onto his words, trying to figure out why he's telling me this.

"The victim was my girlfriend. I was pissed and more than that, I was murderous. I couldn't focus on anything else for days and I wanted so bad to hurt the son of a bitch that when one of the guys found him, I didn't care that I broke my some of my knuckles —"

It had to be more than just a 'mugging'. He must have really hurt her, tried to—

"—on his face, that I was going to get suspended because I used excessive force when he was unarmed. I wanted him to hurt worse than he hurt her. He was in the hospital for about a week and I was suspended, without pay, for about six months because the public demanded retribution. I can't say I didn't deserve it. Probably would have lost my badge if this weren't the first time I lost control. "

I know I'm staring through him, not even looking at him directly, but I can't peel my eyes away from the fish. His word churn my stomach, but it's so easy to him going through something like that, and I push away the thought that crosses my mind as to why that is as disturbing as it is.

He continues, putting the caps back on his fish food and dusting off his fingers, "I should turn you in. But I'm not going to. This is going to turn into a shit storm, so be prepared. Just don't take down Lieutenant Harris with you. He needs to know, too. He'll make the call if he needs to."

I'm not sure what I can say to any of that. I'm not even sure if I should thank him or turn myself in but as I continue to stare at the fish a moment longer, I can feel my body relax. It must have been noticeable to Drake too because the last thing he

tells me before we leave his home is how watching
fish   can   lower   blood   pressure.

20

Then

AJ couldn't contain her excitement to be back at school after the winter break. Not seeing Torryn over the past month had been a slow torture. AJ paced up and down her tiny dorm room, wearing only jeans and a red bra. Various shirts were spread out across from her bed. She looked at the time on her cellphone and groaned. She had less than five minutes left to get ready before she had to leave.

"It shouldn't be this hard," she whispered to herself, wondering if Torryn was feeling just as nervous in her room next door. AJ knew how crucial a first date could be.

The knock on her door made her jump, "shit."

Maybe this was Torryn saying the date's off, she's changed her mind. AJ wouldn't put it past her, considering how hot and cold Torryn was the first half of the school year.

"You ready?" Torryn asked through the closed door.

Shit! AJ thought before she smiled at the sound of

Torryn's voice, the giddy tone that was reserved only for her.

She quickly settled on a white, long-sleeve shirt and covered it with a black vest. She grabbed her black Converse and opened the door to be greeted with the sight of Torryn, who, even in a light-blue flannel, black jeans, and matching combat boots, managed to make it harder for AJ to breathe.

"You look stunning," Torryn told her.

AJ swallowed down her nerves and returned the smile, "you don't look so bad yourself."

"Shall we?"

"We shall."

AJ stepped into her shoes. Linked with Torryn's arm the pair walked out of the apartment. They held hands as they walked in companionable silence across campus to the bus stop that would take them into town.

Now that AJ understood Torryn's reservations, she didn't argue when Torryn subtly pulled her hand free once they were no longer alone.

"I'm glad you're back," Torryn whispered once they were settled in their seats with their passes safely tucked in their pockets.

"Me too," AJ said with a smile as she looked at Torryn, "so where are we going?"

"You'll see."

"Am I going to like this? I'm all for surprises, but if this is the part where you lead me into a darkened alley and kill me—" she couldn't help the smile that escaped, especially at the obvious eye roll that Torryn didn't manage to hide in the reflection of the glass.

"Well, I'm hoping you'll like it. If you don't, pretend you do," Torryn quipped playfully.

AJ nodded and relaxed into her seat.

A few stops into downtown - with AJ looking around the different sizes and colors of the buildings, how their history connected them despite how differently each building came to be—they exited the bus in front of a small French bistro. She allowed Torryn to lead her inside where she took a small moment to appreciate the beauty of the architecture and decor. The dark wood chairs gleamed in the light of the low hanging chandelier light fixtures, as if they were just polished; the floors matched, dark oak wood until it approached the bar on the right hand side, where it gave way to white, brilliant tiles. In front of them laid an array of tables, ranging from larger tables meant for families, to smaller, more private booths spreading back towards the kitchen—which was open to the dinning room. To the left several mirrors and old paintings hung on the wall celebrating the French life.

Several diners were already there, holding private conversations with their glasses of wine and AJ prickled at the thought that she may be underdressed.

A young hostess approached them, and spoke directly to Torryn, flashing a brilliant smile, and looking just as professional as the atmosphere demanded. "Good to see you again, Torryn. It's been a while."

Torryn gave a small one in return. "Yeah, it was a busy semester," she explained with a shrug.

"Yeah, I get how that goes," the girl chuckled as she led the two to a booth that was tucked away in the corner.

"This is my favorite spot in all of downtown," Torryn said, smiling at AJ once they were seated next to each other.

"It's perfect," AJ replied, loving the authentic feel of the place.

Their waiter approached the table, a jug of water that had a black cloth wrapped around the base in one hand and water goblets in the other. He placed the goblet in front of Torryn, and, while pouring the water he turned to AJ. "Good evening. My name is Dmitri and I'll be taking care of you today. May I interest you in a sample of our *Domain Houchart: Cotes de Provence Rouge?*"

Torryn chuckled and AJ was sure that— Dmitri?—would have continued had she not interrupted him. "No, no we're fine without, thank you."

He didn't look surprised. "What would you like to drink, mademoiselle?" He asked as he indicated AJ.

AJ looked around briefly, suddenly worried she was going to order the wrong thing. "Iced tea?"

The waiter left them with a nod. AJ looked at Torryn, sure she had questions dancing in her eyes.

"I've come here often enough," Torryn answered without waiting, "I actually used to work her for a while, until I took a few jobs on campus."

AJ hummed and nodded her head. "Do you ever drink anything other than water?" She teased, though she wondered how many jobs Torryn had and why she had so many in such a short period of time. Maybe an extension of her commitment issues, AJ thought.

Torryn shrugged. "Occasionally I'll have a beer, or a few rainbow shots if given to me by a beautiful woman."

"Oh yeah? And how many beautiful women have given you rainbow shots?"

"Just one," Torryn smiled at her.

The waiter returned a mere few seconds later with AJ's drink. "Did you have any questions about the menu? I would recommend the Cassoulet, today. It's a blend of sausage, duck confit, and delicious haricots with assorted vegetables, baked to perfection."

AJ could admit that it sounded absolutely delicious. She didn't realize how hungry she was until that moment, though, and her mouth watered as she noticed a small loaf of artisan bread pass by.

"I'll have the Chicken Montpellier," Torryn said, without looking at the menu.

"Um," AJ quickly scanned over the menu, pressured to pick something, "Uh, the Coq au vin."

Dmitri smiled, "Delicious choice, mademoiselle."

Torryn collected the menus and handed them to Dmitri, who promptly left their table. AJ blushed slightly when she noticed the look on Torryn's face, like she was impressed.

"When I was in Europe last year I spent some time in France, in each country actually." AJ said in way of explanation.

"I see. Why did you spend a year in Europe? Where was Aidan?" Torryn asked in a way AJ could tell was genuine curiosity and non judgmental.

AJ took a deep breath and prepared herself for the emotions that she was sure were to come when she started to explain, "I couldn't handle life real well after my dad died. Everything reminded me of him, I was depressed, having nightmares. I had to get away, so I left my grieving mother so I could deal with my own shit. I took Aidan with me. I feel guilty about it, instead of just grieving the loss of her husband, she had to deal with losing her daughter and grandson temporarily. She was so understanding though."

AJ braced herself and was surprised when the panic attack didn't come.

"He would have been what...two? That's pretty brave going into a foreign country alone with a toddler. Why Europe?"

"It was as far away as I could think of," AJ shrugged, "and yeah, he was two."

"Tell me more about your life?"

"What do you want to know?"

"Everything."

"Hmm, that's an awful lot for a first date," AJ grimaced.

"Fair point. Tell me more about your parents."

AJ was silent, not sure what to say or where to begin. She didn't really have a difficult childhood, but there were quite a few bumps in the road over the last few years and, with talking about her dad— well, that was overwhelmingly saddening at best, painfully panic inducing at worst. But what could she tell Torryn, the girl who had a traumatized childhood and adolescence, about? Not much ever happened to her.

"Are you okay?" Torryn asked.

"Yeah," AJ cleared her throat, "just, y'know, talking about my parents is sometimes hard. With what happened to my dad and all."

"Oh, right, you don't have to talk about it if you don't want to.."

"No, it's okay. My parents were really supportive and loving, no matter how many times I screwed up and mom didn't really change in that regard after my dad died, but I know it's hard sometimes. Especially because I, apparently, remind her of him. He never met a stranger, so outgoing and playful. He was sometimes like a big kid, which was great."

"I can see how you remind her of him then."

AJ started to talk about her childhood—at the insistent, unspoken urging of Torryn, of course.

AJ informed Torryn of how she met Niki when she was seven and Niki was eight, "Niki moved in next door. I remember sitting on our porch writing a mother's day poem when the car pulled into the driveway. I was so excited to meet the new neighbors that I dropped my stuff and ran to the car before the doors were even open. Then I saw a sad, crying girl who told me she didn't want to play. She was sad her mom recently died of cancer and the next day was mother's day. I told her she could share my mom if she wanted and we've been friends ever since."

AJ told her how Niki was raised by her single dad, resulting in her being the badass that she was now—someone who wasn't afraid to kick the shit out of you, even if it meant getting her nails dirty.

There were a few stories shared over the trouble they would get into—with a few provided by Torryn about her own adventures, including how she emancipated herself at sixteen which led to her habit of having multiple jobs in order to take care of herself. AJ instantly felt bad for assuming that the reason for Torryn's many jobs was commitment issues, when it became evident that the reason was in fact the exact opposite.

Over desert, a set of classic, modest opera cakes, AJ talked about meeting Ava by chance a year after Niki.

"It was the last month of summer. Niki and I were playing at the park. Some boy was giving Ava shit because her parents didn't have the kind of money mine and Niki's dad did and you could tell. Niki grabbed my hand and drug me towards them. She tapped the boy on the shoulder and when he turned around she broke his nose. The three of us became best friends and after that my dad couldn't bear the thought of separating us when we went to different schools. So he helped Ava get into our private school with a scholarship," AJ laughed, "and basically indoctrinated her into the family. He always made sure Ava never felt like she was a burden or someone lesser just because of her situation."

"That must be nice, having family and friends who love you so much and are so welcoming."

"It is. Didn't you have friends growing up?"

Torryn shook her head and shrugged. "A lot of foster homes remember? Makes it hard to build attachments and stay in touch when you're being bounced around."

AJ observed Torryn shift in her seat. She picked up the signals and remained silent.

"Ready for part two of our date?" Torryn asked cheerfully after an awkward moment.

"There's a part two?"

Torryn signaled the waiter for the check and promptly paid for their meal. They left the building and walked down the street to their next destination. AJ told Torryn about the music she listened to as a teenager, her love for Avril Lavigne that put her into a skater phase for all of two months, as they walked.

Two blocks later, Torryn stopped in front of a building that had the words 'Blacklight Laser Tag' printed in white paint on the darkened window.

"I heard this place is a lot of fun," Torryn said, opening the door for AJ and motioning her inside.

When they approached the counter, AJ quickly handed the teenager her card, "for two, please," dismissing Torryn's protests. "You paid for dinner, let me get this."

AJ wanted to comment about how the dinner probably wasn't even moderately priced and she should have offered to split the bill but she didn't want to make Torryn feel bad. Her parents always made it a point to teach her not to point out things like that. She now knew that Torryn kept multiple here and there jobs in order to support herself and was wondering how far the dinner would set her back. She admired Torryn's tenacity and resilience, but also wondered how she could so easily balance so many jobs and the ridiculously good grades she kept. It all made AJ want to work harder on her own average grades.

"The next game is about to start," said the obviously bored, freckle-faced teenager behind the counter as he handed AJ her card back. "Theres two spots left, on opposing teams. Enter the arena through there." He continued to flick his hand.

The kid needs to work on his customer service skills AJ thought as she and Torryn entered the laser tag arena. As per the set-up of the game, both of them had been armed with vests and laser guns in separate rooms. It was dark in the arena, a large dimly lit room, only the walls and obstacles glowed fluorescent. Voices over the PA system spoke of two battling teams and rules. AJ had a hard time seeing the other players running about, only the tiny lights on their vests giving them away.

Familiar to the concept of laser tag, AJ ducked behind a wall and immediately began looking through a cut-out as she searched for her date. She recalled that Torryn was wearing a white tank under her flannel. *If the vest wasn't covering too much of the white it shouldn't be too hard to find her,* AJ thought. The black light would cause the white to glow.

"Hey," a voice boomed from behind her.

AJ turned around. Even in the poorly lit area, AJ could see Torryn's fluorescent smile illuminate the room. She stepped back as Torryn gently pushed her against the glowing neon wall. Her heart thudded with the pressure of Torryn pressed against her, so close she could taste her cherry blossom lotion. AJ bit her lower lip as Torryn reached up and stroked her cheek.

They gave each other time to move away, to back out, but AJ's body trembled with want and she was going to have t. She pulled Torryn towards her by the neck, her hands sure even if her brain was shouting at her to *abort abort abort.*

When Torryn's soft lips touched hers, AJ sighed, parting her lips to fit the shape of Torryn's, to feel more. She moved against the other girl, pressing her body as close as she could with the vests in the way, and was quickly rewarded as Torryn opened up for her, darting her tongue out to tease at AJ's. AJ moaned into the kiss, heat pooling low in her stomach.

An announcement cracked over the PA system that they game had only sixty seconds left, reminding them they weren't alone, and making AJ jump with how loud it was.

AJ nipped at Torryn's lip, one hand still wrapped around her neck and the other underneath the edge of Torryn's shirt. The vest made it impossible to go any higher than the hip. She wasn't even ashamed at that, if she were to be honest with herself. AJ didn't care to move as she watched a devious smile creep across Torryn's face. Torryn kissed AJ on the check before pulling herself away.

She shot AJ in the vest and ran off.

Seconds later, the bright house lights blinked back on, blinding AJ as her eyes tried to adjust. She searched for Torryn as she returned her vest. AJ spotted her waiting at the counter holding up the scorecard. Torryn's cheap shot resulted in her team winning.

"That was one hell of a kiss," Torryn whispered into AJ's ear.

"Tell me about it. It left me completely defenseless," AJ quipped. As first kisses go, that was by far the best she'd ever had.

"Well, I am to please." Torryn quipped in return.

AJ quirked an eyebrow, "Oh do you now? Want to show me more?"

21

Now

Drake knocks on the door to Ava's apartment as I respond to a text from Dax, advising me that Joel got a hit on CODIS but unfortunately was unable to get an ID because it was linked to a sealed juvie record. I show Drake the text, wondering if this was enough for the DA to get a judge to agree to unseal Isabella's records, that was too big a coincidence...

After a second knock, Ava opens the door. "Torryn? Hey, it's been a while."

"Hey, Ava. This is Special Agent Drake, with the FBI. Can we come in?"

"Yeah, sure." Ava moves aside so we could both enter, "I was just getting ready to go to work but I have a few minutes."

Ava led us to her small dinning room table, barely big enough for four. I stayed quiet per Drake's instructions in the car. We agreed that he would take the lead on this interview so my prior friendship with Ava couldn't be used against us in court. I couldn't explain it but I was convinced Isabella was our perp. From day one, I knew Isabella just wasn't right. My hunch, however, is not admissible evidence, and hard evidence was the thing we lacked the most so I agreed this was the best course of action.

"Can I get you anything?"

"No, thank you. Miss Turner, do you know a Miss Adelaide James?"

"Yeah. We're best friends, grew up together. I went to see her at the hospital the other day."

"I'm investigating the attack. Do you know anyone one who would have wanted to hurt your friend?"

Ava shakes her head. "No. Everyone loves AJ, the girl couldn't have enemies even if she tried."

"Well, someone sure has it out for her. Are you sure you can't think of anyone? From her past, maybe?"

Ava shakes her head again...

"What about your sister, Isabella?" He asked as he flipped through his notebook for show. "Could she remember anything?"

"My sister? She barely knows AJ. She wouldn't be of any help."

"We're just trying to find any lead, Miss Turner. Anything at all you, or your sister, could think of that might help would be appreciated."

"Why is the FBI interested in one local attack?"

"We're not...our interest is in serial murder. It's possible this attack could be linked with a string of homicides."

Drake was met by silence as a clouded expression entered her eyes, betraying the calm of her face. Was it worry? Confusion? Fear, maybe? I try to decipher the emotion that was speaking silently through her chestnut eyes.

"Where's your sister now?" Drake asks more insistently.

"I don't know, she hasn't been home for a few

days. I keep calling her but it goes to voicemail."

"You don't seem worried about that."

"Well, that's pretty normal for her."

"So, she lives here with you?" Drake continues.

Ava nods, "just, until she gets back on her feet. Isabella has had a hard time dealing with the separation of our parents—my father had an affair with a much younger woman. Both Isabella and my mother are devastated. What does any of this have to do with AJ?"

"How long?"

"What?"

"How long," Drake says firmly, "has your sister been having this hard time?"

"I don't know. Like two months or so. She lost her job, apartment, everything. Torryn, what's going on?"

I don't respond, instead I just look at her. An hour ago I probably would have felt guilty at the accusing look on Ava's face eating at me but I have to stay objective so I shut those feeling away. But, with Isabella being the best lead we have, it's worth pursuing, friendship be damned.

"And she's been missing since the attack on Adelaide James? That's interesting." Drake continues, folding his hands together in his lap.

Ava didn't answer, she only continued to look at me, obvious betrayal in her eyes. I don't feel anything, I can't. So I force my mind to see Ava as just a stranger, refusing to look away as Drake continues to push.

"Tell me about your sister's criminal past."

"You don't think she's involved in this, do you?"

Ava asks, her voice growing panicky and rising a few pitches. She's worried, sure, but from the way her body is trembling, she scared, too.

"Look, we can do this the easy way or the hard way, Miss Turner. It's up to you," Drake persists.

"She would never hurt anyone," Ava pleads. "She spent a few years in a hospital, but she's better - " She stops abruptly, as though she didn't mean to say that last bit.

"Why did she go to the hospital?" Drake asks, his peaked interest is evident in his tone.

Ava opened her mouth to respond, but then promptly shut it with a snap. She swallows and squares her shoulders, straightening her back.

"I want you both to leave now," she demands firmly.

"Hard way it is then," Drake says as we stand.

Ava escorts us to the front door and slams the door shut once we're on the other side.

"It's her. It's got to be her," I say to Drake as we walk toward the car.

"Get Grieson on the phone. Tell him that Ava Turner refused to play ball, get an APB out on her sister. I'm going to reach out to a contact of mine from the Borough, maybe call in a favor to a judge and see if we can get a warrant to access those medical records. I want to know why she went into a long care hospital. If we're lucky it could shed some light on her sealed record. Ava Turner may have just given us a loophole. And have him meet us for lunch, the three of us need to talk about your involvement in this case."

I call Dax and relay the conversation with Ava.

When I tell him Isabella Turner has been missing since AJ's attack, this piece of information excites him and he agrees to meet us at a little twenty-four hour dinner near the station. Dax greets us by advising that the DA was having a hard time convincing a judge to unseal Isabella's juvenile records.

I nod, feeling disappointed even though this was to be expected. Judges were always reluctant to unseal a juvenile record. If we can get the records unsealed, we'll have a name to accompany the DNA match. If not, I hope that Drake's favor is able to be cashed in to get us a warrant to obtain DNA from Isabella. We needed this piece of information linking Isabella to the murders. Better yet, we find her and get her to confess if she had anything to do with it because right now all we have is theories.

"We need to have a very serious conversation about the situation we're in with this case," Drake says, interrupting my thoughts, as we seat ourselves. "You need to pull yourself off this case, Michealson," Drake continues after we place our drink orders, coffee all around.

I open my mouth to speak but then promptly shut it, not knowing what to say. I know he's right but I refuse to admit it aloud.

"It was bad enough you have a personal connection to the victim." Drake continues, "But now, you also have a personal connection to the prime suspect in this case. That will hurt you in court more than your relationship to the victim will."

I look to Dax for backup but he nods his

agreement with Agent Drake.

"He's right, Torryn. You shouldn't be lead detective on this case; hell, you shouldn't be working it period. There's too much at stake."

"If Isabella Turner is the killer, then you better hope the D.A. can get a plea deal. If not, there's a good chance she could walk. You need to tell Lieutenant Harris, and the D.A.'s office. They need to know what they'll be dealing with." Drake continues.

Our coffee arrives at the table and I immediately take a sip to avoid having to reply right away. Drake and Dax order their food. When it's my turn I just shake my head and ask for a refill of my coffee. Feeling ganged up on, I roll the consequences in my head if I stay on this case. As much as I want to be the one who catches this killer, I know I can't risk letting them walk.

"Okay," I whisper to my friends...unsure when I started considering Agent Drake a friend.

As the guys eat their meal, they discuss the next steps of the case. This will be my last chance to put in my opinion so I pay close attention. Dax throws out the idea to stake out Ava's apartment, thinking Isabella is bound to show up eventually.

"Ava hasn't seen her in almost a week. What makes you think she's going to show up?" Drake asks.

Dax shrugs, "She'll need something eventually and will have to return home. We've already got an APB out."

"I'd recommend checking to see if Isabella's made any credit card purchases of knives. Though, our killer's too smart to leave a trail." I say, "so, in this case, the lack of purchase could be suspicious."

When they finish their meal, I ride with Dax back to the station. We're silent a moment before he speaks up, a hint of guilt in his tone.

"Hey, you know I sided with Drake because I have your back, right?"

"Yeah, I know."

I was about to say more but I was interrupted by the ringing of my cell. I look down and see Niki's name on my screen, thankful I was riding with Dax. If Drake flipped out about my dating AJ years ago, I can't imagine how he'd react to finding out her best friend was also my sister. I answer with a quick 'hey'.

As soon as Niki says she just got off the phone with Ava I put her on speaker so Dax can hear, putting my finger to my lips to indicate for him to stay silent.

"..she's upset that you show up at her doorstep after three years of no contact, basically accuse her sister of...well, I honestly can't repeat all of what she said, you know how she starts spatting out Spanish super fast when she's upset. Anyway, She hasn't seen her sister since right before AJ's attack."

"Yeah, it looks bad, Niki, and I can't—"

"And, look, you and I both know that girl is a pickle short of a picnic basket. But seriously, accusing Ava's sister of murder, to *her face? That's* ballsy Torryn, even for you. *"*

"For the record, *I* didn't accuse her of anything. But, you know I can't discuss an active investigation with you."

"Yeah, yeah. I know. I just wanted to call you and give you a heads up that Ava is really upset about it and if you ask me, and I know you aren't, I think she's a little suspicious of Isabella. She won't admit that to the cops."

"Thanks Nik, I gotta go. I'll call you later, okay?"

"Yeah, sure. When you're not so busy, let's get dinner or something."

"Kay, bye." I hang up without giving her a chance to respond.

Dax says nothing about the phone call. We stay silent the rest of the way to the station as I prepare myself mentally for what I'm about to do.

22

Then

AJ sat on the floor, leaning against the wall, observing Torryn, who sat cross-legged on her bed with a textbook open in her lap and chewing on her pen. She couldn't focus on studying for spring midterms with Torryn sitting a few feet across from her doing a dozen little things that turned her on — like sitting, and breathing, and studying. She chided herself on her raging hormones. She watched Torryn stretch and stifle a yawn.

"Tired?" AJ asked disappointedly, not knowing how much longer she could contain herself.

"Only a little, but I need to study. So, no sleeping."

AJ melted at the smile Torryn shot her way. Pushing her own books aside, AJ approached the bed and knelt in front of Torryn. "Maybe you need a little break. Something to wake you up?"

"What did you have in mind?" Torryn teased, quirking a dark eyebrow.

With a mischievous grin and one swift move, AJ

pulled Torryn off the bed and onto her lap, books and loose papers falling to the floor, "I can think of a few things."

Torryn wrapped her arms around AJ's neck. AJ didn't know why Torryn was so hesitant to take the next step. They had been together for a few months now, and she was not used to having to wait so long to get into someone's pants.

AJ bit her lower lip and held Torryn in place against her. She wanted to rip Torryn's clothes off but understood that she had to let Torryn make the first move. For Torryn, that would be moving dangerously fast.

Loosening her grip, AJ leaned back slightly so that, though Torryn was still strewn across her lap, she could have a better view of Torryn's face and gage her reaction to what she was about to offer.

"What are you doing over spring break?" AJ asked, as she smoothed her palm up and down Torryn's thigh.

Torryn shrugged, "I'll probably stay here and do some community service."

AJ admired how selfless her girlfriend was, but mocked boredom and playfully yawned. "Or, you could come home with me," AJ said, with no hint of hesitation.

Torryn blew air out of her mouth.

"Too soon to take you home with me?"

"Its not that," Torryn said, closing her eyes briefly before she launched into an explanation, "I'm not really good with parents. I told you about what happened with Savannah."

AJ sat up. "Oh babe, my mom won't freak out, I

promise. We had our 'love is love' talk when I was, like, twelve and told her I was going to marry the girl next door."

"Wait, wasn't the girl next door Niki?"

"Well, yeah, but obviously I'm not really going to marry her."

"Did you two...ever?"

"Oh, God, no!" AJ exclaimed. "Niki is gorgeous, obviously. But she's more like my overprotective older sister."

Torryn was silent a moment.

"And she's very straight, so you don't have anything to worry about." AJ said, hoping that her silence meant that she was at least considering her offer of coming home with her and not because of the direction the conversation ended up going.

Torryn had already met AJ's mom but that was before they started dating. AJ knew what it would mean if Torryn agreed; she was ready to take the next step in their relationship and wanted Torryn to be ready, too. AJ lightly kissed the base of Torryn's neck. Smiling, she left a trail of soft kisses as she moved her lips up Torryn's skin, across her jaw line, and then finally to her ear.

"Please, come home with me," AJ whispered, unashamed of the Cheshire grin that spread across her face.

"Okay," came a whispered and fragile response.

AJ pulled back and looked into Torryn's eyes. "Perfect. I can't wait."

****

A few days later, AJ, Torryn, and Ava piled into Niki's Mustang. Although it was only Thursday morning, their spring mid-term exams were over so for them it was officially Spring Break.

After three hours traveling in the car, Niki dropped Ava off at her parent's apartment. A few minutes later, Niki pulled into the driveway of her childhood home.

AJ leaned over and whispered to Torryn, "you ready for this?"

Torryn smiled and kissed her forehead in response.

Niki rolled her eyes in the rear-view mirror. "Alright, love birds, let's get moving."

The three girls climbed out of the black convertible. They each grabbed their bags from the trunk.

"You crazy girls have fun. Come by later if you want," Niki said to them before darting off towards her front door.

AJ grabbed Torryn's free hand and led her next door. AJ always loved how modest her home was. It was never flashy or showed off how much money her parents made. She opened the door and walked inside with Torryn on her heels.

"Mommy," came a voice of a little boy as he ran from the couch to the foyer where the girls stood.

AJ dropped her bag and caught Aidan as he lept into her arms and buried his face in her neck. She kissed the side of his head and was suddenly happy her mom had taken the day off work and allowed Aidan to stay home from pre-school despite her original protests. *He hasn't missed a single day all year so it's not as if he'd lose his spot,* her mom had told her on the phone.

Aidan lifted his blond head and gave a toothy smile, "Hi, Torn."

Torryn chuckled at what had developped into her nickname from the boy. "Hello Aidan."

Aidan slid down AJ's body, took the hand of both girls and led them through the living room and into the kitchen. "Look, Gram, mommy's here. Torn, too."

Hailey James looked up from her task of preparing lunch for the boy and smiled. "Girls, I'm so happy you made it. How was the drive?"

"It was great, mom."

"Well, go put your things away. Are you hungry? I was just making subs for Aidan and myself. I didn't know what you two wanted for sleeping arrangements so I made up the guest room…just in case." Hailey James said, with a wink at her daughter.

"That's very thoughtful of you, Mrs. James, thank you." Torryn spoke up.

AJ heard her mom usher Aidan to the kitchen table as she and Torryn went back to the hallway to retrieve their bags. AJ led Torryn her bedroom upstairs. She noticed how Torryn immediately looked around the room. AJ soaked in the memories of a happy childhood that adorned the walls while Torryn walked over to the picture collage on a cork board. She couldn't help the pang of guilt that resided low in her belly, though, knowing that Torryn didn't have the same experiences she did.

"Is this your dad?" Torryn asked.

AJ walked over to stand beside her, "Yeah, that's him. That was from one of our camping trips. I think he was teaching me how to fish or something."

"Sounds like fun."

"Have you ever been? Camping?"

"Never."

"I'll have to take you some time," AJ responded with a broad smile.

Torryn continued examining the pictures, trophies, and memorabilia that showed off AJ's life. AJ followed Torryn's gaze until it landed on the bed.

AJ cleared her throat. "So, no pressure or anything. I'm okay with wherever you want to sleep."

"We've slept in the same bed before, AJ," Torryn smiled.

AJ relaxed. They slept in the same bed more and more often over the past few weeks. It had become common practice for one of them to find their way to the other's room, sometimes even running into each other in the hall. The fact that they slept together without sex somehow made their relationship more intimate, but the more often they woke up in each other's arms the greater AJ's desire to take it further became. The idea of not sleeping in the same bed as Torryn made AJ feel anxious.

"Well, in that case," AJ said, taking the bag from Torryn and dropping it on the floor. AJ pulled Torryn on top of her as she fell backward onto the bed and brought their lips together.

The kiss quickly deepened as AJ slipped her tongue into Torryn's mouth, pressing their bodies together and moving her thigh between Torryn's leg.

She slowly slipped her hand under Torryn's shirt and felt her stomach muscles stiffen at the touch.

Torryn broke the kiss first. "Your mother—" a small peck landed on AJ's cheek, "—and Aidan—," another kiss on the other side, "—are waiting for us."

"Right," AJ agreed, willing her body to calm down, "lunch."

AJ was hungry but not in a way that her mother's food would be able to satisfy.

****

The next morning, AJ woke with Torryn's arm draped across her torso and a wet, tingling sensation between her legs. She clenched her teeth as frustration bubbled inside her. She was trying to be patient with Torryn, respect her boundaries, but it was proving to be a lot harder not to give in.

Torryn stretched out, pressing her body impossibly closer to AJ's, eliciting a light moan from her full lips. The movement, and Torryn's moans, sent a jolt through AJ's already heated body, making her want to scream. The feel of Torryn's body against hers was too much to bear so she slipped carefully out of the sleeping girl's grip.

She quickly brushed her teeth in the hallway bathroom before going back to the bedroom to change her clothes. She dressed in some sweats and a tank before bending over to tie her sneakers.

"Good morning!"

AJ jumped at the unexpected voice calling out. "Jesus Christ, what the hell," she breathed out, putting a hand to her heart, laughing, before playfully swatting at Torryn, "I have a weak heart, you can't just scare me like that."

Torryn rolled her eyes and AJ leaned over to peck a kiss to her lips. "Anyway," she continued, "I'm going to go on a run. Want to join me?"

Torryn looked at the clock on the bedside table, "It's pretty early for you, but yeah, I could use a run."

AJ watched as Torryn slipped out from beneath the covers to revel her toned thighs under her pajama shorts, her abs barely contained beneath the edge of her short cut pajama top. She adored how the honey bronze tint of Torryn's sun-kissed skin complemented her chestnut curls. AJ continued watching as Torryn rummaged through her bag, searching for appropriate running attire.

Running, AJ had quickly discovered, was something they had in common, even though their reasons for doing it couldn't be more different. AJ ran because it allowed her to clear her head, making it possible for her to forget her problems, avoid the stress of everyday life, let out her frustrations in the setting sun. It allowed her to get away from it all for a brief moment in time.

Torryn preferred her run to be first thing in the morning and worked out in order to prepare her body for the police academy she hoped to enter after she graduated at the end of this semester. Torryn was all business and AJ would often wonder if that was why their relationship was moving at turtle speed, because Torryn was planning on leaving after graduation, her heart and mind set on her career.

This led to AJ wondering if she was setting herself up for heartbreak. These thoughts, along with the constant desire of simply *wanting* Torryn is exactly why AJ needed this run.

The two girls were out of the house by five forty-five. Torryn easily kept pace with AJ, though she was not familiar with the neighborhood. They ran, the music playing in their ears the only sound, for five miles before crashing through the front door of AJ's childhood home an hour later.

Aidan bolted up from his position on the living room floor where he watched some educational cartoon. "Hi mommy," he squeaked.

"Hey, baby," AJ replied, out of breath.

Mrs. James entered the living room and turned off the TV, to which Aidan groaned in protest.

"Grab your bag, it's time to go," she said to the three-year-old before turning her attention to the sweaty girls standing in the hallway. "Hi girls. Enjoy your run?"

"Good morning, Mrs. James. We did, thank you," Torryn replied politely.

"Please, call me Hailey. There's breakfast on the table, help yourself. And AJ don't forget the preschool lets out at noon today and I let the nanny have the week off."

"We'll pick him up, don't worry." AJ said as she crouched down to give her son a big kiss.

"Oh, and AJ, I washed some towels but I didn't have the time to fold them. Can you take care of it? They're on your bed." Her mom said as she rushed out of the door, holding Aidan's hand, who was tugging her along.

After Mrs. James and Aidan left, the girls ate their breakfast is silence, sneaking glances at each other. AJ doused her pancakes in syrup and watched Torryn eat a selection of fruits and cereals. Torryn had her own particular way of eating - slow, composed, meticulous - she really did fascinate AJ.

AJ was halfway through her large pancake stack when she lost her appetite, the smell of sweat and dirt hitting her differently. Maybe because she didn't immediately shower afterwards. She scrunched her nose and abruptly stood up, declaring that she would be in the shower. Before turning completely, she winked at Torryn. "Feel free to join me, it'll save water." She left Torryn sitting alone at the table.

When AJ entered the shower, she rolled her eyes at herself, not quite believing she just said that to Torryn. If that wasn't forward enough, then she didn't know what was. Honestly, at this point, she was sexually frustrated to the point of combustion.

AJ's thoughts kept whirling — should she feel guilty for ditching Torryn during breakfast? Should she feel bad for her lame comment? — once calmed down and she could no longer stand the frigid water she quickly turned the hot water on and washed her body. The scent of rosemary and mint filled the shower as she messaged shampoo into her hair. When she was finished and stepped out of the shower, she immediately regretted forgetting her clothes. And a towel. *Great,* she chastised herself, when she remembered her mother's earlier words and opened the cabinet to confirm that it was empty. AJ quickly darted for the bedroom hoping that

Torryn would still be in the kitchen.

To her dismay and horror, Torryn was sitting on her bed when AJ entered the room, hair still dripping wet and body completely on display.

"Are you okay?" Torryn asked, after a moment of silence. Her eyes darted back and forth, as if unsure where to look.

AJ nodded slowly. "Um, towel," she said as she pointed to the pile next to Torryn, who threw one immediately in AJ's direction.

"Thanks," AJ muttered as she wrapped herself in the thick cotton. "Are you...okay, I mean?"

"I'm not the one who abruptly took off in the middle of breakfast," Torryn teased in response.

"Sorry about that, I just really needed a shower."

"Come here," Torryn said, pulling AJ onto her lap, their mouths inches apart. She leaned her forehead against AJ's and closed her eyes, "It's not that I don't want you," she said as though she could read AJ's mind, "because, believe me, I do, more than you know. It's just..."

Torryn paused, sighed and pulled back slightly.

"What is it?"

"Sex complicates things, AJ. I just want to make sure that our feelings are real and not just some after-sex glow."

"And are you? Developing feelings?"

A smile teased across Torryn's face, "Maybe."

"I suppose I could live with that for now."

"I hope so, because girls like you are dangerous," Torryn mocked.

"What do you mean girls like me?" AJ played at being offended, making Torryn chuckle.

"Beautiful. Smart. Extremely sexy," Torryn said as she glances down.

AJ's towel had become partially undone, exposing a fair amount of cleavage. AJ noticed a sudden change in Torryn. There became a dangerous and feral glint in her eyes.

"We don't have to do this," AJ whispered in response, her pulsating body disagreeing with her words.

Torryn pushed aside the half of the towel that had already begun to slip, exposing AJ's naked body. The towel pooled around her lap. AJ held her breath as Torryn caressed her face then slowly traced along her jawline and down her neck. AJ's body shivered at the touch as Torryn's finger grazed her breast and continued its journey to the top of her thigh.

Torryn let out a heavy breathy as she grasped hard at AJ's hip and fell backwards onto the bed, pulling AJ down with her.

****

AJ awoke for the second time of the day, blissfully wrapped in Torryn's arms. She couldn't recall a time she'd ever felt this good, her body pleasantly satisfied. AJ picked up her phone and looked at the time. She turned to her side and faced Torryn, softly rubbing her hand over her girlfriend's naked body.

"Time to wake up, sleepy head," AJ said as she kissed Torryn's temple before she slipped out of bed.

AJ got dress and turned to face the bed when she heard Torryn's movements. She smiled at the sight of Torryn topless on her bed, blanket pooled on her lap.

AJ rushed over to the bed. "After sex glow looks good on you," she whispered onto Torryn's lips before kissing her, "I have to go pick up Aidan."

23

Now

We arrive back at the station at the same time as Drake. We start to walk towards the building together, but I pause mid-step.

"Hey, guys," I call out to them, "before we go in and I destroy my career, I've got an idea."

They stop and turn to me expectantly.

"Let's presume that our suspect doesn't know that AJ's alive. Considering AJ's somewhat of a celebrity, we've miraculously been able to keep much of this out of the press. However, if the news were to leak to the media that AJ was the sixth victim and is still alive then whoever attacked her will find out."

"So, you're wanting to use your ex-girlfriend as bait?" Drake asks.

"No, not exactly—well, actually, a little bit, yeah." I reply as I dig my fingernails into my palm.

"It's too risky," he replies.

"Tomorrow is Tuesday; we're out of time. If we don't catch the killer soon, we may end up with another victim in a few hours," I implore.

"It's worth bringing the idea to the Lieutenant," Dax says after a moment.

I nod and take a deep breath, "okay, let's get this over with."

The three of us continue on our way to Lieutenant Harris' office, where he's found on the phone when we arrive. From the red tones of his face, he wasn't having a pleasant conversation. Now, I'm not so sure this is the right time to add fuel to the fire.

"That was the mayor's office," Harris states firmly once he hung up, "She's not very happy with the lack of progress on this case. Frankly, neither am I."

"That may be changing today sir," Dax replies. "We believe we have a solid lead on the case. Isabella Turner is a prime suspect."

"Which is why I need to speak with you, sir," I add before Harris can ask Dax to elaborate. I briefly glance at my partner, who gives an encouraging nod. I stand up straighter. "I'd like to excuse myself from this case."

"Excuse me?" He asks incredulously, jaw snapping shut with an audible snap.

"I knew our last victim, Miss James, a long time ago. We haven't seen or spoken to each other in years and so I didn't think there would be any conflict." I pause as the anger etches itself on his face. With my heart racing I push forward with my explanation. "With this new suspect being the younger sister of an old friend that is connected to both the victim and myself, it's evident that this is no longer the case."

Lieutenant Harris stands, watching us for a

moment. When he finally speaks he looks directly at Dax, "You knew about this?"

"Yes, sir. I agreed with Detective Michealson that with the lapse in the time that the personal connection to the victim wouldn't be a conflict, however, as it became so I, along with Agent Drake, encouraged her to remove herself from the case."

"Agent Drake?" Harris prompts, turning his attention to the FBI agent without so much as a glance at me, which was impressive considering that I was standing between them.

"I agree with Detective Grieson's assessment of the situation and choices he made. In a small city like this, it's unlikely that a cop wouldn't come across a victim they knew personally, at least once in their career. It's my opinion that Detective Michealson has been able to be professionally objective throughout this case. There is only a conflict now due to the various connections between the victims, the suspect, and the Detective."

Lieutenant Harris scrutinizes the three of us, expressionless. Finally he speaks, his voice echoing slightly in the small space, "Alright, Detective Michealson. I'm placing you on administrative leave for ninety days—"

"Ninety days?" I blurt, unthinkingly.

"Yes!" He shouts back, unaware of the shock it causes, "and that's the minimum so don't push your luck."

"But, sir—"

"Torryn," Dax interrupts at the same time Drake places his hand on my shoulder, "it's better than the alternative. Don't get yourself fired."

I open my mouth to protest further but the heated glare Harris was cutting me with stopped any vocalization.

"Go home, Detective, and I want you here at nine o'clock for the paperwork. You'll need to hand over your badge and gun to the clerk down in holding."

I nod firmly, once, and Drake mirrors the motion, shooting me a small, forced smile. Dax sighs and gives my should a squeeze before dropping his hand back to his side.

"Maybe next time you'll be more forthcoming with information that may jeopardize a case. Be grateful I didn't say without pay, Detective. If it weren't for Agent Drake's opinion of you, it would have been. Now get out of my office before I change my mind."

"Yes, sir."

I turn and quickly leave his office, not bothering to stop by my desk to collect my personal things or to clock out. My lungs feel heavy, like someone is sitting on my chest, and I can't help but shake out my hands, hoping that it will get rid of this feeling of being kicked like an unwanted puppy. I'm on autopilot, not exactly sure how I made my way down to holding, but my hands shake as I remove my badge from around my neck and my gun from its holster.

The middle-aged clerk at the desk gives me a frown and begins typing on her keyboard. "I don't have anything in the system on you yet, Detective."

"Not yet, but you will," I respond, emotionless, numb. "I'm coming back for the paperwork in the morning."

"I see," she looks at me with knowing eyes, "how long?"

"Ninety-days, minimum."

She resumes her typing and prints out a few sheets of paper. I sign all the spots she indicated for me to sign and watch as she locks away my gun and shield. I hand her the forms and without another word, I turn my back and make my way to the parking lot.

The moment I get into my car my phone pings with a text from Dax.

I'm not supposed to, but I'll keep you posted.

I reply back with a quick 'thanks' before starting the engine, intending to go home and get caught up on some much needed sleep. Instead, I head to a local bar I became acquainted with during my first case as a detective.

The drive was relatively quick, not hitting a single red light. When I walk in the the dimly lit bar, I make my way to the end of the wooden countertop.

"Good afternoon, Detective," says the cheerful bartender, "It's been a while since I've seen you around here. What can I get you?"

"I'll take whatever you have on tap."

"Bad day?"

I scoff and roll my eyes. "Got suspended."

The bartender gasps, obviously just as surprised as I am, even though I saw it coming. "For what?"

"I don't want to talk about it."

"Say no more. I got the perfect beer for you, then, if that's how your night is going."

Soon there's a glass of dark lager in front of me, the aroma of heavy oak, hops, and something sweet hits my nose even before I bring it to my lips to take a sip.

I almost gag as the beer hits my tongue, the burning sensation of the alcohol unexpected. "Jesus Christ, what the hell is this?"

"It's Armageddon. It'll knock you on your ass."

My eyes were wide for a moment, looking the brand up on my phone and reading the alcohol content I realize this was probably the worst decision I ever made…well maybe second worse.

I shrug and take another gulp, scrunching my nose against the harsh taste. I minute goes by and I decide it's not actually that bad once you get to the third sip.

I finish drinking my beer in silence and order another. I caught my first criminal as detective in this bar. It seems only fitting that I spend my last day as a detective in this place.

24

Then

AJ returned to the dorm suite after her writing class. As soon as she opened the door, she was greeted with an armful of Torryn. The rest of her roommates were probably not here.

"I have the best news," Torryn said.

"Well," AJ replied, "what is it?"

Torryn released her and handed her a letter. "I got in. I start training at the academy the week after graduation."

AJ entered a state of shock as she read Torryn's acceptance letter. She looked from the letter to Torryn's face, with her eyes swimming with obvious delight, and her lips parted wide in the biggest smile that AJ had never seen. It made AJ's heart flutter and her stomach drop.

AJ swallowed, realizing she had taken too long to reply. "That's great!" She exclaimed with enough excitement to save the lapse. "Congratulations, babe!"

"Thanks. I have an eight o'clock class tonight but after that we should celebrate."

"Yeah, absolutely. I'm meeting the girls at Epic Underground. You should meet me there afterwards," AJ suggested.

"I'm free until then, so we have a few hours for a more private celebration," Torryn raised her eyebrows mischievously, snaking her arm around AJ's hips and pulling their bodies together

"I, uh..." AJ began, a bit flustered, too shocked that Torryn initiated the contact this time to really do much other than ride with it.

Soon, soft, insistent lips crashed against hers. Torryn's tongue immediately seeking entrance. AJ's breath caught in her chest as she arched into Torryn's grip, the other girl moving them along to the bedroom, leaving a trail of clothes along the way. AJ's breaths came faster, moans slipping out as Torryn moved her hands along her body, gripping, pulling and digging into the flesh as they both fought for control, wanting to both dominate and be dominated.

The sound of the door slamming shut startled AJ, whose lips were red and swollen from Torryn's efforts, and whose body ached.

AJ locked eyes with Torryn, lips parted on a breath, but before she could do anything herself, Torryn toppled them onto the bed.

****

When AJ woke, she was alone bed. A note was left on the pillow advising to drink some water, and stating that Torryn left for class and would see her later tonight.

AJ searched in her jean pockets for her phone and sent a text to her two best friends asking them to meet her at the shady dive bar a few blocks away from campus. Niki responded immediately with an offer to pick both AJ and Ava up but AJ declined.

She needed a good run.

An hour later, AJ was deep into an alcohol buzz when she received a text from Torryn informing her that she just left class and would head to the bar soon. AJ picked at the fries on the plate in front of her.

"It's not that I'm not happy for her," she said, looking between Ava and Niki, "it's just that everything is going great, we just started dating, and now she's leaving."

"Well, what did you expect?" Niki inserted bluntly.

Ava shot her a pointed look, "Niki."

"What? AJ's an adult, no need to sugarcoat things," turning her attention back to AJ, "Honestly. You're a freshman, she's a senior. You knew what you were getting into when you started this whole thing. Did you expect her to just put her career on hold, stick around campus, and wait until you were done?"

"Well, no, but I also didn't expect to fall in love with her, either, and I don't know if long distance will work. What if we just, I don't know, fizzle out?

Ava cupped AJ's hand with her own. "Maybe that is a conversation you should have with Torryn."

AJ nodded.

"Speak of the stoic devil," Niki said, nodding her head in the direction of the entrance, "and she shall appear."

Ava moved to the other side of the booth and sat next to Niki when Torryn approached.

AJ moved over a little bit to make more room for Torryn, automatically leaning into the kiss that was placed on her cheek.

"You okay?" Torryn asked in way of greeting.

AJ smiled politely and ducked her head a bit.

Torryn turned towards the other girls, "hey, thanks for letting me crash your plans."

Ava played along, "oh, no problem, you're always welcome. You know that."

"I hear congratulations are in order," Niki chimed in, "so you'll be taking off for what, six months or so?"

"Thank you, and yes something like that," Torryn responded.

"Can I get you anything to eat and drink? It's on me, as a congratulations gift," Ava piped up.

"Oh, you don't have to."

"I want to. Wings and a beer?" She asked, pulling Niki with her as she left without giving Torryn the chance to decline her offer again.

AJ inwardly groaned, knowing that Ava was trying to given them space to talk. But AJ didn't want to talk about this now, not here.

"Are you sure you're okay? You seem…distant."

AJ forced a bigger smile and cleared her throat. "Yeah, I'm fine now that you're here."

Torryn stared at her, waiting. AJ stared back.

"We should talk later, about some things, y'know."

AJ actually did groan aloud this time. "Infamous words there."

Torryn rolled her eyes. "I'm serious. We need to."

"Sure, sure, but later. Tonight, we celebrate!" She shouted before shooting back the rest of her cocktail in a few gulps, ignoring the look on Torryn's face.

****

Later, that evening, and AJ was unsure how much later, they arrived back at their apartment. She very much wanted to get out of her clothes and into bed so that she could sleep. The bed looked nice.

"What's wrong?"

AJ glanced back at Torryn, then turned to the bed and threw the blanket off the top half. "Nothing's wrong. Why would, why would something be wrong?"

"Because you're drunker than I've ever seen you and you kept avoiding me tonight as if I did something to you."

"You didn't do anything, don't worry about it." AJ sat at the edge of the bed and stare at her socks. "You got in, congrats," She slurred as she bent over to remove the offending garments.

"So, that's what this is about?"

AJ sighed and flopped back onto the bed. "Just break up with me, already, you don't have to be nice about it."

She thought she heard Torryn laugh, then sigh. She could almost hear the girl roll her eyes.

"I'm not going to break up with you, you silly, paranoid girl. Is that what you were thinking about all night?"

AJ tried to nod but only managed a grunt. She heard some rustling around and grew curious. She lifted herself into a sitting position, which took too much effort for her, and tried to see where Torryn went.

Oh, the desk. To grab the letter.

"Read it again, knucklehead."

"No."

"Yes."

"Fine." AJ held out her hand to take the proffered letter. Her eyes swan and couldn't focus. "Yeah, I can't, I can't read that."

She definitely heard Torryn chuckle that time.

"It says, 'We are pleased to inform you that you have been accepted into the Parker Heights Police Academy.''

AJ was silent for a few moments, not understanding why Torryn was reading the letter to her. "And?" she finally asked. "Means you're leaving'."

"The *Parker Heights* Police Academy."

AJ perked up. "Oh! My hometown!"

"Yes, silly, your home town."

AJ smiled, then crinkled her eyebrows together, "But, that means that—" she motioned between herself and Torryn with excited hands.

"Yes, of course. I chose Parker Heights, why would I have chosen that location if I were planning on breaking up with you. It's only a three hour drive so the commute won't be so bad."

AJ beamed, standing upright and throwing herself at Torryn, arms circling around her shoulders and whispered, "I love you."

"I love you, too."

25

Now

I wake up with a splitting headache and Atlas' wet nose nudging at my feet.

"Okay, okay."

Picking up my phone, I groan at the time. "No time for a run boy, do your business and back inside. Got it?"

Atlas whines and leaves the room, me on his tail. I shiver when we get outside, the air frosty against my skin and I wish I had taken the time to grab my robe instead of coming outside in my shorts and tank.

Atlas is moving in slow motion and I swear, it's been an eternity when we walk back into my toasty apartment. The time on my phone confirms it's only been three minutes. I put on a pot of coffee then jump in the shower to quickly wash away the smell of formaldehyde. After I have successfully showered, brushed my teeth twice, dress and drank an entire pot of coffee I grab my keys.

"Shit," I whisper to myself, remembering that I took a Lyft home. I look at the time and realize that there's not enough time to get my car first so I call for a Lyft to take me down to the station to pick up my paperwork.

Lucky for me there is a car nearby so it doesn't take long before I'm in the back seat. Once I arrive at the station I make my way to Lieutenant Harris' office and knock on the door. He motions me in and he's accompanied by our Sargent and another higher ranked officer whose name escapes me at the moment. My mind is still a little fuzzy from drinking the night before but I force myself to focus.

I listen to Harris as he explains what I already know. I'm suspended for ninety-days with pay, pending a reinstatement hearing after the three months is up to determine if I'm fit to return. If, at the conclusion of this case, my actions have a negative impact, it's possible my suspension could be extended until everything clears.

I want to lash out, but I keep my composure, not wanting to make things worse. I quickly scan over the document handed to me that outlines everything Harris just went over and I sign it. The weight of the pen heavy in my hand.

"I've already turned in my badge and gun, sir." I advise him, showing him my copy of the signed paperwork from the holding clerk.

"See you in ninety days, Detective," Harris says to me as he hands me my copy of the paperwork, his way of dismissing me.

I pass by my desk, and my partner, without a word. Dax probably would have followed me had it not been for Lieutenant Harris calling him into his office. Drake will most likely continue working with Dax as his partner until the case is over. After that he'll either work without a partner until my return or get assigned a temporary partner. I feel selfish for a moment as I briefly hope he choses the former.

I call another Lyft to take me to the bar so I can retrieve my car. On the radio, the DJs are talking about the latest news to hit the media outlets. I ask the driver to turn up the volume.

"I'm not sure how You Heard It Here First dot com got wind of the story," the voice coming through the speaker says. "But the news is spreading like wildfire. Hometown author, A.E. James, is currently in critical condition after being attached by what sources say is a serial killer—."

"Damn it," I whisper to myself.

"—five other victims—" I continue to listen in horror as they discuss the case. The case that was supposed to be kept out of the news. I can't help but wonder if someone from the department leaked the news.

"I don't know how the police haven't been able to catch the guy—"

And then it hits me. Dax, Drake, and I were discussing this very scenario. We put enough information out there to piss off the killer, hoping that it'll make them give themselves away.

I only marginally relax and decide exactly how I'm going to spend my day off.

Once we arrive at the bar I jump into my car and take off towards the hospital. I'll probably have to take the back entrance as the main entrance will most likely be swarmed with reporters from all major news outlets by the time I get there.

****

I make my way through the ICU floor, scanning the lay-out of the floor and sneaking past the officer who is flirting with the young nurse behind the registration counter instead of standing watch outside of AJ's room. I clench my jaw and move on. I, technically, don't have a reason to be here on a professional capacity due to my suspension. I realize that my being here is solely on a personal level, they were right about me being to close to this case.

I pull a chair up and sit next to AJ's hospital bed, out of sight from the door.

"Hey, you," I whisper in her ear, "I don't even know if you can hear me, I mean, that's what everyone says right? That you can hear people when you're in a coma. But, anyway, I'd really like it if you could wake up."

I relax into the chair, holding her hand and staring towards the door. It comes as a surprise when my phone jingles with a call. I answer quickly, the sound tooled in the quiet room.

"Michealson."

"Hey," it's Drake, "I just wanted to let you know that the favor I called in…it worked."

"So, you got the juvie records unsealed?"

"Yeah, the DNA under AJ's fingernails is a match for Isabella Turner."

I breathe out and run my hand through my hair. "Must have been some favor he owed you," I reply, relieved that I didn't get myself suspended for nothing. Isabella is our killer, we finally have the evidence we needed that she attacked AJ. Now we just have to figure out how to connect her to the murders.

"Hey, Drake, did the team leak the case? I heard about it on the radio."

"Yeah, we did. It was your idea and Harris thought it was a good one. We're hoping it works, though."

"That would be great. You've got a warrant?"

"DA's getting it signed as we speak. We'll head back to her sister's apartment—"

"You need to search—"

"I know, Grieson and I are headed there as soon as the warrant is in our hands."

"I'm uh, at the hospital now actually—" I hear the sigh he lets out but press on, "I know, I just, I had to see her. Anyway, there's a uniform here so if anyone shows up that hasn't before, he'll let you know."

"Yeah, okay. Grieson and I will keep you updated."

"Okay, thanks Drake. You're not so bad after all."

I end the call before he has the chance to respond and shake out my shoulders. Now, I wait.

After a few anxious hours, where I paced the room, tapped my feet, awaiting a call or text to let me know they arrested Isabella, wishing I were in on the take down, and dozed off for a bit, I hear someone approaching the room. I look up at the door as it opens.

I'm greeted with the sight of Isabella Turner, her

Latino features more prominent than Ava's but they are still similar enough to carry a resemblance.

I slide my phone out of my pocket, careful to keep it hidden. I send Dax a blank text, our code that one of use is in trouble. I'll follow it up with a call, which he'll answer without a word and immediately put his end on mute.

It takes Isabella a moment to notice me in the dim lit room. "Oh, sorry, I didn't realize anybody else was here. I should go and give you your time with her."

I cock my head to the side and smile. "No, no, it's fine, come in. Did the officer ID you too?"

Her eyes flicker briefly and I notice her shoulders stiffen. "He's sleeping on the chair."

The hairs on the back of my neck stood at the way Isabella said the word sleeping. I swallowed. I hit the call button and place the phone next to AJ as I stand, raising my arms in a stretch. "Do you want to sit?"

"No," she replies too quickly, locking eyes with me. They are the same dead eyes I remember by the lake. A gaze that isn't afraid of death. "I mean, I've been sitting down all day, I'd like to stand."

I stay silent but refuse to take my eyes off her.

"I just heard about AJ. It's a shame. Such a horrible thing to have happened," Isabella says, the sympathy in her voice outweighed by the upward tilt of her lips. "You're Torryn, right? We met a few years ago, remember? I heard you're a cop now."

"I am," I reply, keeping my cool, and placing my fingers lightly on AJ's wrist as I lean against the frame of the bed. "I'm actually a homicide detective now."

Isabella's left hand runs over her neck, where there are faint, red scratches.

"What happened there?"

"What do you mean?"

"Your neck. I don't mean to pry, but...did you get scratched recently?"

"Oh, yeah, mhmm, by my cat."

I nod and accept the lie. Her left hand comes to rest at her hip, her right is tightly clenched and turned away from me.

"Who could have done this?" Isabella says, creeping slowly forward. "Do you...have...any suspects?"

I shrug my shoulders, "I'm sure they have a few."

"They?"

"Yeah, I'm actually not on this case."

Isabella visibly relaxes at this news as the beeps on the machine monitoring AJ's vitals spasm violently. As if AJ's body was reacting to the sound of Isabella's voice, "oh, I would have thought-"

I don't hear anything else because I see a syringe in Isabella's hand clearly now and it all happens so fast.. *This is it,* I think as Isabella lurches at AJ. *Time to move.*

Moving faster than Isabella, I grab her left hand just as she reaches out to AJ, yanking her backwards.

She twists and throws her two arms around my waist, trying to lift me off my feet but I bend forward and we fall to the floor. I twist and move out from underneath her weight, wrestling her onto her back.

Adrenaline gives me the strength to pin Isabella's arms down.

I knock the syringe from her hand in one swift move and it skids across the cold tile. Isabella jolts forward and head butts me, my teeth clacking together by the impact and I stumble backwards, spots swimming in my vision, and an obvious ache already starting.

"Fuck," I curse under my breath just as I come out of the brief stupor.

I use all my strength to charge at Isabella, tackling her back to the ground. I press my knees into her thighs, and lock my ankles around hers. I grab Isabella's hair and knock her head to the floor, a thick thud, and pin it there. She lays there, weakened and disoriented, but I still clamp down on her elbows, making sure she can't surprise me.

I breathe out, long and hard, trying to control my rage. It's only then that I notice a sharp searing pain in my side. I look down to see a large stain of blood appear on my shirt.

"Oh, shit," I mutter, my eyes fluttering.

Isabella groans and starts to move underneath me.

"Stay down, bitch," I grunt out as I throw my full weight into her abdomen, knocking the breath out of her.

Dax and Drake burst into the room, the door flying open and banging against the wall.

Drake lunges down to Isabella, picks her off the floor and pins her against the wall.

"Shit, what happened?" Dax says when he sees me clutching my side, blood seeping through my fingers.

"I…" Is all I can manage before falling onto my back, familiar signs of shock overwhelming my body. My lungs start to hyperventilate and spots blur my vision.

"You're fine, breathe," he says as he adds his hand to mine, keeping pressure on the wound.

I think I hear Drake call out to the nurses in the hall.

I shoot Dax a glare, though it's most likely ineffective. "Easy for you—to—say," I groan out, feeling weaker as the seconds tick by.

I look at Isabella, with blood dripping in patches over her face, and the wide, vicious grin spreading across her lips. It's enough for me to want to punch her straight in the face.

Nurses barge into the room, then, their shoes squeaking on the linoleum.

"I think…I could use… some…help," I say, my voice sounding far away, as I finally give in.

26

Then

"What the hell, Torryn?" AJ fumed, pacing in and out of the camera's view.

"I'm sorry I didn't tell you first, but this *is* a good thing," Torryn said defensively, her face illuminated by the glow of her computer.

"How is this a good thing? Instead of coming back after you graduate from the academy, you're staying there. I still have two and a half more years before I finish school."

"I understand this has been hard on you, it's been hard on me, too. But—"

AJ did not like that tone. It was a tone that meant Torryn was beyond her patience.

"—this is my job, my career. Not all of us have a rich mom to live off of while we chase after a dream, AJ."

AJ's mouth dropped wide open.

"Look, I'm sorry," Torryn apologized, her heavy breath escaping, "that was out of line."

"*Way* out of line."

"We can handle the long distance thing for a bit

longer, right? We've made it this far."

"Yeah, and the whole six months have been hell," says AJ, tears welling up. "I just thought when you finished you'd move back here…like we discussed. Like you promised."

"I know…I know. But when they offered the job, they also offered to pay off the loan to attend the academy. I could't pass that up."

"I just want you here with me."

"I'll still come visit every chance I get. And you'll be here on breaks. We'll make this work AJ, I promise. Look, I have to go. I'll see you this weekend, right? I love you. Always."

Incensed and unhappy, AJ did not respond, instead she disconnected the call by firmly closing her laptop shut.

****

The week dragged. AJ was still upset over her last conversation with Torryn. They hadn't talked since. She placed her bags in the trunk of her car. Having her car now that she wasn't a freshman meant that AJ more freedom to come and go as she pleased. Meaning, she didn't have to wait until finals were over in order to head home for the weekend, be back by Tuesday to take a few tests and then home again by Friday for winter break.

She was looking forward to seeing her mom and Aidan, still debating if she was feeling the same towards Torryn. She waited in the parking lot of the off-campus apartment she shared with Niki and Ava, who were joining her for the ride home. As she was about to put the key in the ignition, AJ's phone chirped alerting her of a received text.

Speak of the devil, AJ thought when she saw Torryn's name appear on her screen.

Hey. You're still coming right?

Yeah, on my way now.

Can't wait to see you. I have a surprise.
I miss you. We haven't talked since our video call.

Just been really busy.
See you soon.

Still mad at me?

I got over it.

I'll pick you up.
Love you.

...Pick me up?

Torryn didn't respond to AJ's last text but as promised she did pick up AJ from her mother's house later that afternoon. AJ sat in the passenger seat, inhaling that new car smell. Torryn's new job meant she now had a regular influx of money and AJ could tell that Torryn was proud of that. This car was probably the first thing that Torryn ever really owned, AJ realized as they sat in silence, AJ's own pride slowly replacing her infuriation. AJ smiled as she looked out the window and wondered where Torryn was taking her.

"Can you put this on," Torryn asked, handing her a sleep mask, "we're almost there and I don't want to ruin the surprise."

AJ took the mask and positioned it over her eyes without saying a word.

A few minutes later AJ felt the car being parked and the engine being turned off. She sat still as she heard Torryn exit the car only to return to the passenger side and open AJ's door. She was guided up a flight of stairs, after which she heard Torryn unlock a door, then continued walking a few more steps. AJ felt Torryn carefully lift the mask and found herself standing in the middle of a spacious, but semi-bare, apartment. Only a few large cardboard boxes, tucked away in the corner of the room, occupied the living space.

"I know there isn't much stuff in here yet," Torryn said, observing AJ's reaction, but once the paychecks start rolling in more, I'll change that.

AJ couldn't quite grasp what was happening. She stuttered as her nostrils flared at the aroma of garlic and spices in the air. She looked at Torryn, and tried to absorb the new surroundings.

"I'm cooking you dinner," said Torryn happily.

AJ smiled as she walked and twirled around the massive living room, mesmerized by the French doors that led out to a balcony. Torryn followed her through the doors. The balcony overlooked a garden with a pond filled with orange-gold koi.

"Torryn, it's beautiful." AJ whispered.

Torryn reached for AJ's hand, lacing their fingers

together. "I'm glad you like it. I was hoping you and Aidan would live here with me."

"Seriously?"

"After you graduate, of course, but when you come home on breaks, I want this to be the home you come back to,"Torryn added.

AJ stood in front of Torryn, stunned. She hadn't thought they were at this stage, yet. Sure, she had imagined a future with Torryn, but not so soon, even if she was a romantic.

"Question."

Torryn opened her mouth, then stood straighter. "Okay."

"If Aidan were to wake up in the middle of the night and throw up, would you be willing to help take care of him?"

"Yes."

"Would you be willing to pick him up or drop him off at school if I couldn't?"

"Of course."

"Indulge in movie nights with us?"

Torryn rolled her eyes but smiled. "Obviously."

AJ grinned, her stomach slowly unraveling the knots it formed earlier. "I know. I was testing you."

"I figured. But you don't have to worry. I gave this a lot of thought."

"You must have." AJ realized what a big step this was for Torryn. She kissed Torryn gently on the lips and moved her fingers to intertwine with Torryn's. "I'd love to, in answer to your question."

Torryn smiled a wide grin. "Come on, you have to see the rest of the place."

Hand in hand, AJ was whisked away to the

doorway of an adjacent room.

"I thought this could be Aidan's bedroom," Torryn said as she opened the door to reveal a racecar bed next to the window, and a bright blue dresser.

"You already bought things for him?" That was a little cocky," AJ teased.

"I had hoped you'd say yes. I know it's not much but...it will be."

"Babe, it's perfect," AJ interrupted her, nuzzling into her neck.

"Ready to see our room?"

Without waiting for an answer, Torryn whisked her away to the master bedroom. A blow-up mattress had been inflated and positioned in the middle of the floor.

"I, um, thought maybe you'd like to pick out our bed together."

"Gee, such a romantic," AJ quipped playfully.

Torryn pulled AJ close to her, and wrapped her arms around her waist, "I've missed you."

AJ tenderly kissed Torryn a dozen times on her lips. She heard a faint beeping sound as Torryn pulled back slightly.

"Ready to eat?"

"Oh, you have *no* idea."

Torryn rolled her eyes and led AJ to the dining room, adjacent to the kitchen. She motioned for AJ to sit at the table.

She watched as Torryn grabbed a bottle of wine out of the fridge. AJ saw enough of the bottle to see the brand as Torryn set it on the counter.

"Mmm, my favorite! You know, I don't turn

twenty-one for another few days. Now that you're a sworn police officer should you really be contributing to the delinquency of a minor?"

Torryn came out of the kitchen carrying a glass baking dish. "Funny girl, aren't you?"

Steam wafts from the dish.

"Oh, I'm a hoot," chuckled AJ.

"Baked spaghetti, and I'm pretty sure this is your favorite too," Torryn replied. She placed the dish onto a heat mat on the table. "I asked your mom to teach me how to make it."

"Isn't this against your diet?"

"Not tonight."

AJ watched Torryn retreat back to the kitchen and retrieve the bottle of wine before she returned and took a seat at the table, her smile never leaving her face and her eyes glistening in a way that AJ didn't recognize.

"What have you done with my Torryn?" Asked AJ, laughing.

Torryn scooped up a portion for AJ's plate, and then her own, before pouring wine into the glasses.

AJ immediately funneled a fork of cream cheese and the melting garlic meat sauce into her mouth, "oh my God, babe, this is incredible."

"To us," Torryn said, raising her glass, and looking deep into AJ's eyes.

"To us," repeated AJ, chinking the glass and returning Torryn's gorgeous love-filled gaze.

****

After dinner and much giggling and declarations of love, AJ insisted they start to unpack Torryn's boxes. With her wine in hand, AJ ran over to the stack of boxes and began to tear off the tape at the top. She loved how Torryn watched her. Feeling giddy and tipsy, AJ pulled out the textbooks, and detective novels, to fill the room's built-in bookshelf.

As AJ lifted a book up - one of Torryn's favorite Agatha Christie novels - and goes to place it on the shelf, a photograph fell out of the book onto the floor. AJ picked up the photograph and stared at it.

"What's this?" AJ asked Torryn, showing her the worn photo.

Torryn looked up at AJ and quickly tensed when she noticed what AJ was asking about, "That's my, uh," Torryn swallowed, "birth parents. That photo is all I have of them. I never got the chance to meet my father and she abandoned me, but—well, I know it's stupid to keep them when they didn't want to keep me—"

"No," AJ says quickly, "It's not."

As AJ said these words, she crooked her head to the right and slowly sat down on the floor as feelings of disbelief swept over her, tears welling up in her eyes. She was about to give Torryn either the best gift she could give or her worst nightmare. She hoped it wasn't the latter.

"Are you okay?" Torryn asked. "You look like you've seen a ghost."

"I know this man, Torryn."

"What? That's impossible."

"No, it's not," AJ shifted, tucking her feet

underneath her as she sat on the floor, motioning for Torryn to follow her lead. "This is Niki's father."

Torryn stared at AJ. Her mouth fell open as her chest began to rise and fall rapidly. "What, did you just- - *what?*" Torryn said, noticeably trying to desperately string her thoughts into words.

AJ had never seen Torryn so at a loss for words and it worried her. "In all of the time spent at my mom's how have you not run into him?" AJ asked incredulously.

"I've been rather busy!"

Torryn's response sounded distant to AJ's ears, an unrecognized expression on Torryn's face that made AJ feel useless, unable to help Torryn through whatever emotions she was going through, until she thought of someone who might be able to help.

"I'm going to text Niki to get over here," AJ declared. "If this if your dad then you two should talk."

Torryn nodded as AJ went to grab her phone. Less than an hour later the three of them sat on the living room floor. Niki held the photo of Torryn's parents. AJ had wanted to give the two of them privacy, but Torryn had pleaded with her not to. AJ stayed knowing that both her girlfriend and her best friend would need her support.

"He didn't know about you," Niki said in a hushed whisper that unnerved AJ. "If he had, he would have never let you grow up without him."

AJ felt Torryn's grip tighten round her hand. Torryn had been silent since Niki's arrival, forcing AJ to explain the photograph of her father—their— father. She didn't know what to do or say in this situation. AJ was used to this behavior from Torryn. It was Niki's demeanor that gave AJ pause and had her on edge. She had never see her best friend so unsure and hesitant. Torryn and Niki had butted heads so often, usually because of her, that AJ was unsure how either of them were taking the news.

"Holy shit," Niki exclaimed, finally becoming her normal self before AJ was forced to break the tension. "I have a sister. Do you want to meet him?"

"No," Torryn deadpanned.

"It's probably too soon," AJ placated, she recognized the disapproving look that appeared on Niki's face at Torryn's response.

Niki nodded as she stood and handed the photo to Torryn. "You're probably right. Come on, I need a drink."

AJ stood and pulled Torryn up beside her, "Niki, I don't think I can get away with underage drinking in a bar in a town that everyone knows everyone."

"Good," Niki replied as she pulled Torryn's arm. "Because you're not invited."

AJ stood in shocked silence as she watched the girls exit the apartment. She wasn't sure if she was more shocked over Niki telling her she wasn't invited or the fact that Torryn didn't offer any sort of protest. She looked around the bare apartment and then called her mom to pick her up, explaining what happened. After she hung up she realized that her mom didn't ask for the address. AJ smiled, *of course mom would already know.*

A few minutes later in the front seat of her mom's car, her son in the back asking where 'Torn' was. She pulled out her phone to send a quick text to

Torryn.

> *Going to a movie with mom and Aidan.*
> *Text me when you get home*
> *Have fun & try not to kill Niki.*
> *Love you*

I'll try. Love you.

27

Now

I wake up groggy, my mouth filled with cotton and my lids heavy with sleep. My body itches and I can feel the stiffness of the hospital bed underneath me. I groan at the discomfort that makes itself known to me. I refuse to make eye contact with a tired looking Dax who sits beside the bed. I see Drake in front of the door and I have to force myself not to roll my eyes at the thought that they both stayed. Don't they have jobs to do?

I push down the hospital blanket and pull at the seam of my hospital gown to look at several red and raw stitches holding my skin together on my abdomen.

"What the hell, Dax," I finally croak out, my throat dry. "Why aren't you at the station?"

He gives me his best 'are you stupid' look and I can't help but smile. "We have other officers who are looking after Isabella until Drake and I arrive to interrogate her," replies in lieu of actually answering.

"How bad is it?"

"Little bit of blood loss, twelve stitches. Missed any major organs. Quick surgery fixed you right up."

"Great, let's get out of here," I say, forcing myself to sit up. I clench my jaw and force the nausea that threatens to overpower me away as pain sears throughout my body.

Dax holds his hand out to help steady me but I swat him away.

"I don't think the doctor is going to agree to that."

"Yeah, yeah, whatever, I'll leave against medical advise. We've got work to do."

"You're suspended, remember? So there is no 'we' here Torryn," he says, turning away enough for me to grab my pants that were left on the bedside table and pull them on.

"Doesn't mean I can't watch you interrogate the hell out of her. Besides, she assaulted a police officer, I have a statement to make." I say once I am no longer cringing at the sharp pain emanating from the stab wound.

"Technically, you didn't have a reason to be here—"

I pull on my socks and shoes, "She's a friend—"

"—so it's going to look like an awful big coincidence that you were here just as our main suspect—"

"Yeah, I know."

"—It's not going to look good on or off a report," Dax finishes, dead-pan.

I let out a sigh. "Then we can say I was visiting another patient and heard something."

"That won't work. You're not going to get in trouble, not really. The brass can't control what you do off duty, but this is still not going to go over well with the Lieutenant."

"You're right, but feel free to tell him to look at it this way. My being here prevented a murder. As a good samaritan, I had to act. "

"You tell him," He smirks.

"Absolutely not, he'd kill me."

He laughs and I finish getting dressed, hissing at the strain pulling my shirt over my head causes and groaning once I see and smell the dried blood.

"Still wanting to leave AMA?"

"Obviously. I want a new shirt."

"We thought you might say that," says Drake as Dax hands me a bunch of completed discharge papers.

"All you have to do is sign them and we can go."

"I smile at Dax and sign the papers without care. My smile fades when a memory hits me. "Officer Cage?"

Dax looks at me, a sadness in his eyes that comes from a deep loss but it was Drake who answered, "he wasn't as lucky."

I take a minute, breathing deeply and slowly until my lungs are so full that I am forced to let out my breath in a hard exhale, then hand the papers back to Dax. "Let's go."

He stands and places a bag on the edge of my bed.

I blink and open the bag. "You let me put on my bloody clothes when you had fresh ones this whole time?"

"We'll be right out there if you need us," he sings as he heads towards the door.

"I don't really think this is the time for jokes,

Dax."

He shrugs his shoulders and leaves.

After I painfully get re-dressed I join them, refusing their offers of assistance. As we're walking towards the elevator, me clutching at my side, I ask Dax and Drake to wait for me outside. "I'd like to go check on AJ," I explain.

Drake gives me a pointed look as Dax sighs and pretends like her doesn't hear me. Dax steps into the elevator to go down to the lobby. He and Drake share a look over the threshold.

"I'll be quick. I just need to make sure she's okay."

Drake nods at Dax, as if they came to a silent understanding. Dax presses a button and the elevator door closes, with Drake still beside me.

"Good to see you boys bonded in my absence," I say, not bothering to hide the irritation in my voice as I press the call button again and wait for an elevator to take me up to her floor.

"You're injured," Drake says in response, "we can't let you roam the hospital alone."

I nod as we step into the elevator. Maybe I'm crazy and the pressure on my hand was nothing. But maybe she did react to Isabella's voice; it's not uncommon for coma patients to hear things, so there's a chance. But more importantly, maybe she had started to wake up. I refuse to let myself get excited at the idea.

When we approach her room, he stays near the nurses station. I notice that Officer Lipscomb is stationed outside the door. After a quick glance at Agent Drake he nods and allows me to enter without signing in. No proof that I returned today.

AJ is still asleep and I try to ignore the pain that sight causes me.

Gently interlacing the fingers of AJ's right hand with my left, I whisper "Hey, you," into her ear. I take a deep breath to control myself before continuing.

"I'm pretty sure you can hear me. I want you to know that I think we caught the person who did this to you, You need to come back. Your son needs you. Your mom needs you," I break off, my voice beginning to crack, "I need you."

I watch AJ's chest rise and fall. I look at her, for the first time in a long time, really *look* at her. She seems so fragile. Her face still bruised and swollen. *Why would Isabella want to hurt this beautiful person,* I think, as I blink back the tears that fill my eyes, unable to stop myself from sobbing.

The pain in my side creeps up, crushing my lungs and wrapping its tendrils around my heart. My head collapses gently onto her pillow and I kiss her cheek. This is the second time I truly allowed myself to cry for her and it doesn't even compare to the empty apartment and note.

It's at this moment , I realize that all those years when I was afraid, or too proud, to stubborn, to let myself love, or be myself around AJ, that I accomplished nothing. I let AJ walk away three years ago when I should have gone after her and begged her to stay. I love my career but now I know that I love her more and maybe, if I just try harder, I can still have both. I made the wrong choice then. I can only hope that if—when—she wakes up, AJ is willing to give us a second chance. Because at this moment, I decided that if she does, I'll never let her go again.

"I'm sorry for everything," I whisper, the years of regret push the tears out from behind my eyes. "Please. Wake. Up."

I slowly bring her hand to my lips, caressing it softly. Despair caresses me and I want to just lay there, on the cold, hard floor and let it consume me, But there is also hope and I know that is what cradles my head, pacifying my swirling emotions.

I force myself to get up and walk away, to resume my normal resolve. Even though I'm on leave, I have to see the case through. After that, it all depends on if AJ wakes up. I rub my red and wet eyes with my hands as I walk away. Without a word, Drake follows me into the elevator and through the lobby where my partner awaits just outside the sliding doors.

"Shut up," I tell Dax before he has the chance to say anything, my voice thick.

He just smiles, knowing my tone meant I was not in the mood for teasing, "Let's go get this bitch."

When Drake walks to the driver's side of my car and opens the door, I realize that I don't have my keys.

"Sorry Michealson, but there's no way in hell we're letting you drive in your condition." Drake says as he gets in the driver's seat. I groan and get into the passenger seat as my partner gets in his own car.

"I'm not a baby, Drake, I can take care of myself."

"You're right. You're not a baby, so don't act

like one. You're my friend and you don't always have to be alone."

The corner of my lip twitched as I look out the window as we pull away from the hospital.

28

Then

It was spring break of her junior year of college. In the living room of the off-campus apartment she shared with Niki and Ava, AJ went over her mental checklist, comparing it to the items carefully laid out on the floor.

Blankets - check.

Sleeping bag for two - check.

Sleeping bag for Aidan, hiking boots, first aid kit. Check. Check. Check.

All the essentials for a weekend of camping and fishing were present.

Wait.

Tent, tent poles, fishing rods, bait and tackle box, wipes, fire starters, pots, pans

The list continues and AJ decided to actually write everything down lest she forget something essential. Like toilet paper.

Eventually, AJ packed everything into several bags and called Torryn but didn't receive and answer.

Ava enters, carrying her own bag of supplies and

clothes.

"Hey, have you heard from your sister?" AJ asked, looking up at Ava.

"She sent me a text a few hours ago when Torryn picked her up. It was really kind of her to bring Isabella here, too."

Ava's words hung in the air and Niki walked into the apartment, throwing open the door in a flurry of motion. "Hey, look who I found lurking in the parking lot like a bunch of creeps."

Liam and Ryder followed her quickly into the apartment, moving around all the supplies strewn about as they made their way to the couch.

"Only one of us is a creep, love," Liam said defending himself.

Ryder visibly perked up at the site of Niki, AJ and Ava.

"Only sometimes my friend," snarled Ryder. "I took care of all the grubbage, by the way. I packed the beer, too. You girls better be ready to go? Spring break waits for no one. I want to start loading everything in the truck."

"What did you get? Actual food or just junk?" AJ was quick to ask.

Ryder rolled his eyes. "Don't worry, I have all the camping essentials. High Fructose corn syrup smothered in artificial flavors and colored dyes, all the fixings for smores, highly preserved hot dogs and cans of beans, and even some real fruit for all you queens," he finished with a playful bow, a laugh bubbling through.

The girls grabbed their camping gear and chatted excitedly about the trip as they headed down the stairwell towards the truck. Liam took Niki's bags, wrapping his other arm around her and admitted that he had never been camping. In the parking lot, they loaded their gear into the bed of Ryder's father's Chevy.

Right then, a silver Dodge Durango pulled up beside them. In the back seat sat a dark-haired teenage girl. Torryn jumped out of the driver's seat just as AJ ran over to meet her. AJ wrapped her arms around Torryn and pulled her head close for a kiss.

Niki opened the back door. A five-year-old Aidan squealed with excitement.

"Hey, little man," Niki said to the boy in the booster seat.

Niki went in to hug the boy, but instead started to tickle him.

"Stop it, Aunt Niki," Aidan said between fits of giggles. Niki unclicked the booster seatbelt and picked up the boy, before handing him off to AJ.

"Hey, baby," AJ said, hugging her son.

"Hi, mommy. Look! We took gramma's car."

"I see that. You ready to go camping?"

He nodded his head vigorously.

Ava loaded their remaining bags into the back of the vehicle. "Torryn, thank you so much for bringing my sister along."

Torryn nodded, a smooth but clipped notion.

"Let's get on the road," Liam called from his seat in the truck.

Niki went over to Liam and kissed him on the cheek, "see you there."

"Not riding with us, then?"

"Sorry, babe, I'm going with my girls."

The girls piled into Mrs. James' car. Ava climbed in the very back next to her sister, while Niki played with Aidan in the middle. AJ glanced into the rearview mirror and smiled at the sight of her son looking happy. *He's growing up so fast*, she thought.

The four-hour drive to the campsite passed quickly, mostly with conversation amongst the girls and playful banter that filled the air heavy with laughter. Aidan kept to himself, occupied with toys and books and Niki, who indulged in all his questions about her life, as if he'd never seen her before. Torryn kept mostly to herself, focusing on the road, and AJ basked in the companionship amongst her friends. A few times she tried to start a conversation with Isabella, but ceased her attempts when the other would ignore her completely or give short answers that brooked no conversation. She asked Torryn at one point if anything was wrong and Torryn merely shrugged, stating that she had been somewhat distant the whole time.

Upon their arrival at the campsite, the group began unloading their bags and setting up tents. The tent itself was the perfect size for the three of them: a large compartment for them with enough height that they wouldn't have to crouch down, and a smaller one on the side for Aidan.

After the group finished—with plenty of breaks for pranks between the boys and moments of frustration felt by everyone when their tent fell down— they gathered their fishing equipment and hiked down to the lake. AJ and Torryn were walking at the back of the group. Liam carried

Aidan on his shoulders as he called out to everyone that he was now the tallest, with AJ exclaiming how she didn't know how he got so tall and what was she going to do about the doorways at home.

"Have you ever been fishing?" AJ whispered to her girlfriend after Aidan's laughter bubbled down.

Torryn shook her head.

"Don't worry, I'll teach you."

Once at the lake, AJ strapped a life jacket tightly around Aidan. He wriggled out of her grasp the moment the last clip was done, flapping his arms wildly with excitement as he ran to the edge of the lake, waiting for everyone to join in.

Running up behind him, AJ knelt beside her son. "You know, I was around your age when your grandpa first took me fishing."

"Really?" Said Aidan, eyeing up the water for fish.

"Really," AJ said as she searched for the bucket of worms and surprised when it was handed to her by Ryder. In a moment, she had a worm from the bucket and watched as Aidan's eyes grew large with curiosity. "You take the worm and you pierce it with your hook like this," AJ explained as she stabbed the hook through the body of the worm and twisted the rest of the squiggle creature enough around the secure it. "Got it?"

Aidan nodded, confident in his ability to mimic his mother.

"Then you press this button down, put the rod over your shoulder, then flick it out in front of you—but don't let go of the pole, that's important," she winked at Aidan and he giggled. "Then, you let go of the button when the rod reaches here," AJ instructed Aidan as she demonstrated the movements of throwing a cast.

"I got it, mom. Can I have a go? I wanna try!" Her squealed with delight and impatience.

AJ handed Aidan the pole and took a video on her cellphone of her son's first cast. She then turned her attention to teaching Torryn how to hook the worm and cast her line. AJ stood behind Torryn, one hand on her hip and the other wrapped around Torryn's hand on the rod.

Together they moved their arms up and out, casting a line out into the water. AJ whispered in Torryn's ear when it was time to release the line. AJ watched Aidan and Torryn standing side by side and snapped another picture from behind them. AJ saw Torryn's bobber dip beneath the surface.

Gripping Torryn's hand she yanked the rod, "Reel it in!"

After much splashing and struggling, Torryn reeled in a fish out of the water. A six-inch trout flopped and flapped on the line.

"Hold it up," AJ encouraged Torryn, snapping a picture when she did.

"Wow!" Aidan cried out, jumping up and down and abandoning the rod on the ground.

"Hey, don't lose the rod," AJ snapped out automatically even as she made a reach for it herself.

"That's a big fish! Can we keep it?"

Torryn smiled and shook her head, "We have to put it back in the lake."

"So we don't getta eat it?"

"No, he belongs in the water."

Aidan frowned, "but I want fish sticks."

A round of laughter erupted from the group, save for Isabella, who looked murderous, as if the lake had offended her and everyone was at fault for it.

Aidan helped Torryn unhook the fish and release it back unharmed into the lake. They continued to fish until the sun began to fade in the sky. When the large group returned to the campsite Ryder announced that he was going to gather firewood in order to cook dinner, at which point Aidan begged to go too. Ava must had read the concern on AJ's face because she offered to go as well and keep an eye on him and Ryder. When they returned to camp, Aidan carried as much firewood as his little arms could manage, looking rather pleased with himself and his small hoard of firewood.

Torryn taught Aidan how to build a fire, "Did you know that Aidan is Irish and means 'little fire'?"

"Cooool." Aidan said with an excited, toothy smile.

"My name is Irish too, it means chief," Torryn continued, " But it's also Norse and derived from *Thor*—" she raised her right arm into the air, pretending to raise Mjolnir and summon lightning"—*God of Thunder!"*

Aidan squealed with delight and mimicked Torryn before delving into the role of Loki and pretending to attack Thor.

AJ watched with a certain look in her eyes, a warmth blossoming in her chest at how easily they've connected over the last couple of years, despite the long distance.

She watched the two loves of her life play.

Torryn, who was usually tense and serious around others, was completely at ease with Aidan. When Aidan had successfully taken down Thor and won the battle, we wrapped his arms around Torryn and squeezed tightly, forcing her to gasp in a breath of air and fall to the ground in a fit of comical dramatization.

AJ's smile couldn't be contained and she was aware, briefly, that her cheeks had started to ache. Deciding to move in with Torryn was a big step, but involving her in Aidan's life was even bigger. AJ thought about the life the three of them could have together—how AJ would pick Aidan up from school and they'd get home in enough time to cook dinner and Torryn would walk through the door, toss her keys on the stand and give Aidan a hug first, kiss the top of his head, then do the same with AJ and they would eat together and laugh and enjoy the moments, and then they'd put Aidan to sleep. Torryn would read a story about Norse gods and Aidan would pretend to be Loki before he fell asleep; they'd go to bed together, talking about their day and their respective work, they'd hold each other and repeat the next day. And the next. And the next.

"Huh?" AJ responded, coming out of her daydream to Torryn's hand waving in her face.

"You looked lost for a minute and then you wouldn't stop smiling. It was kind of creepy," Torryn replied playfully.

"Oh, I was just thinking of the three of us: you, Aidan, and me being here together. It's nice," AJ smiled.

Torryn leaned down to plant a chaste kiss on AJ's cheek before resuming pretend play with Aidan.

AJ shook herself, adjusting her position on the lawn chair she brought along with them and moving closer to the rest of the group, who all, at this point, had collected themselves around the fire in their own chairs or the hollowed out log that Ryder probably found and brought back. She glanced at her friends—Niki and Liam were cuddled close with a blanket on their laps on the log, with Ava on Niki's opposite side, and Ryder next to her in a chair, poking at the fire to aerate it, making embers fly out in all directions, and next to him sat Isabella, who made eye contact with AJ instantly.

Something about her, AJ thought, wasn't right. Had she complained about being outside, AJ would have chalked it up to her not being a fan of the outdoors. But she hadn't said a word the whole time and now AJ could see that her arms were crossed tightly across her chest, her ankles crossed underneath the chair. If she didn't want to talk to anybody, that was fine; a little rude, but fine. If she didn't like the outdoors or camping, then why come?

It was the stare, AJ decided, that really set off the alarms for her. It was unblinking and cold, the small remnant of daylight casting dark shadows around them, making them deeper and harsher than they had any right to be. The flicker of the flames danced in her eyes, and AJ couldn't look away. She was held fast by the intensity of Isabella's gaze, the sensation of a tight voice wrapping around her, cold fingers clamping on her throat and squeezing, harder and harder, the longer her gaze was locked onto AJ's.

"Hot dogs!"

AJ jumped, unprepared for the announcement but thankful that it came. She let out a shaky breath and turned her attention to the stick that Liam handed her, refusing to acknowledge Isabella's continued stare, even though she saw, out of the corner. Of her eye, the other girl take a roasting stick.

When Aidan grabbed his, he made a run to get as close to the fire as possible. AJ and Torryn both grabbed him by opposing arms.

"Hold it right there, mister," Torryn said to the boy, causing him to freeze his attempt to break away from the girls, "Fire is dangerous—"

"You could get hurt!" AJ interrupted.

"—It's really hot and it could burn you. You can't run towards is like that."

"What if you tripped and fell in?"

Satisfied that Aidan now looked properly chastised, AJ let go of his sleeve and nodded at Torryn, who positions Aidan between herself and AJ on the last remaining chair, close enough to roast his hot dog, but far enough away that he wouldn't get too hot or risk burning himself.

****

AJ jerked awake to the sound of muffled screaming in the distance. She could swear she heard Aidan's voice call out 'Mommy.' She unzipped the side compartment of Aidan's tent to reveal an empty sleeping bag and her blood ran cold instantly at sight.

"Oh my god! Torryn wake up!" AJ yelled, her voice echoing in the small space shared between them. She didn't wait for Torryn to move, instead immediately throwing off the blanket, slipping on her shoes, and making her way out of the tent.

AJ was halfway out when Torryn sat up in bed, looking around with furrowed brows, "AJ, what's wrong?"

"Aidan's gone!" She cried, panic setting in too early. *He could have needed to pee and didn't want to wake us because he wanted to be a big boy. Maybe he just wanted to sit outside. Maybe he's playing in the dirt with some sticks.* "He—I didn't hear him wake up," AJ ranted in a whisper to herself, "he's probably just playing, right?"

AJ stepped the rest of the way out of the tent with Torryn on her heels and looked around. No one else was awake and she couldn't see Aidan in her immediate sight. She called out for him, hands around her mouth to help the sound carry.

Torryn did the same and they walked the perimeter of the campsite, going past the tents enough to see if maybe Aidan was in the woods or wondered off to other spring breaker's campsites.

"Hey, what's going on?" A very tired, still half asleep Niki asked, poking her head out of her tent.

Torryn turned towards the other girl and started to explain, Aidan's go-" before she was interrupted by another muffled cry into the night, the faintest of echoes reaching them.

AJ didn't wait to hear it again, to be sure of the direction it came from. She bolted, not caring if

Torryn was following her, and not stopping until she reached the deck that they had all fished on earlier that day.

The black lake glistened under the moon, mocking and sneering with its dangerous beauty, and AJ knew before she even asked the shadowed figure what happened that Aidan was trapped underneath. "Isabella, where's Aidan?" AJ's voice rang out.

"I—I—I didn't know he follow me until I heard a splash."

AJ ran closer to the water, preparing to dive in until she saw Torryn already diving beneath the water's surface. Her chest tightened in fear at each passing moment as panic gripped her lungs.

This can't be happening, she thought, *please save him.*

Her legs felt weak when she tried to stand, having collapsed when, after thirty seconds, she didn't see any movement.

"Where are they?" She cursed even as she made a move to follow Torryn into the cold water. Not a breath later, Torryn breached the surface, gasping harshly and coughing out water, bobbing and struggling to get back to shore. AJ ran back to the bank, jumping off the deck as soon as she was above land to reach them. Niki and Ava called out to her, but she didn't bother stopping to explain, she needed to get to Aidan.

Torryn dragged Aidan onto the shore just as AJ reached them, and laid him flat on his back. AJ kneeled beside him, crying his name and brushing his hair out of his face as Torryn began check his pulse.

"AJ, move," Torryn snapped, tilting the boy's head up enough to open his airway and deliver a lungful of breath to him.

"Oh, god," AJ sobbed, "c'mon, baby, c'mon."

"Niki, get her back," Torryn said as she delivered another breath, Aidan's chest rising with the inflation, but still nothing. Another breath. And another.

AJ became vaguely aware of Niki's arms around her as the rest of the group made their way to them, looking at the scene with varying degrees of worry and concern, but when AJ looked to Isabella, she was met with the same distant, cold look as before. She raged inside and was about to pounce on the girl, hands already balled into tightly clenched fists when Aidan sputtered out a ragged breath, water gurgling in his throat. Torryn and AJ lifted the boy into a sitting position, Torryn hitting her curved hand hard on his back.

"Thank God, Aidan, you're okay, you're okay," AJ said, even as Aidan continued to cough.

"Mommy," the boy barely whispered, throat unable to work properly.

AJ gathered Aidan into her arms and kissed the top of his head, stroking her hands over his back and refusing to let go or lessen her grip. "You're fine, you're okay. I'm here, you're alright," She whispered to him as his gasped in a breath every so often and sobbed into her shirt.

AJ looked up at her dripping wet girlfriend and mouthed the words, "thank you."

A blanket was produced a few minutes later and

draped around them. Torryn had one herself and AJ looked to see that Liam and Ryder must have gone back and returned with them, with equal expressions of sympathy and concern.

"What were you doing out here?" AJ questioned but was not given an answer. Aidan only shook his head and cried a little harder. "You can't just wander off like that! If we didn't wake up—"

Torryn put her hand on AJ's shoulder, "We should get him back to the fire to warm him up."

AJ nodded as Torryn scoop him up into her arms and everyone, including the random groups of strangers that gathered, made it back to their campsite.

"What the hell happened?"

"I woke up and Aidan was gone."

"Yeah, I got that part, why'd he go down to the lake?

"He followed Isabella," Torryn interjected, the words heated, as if she thought the girl was at fault.

AJ couldn't blame Torryn for that because she was wondering the same thing. The situation didn't sit right with her. Everything seemed off.

Liam and Ryder gathered more wood for the fire as Niki and Torryn found lighter fluid and starters.

"What happened, Isabella?" Ava asked her sternly.

"I just wanted to go for a walk. I didn't know he followed me. I swear. I heard the splash. Then the screams. Next thing I know, AJ and Torryn showed up."

"Why didn't you try to help him? You were just standing there," AJ accused.

"I froze," Isabella defended herself. AJ was fixed in her glare.

"You didn't think to come get help?"

"I couldn't...I...I didn't want to just leave him."

"You could have called out to us, you could have—" AJ breathed deeply, closing her eyes, and biting her tongue. She looked to Torryn, "I think I'm ready to go home."

Torryn nodded, "First thing in the morning."

No one else said anything, just silently agreed. Once the fire was high enough not to need attention, the group dispersed, sloping back to their tents and re-packing their belongings.

At some point, Torryn had changed clothes and brought out extra pairs for Aidan and AJ. AJ worked on autopilot and kept Aidan close to her for the rest of the night, eventually moving back into the tent and huddling underneath the blankets, her arms secured around her son. Her heart still ached at the thought of losing Aidan and her eyes were swollen, but she found sleep, knowing that he was fine now and soon they were leaving to go back home.

29

Now

The three of us arrive at the police station where I make my statement. We walk into a conference room and are greeted by Assistant District Attorney, and friend, Eric Harper. Eric stays quiet as Dax questions me about the events that took place at the hospital.

"Why were you in Miss James' room?" He starts off, not accusingly, a routine question as to what I was doing there.

"I went to visit an old friend. As you're aware, I excused myself from this case so my being there was strictly of a personal nature."

"And you're aware, it is the reason behind your suspension."

Eric jumps in, "Detective, maybe we should leave that bit out of the statement."

"Can you tell me what happened?" Dax resumes.

"I was sitting next to Miss James when I heard someone approach the room. I looked up to see that the person who arrived was Isabella Turner. I knew that Miss Turner was a person of interest so I sent you a blank text as a way to alert you that I may be in danger. Then I called you so you could hear what was going on, with the hope that you'd figure out where I was.

I saw Miss Turner slip a syringe in her hand and reach towards Miss James. I had to stop her so I pulled her back. She began to fight, we tussled, which at some point she stabbed me. Then you and Agent Drake arrived. Next thing I knew, I woke up in a hospital bed."

"Did you announce yourself as a police officer?"

"I didn't. She already knew who I was, stating she heard I was a cop. I confirmed she was correct. She questioned me about this case, at which point I informed her that was not working it."

I conclude my statement and Eric gives his nod of approval. I ask Dax if I can watch Isabella's interrogation. He doesn't answer, instead looking to Eric to do so.

"As long as you stay on the opposite side of the two way mirror, I don't see a problem with it."

I'm satisfied enough with this answer, as it allows me to know what is going on without further jeopardizing the case.

They escort me to the observation room and I position myself close to the glass, my skin itching with the need to be in the same room as Isabella, to interrogate her myself, but watching through the glass will have to do.

Isabella sits in an uncomfortable chair with handcuffs around her wrists that bind her to the table in the center of the room. She leers at Dax and Eric's arrival and it makes my blood boil. I remember that look from years ago. Her face gave me the same unsettling feeling then as it does now.

Dax sits on the same side of the table as Isabella, facing her but far enough away that she wouldn't be able to reach him with her limited mobility should she try to attack. Eric Harper sits across from her on the opposite side of the desk.

"I'm Detective Grieson. Before we get started, can I get you some water? Coffee?"

She shakes her head, "no."

Dax places a recording device on the desk and pushes start, "I'll be recording our conversation today. I'd like to take a moment to remind you that you do have the right to remain silent and anything you say can and will be used against you in court. Now, it is my understanding that you have waived your right to have an attorney present. If you want to stop at any time to request an attorney you may do so and we can have one appointed to you," Dax finishes, years of repetition making him sound bored with the whole thing.

I can see Isabella smirk and I fight back to desire to storm into the room on the other side of the glass and slam her face against the table.

"Could you state your full name for the record?"

"Isabella Marie Turner."

"Miss Turner, do you understand your rights?"

Isabella nods.

"Would you mind verbalizing your answer? Please?"

She smiled a wicked smile, "Yes, I understand my rights."

"I see you were working at a laundromat up 'til a

few weeks ago. What happened?"

"Owner was a jackass."

"It must have put you in a tough spot, losing your job."

"Not really. It was a laundromat. I wasn't exactly rolling in the dough."

"So you've had some financial hardships, then? You've had, from what we could find, seven different jobs in the last five years."

"Come on, Detective, I'm sure you didn't go through all the trouble of bringing me here just to talk about my job history," she shifts in her chair, her smirk firmly in place, to cross one leg over the other.

"Okay, you're right. I guess I want to talk about Adelaide James. What were you doing in her hospital room?" Dax asks.

"Visiting my sister's friend. That's not a crime, is it?" Isabella asks coyly and it sickens me.

"No, but attempted murder is as well as murder and assaulting a police officer. Those are felonies, y'know, Miss Turner."

"She grabbed me first," Isabella shrugs. "It was self defense."

I grit my teeth at the accusation.

"She had reason to believe that both Miss James and herself were in danger. What was in the syringe?"

He was met by a silent shrug.

"That's okay, you don't have to answer. My guess would be succinylcholine, but we'll find out soon enough." Dax says as he pulls out pictures of the other five victims. "Do you know any of these women?"

A glint of recognition flashes in Isabella's eyes, along with something else. Pride, perhaps, at a job well done, at being reminded that she had succeeded at something?

Everyone has a tell when they're lying, it's just sometimes hard to spot if you don't have a solid base line. I try hard to rely on facts, hard evidence, and truths, but sometimes, when those fail to provide answers sufficient enough, when there's something nagging at me, I have to believe that it's for a reason. So, when I see Isabella's features morph into something I can't quite place, and there's this sinking feeling making itself known in my stomach, I have to believe that it's because she really is the killer we've been looking for, that she's a dangerous sociopath and would try again.

"I don't know who they are," Isabella says calmly and confidently.

"You have a history of violence, don't you?"

"I'm sure you do, too, Detective. Isn't that why you're a cop?"

Dax pauses, and I don't have to see him to know that he has a hard gleam in his eye, but he doesn't take the bait. "Want to talk about that?"

"Why? There's nothing to tell. You have my file." She nods at the case file in his hands.

"I do and it says that you were ordered to attend youth therapy because you couldn't stop hurting animals, and that you were suspended numerous times for getting into fights with your classmates when you were younger. Curious though, you always lost those fights. Was that on purpose?"

The smirk that Isabella wore slowly left, replaced by something more akin to faint disinterest. She didn't reply.

Dax flips a page of his file, making sure to keep it out of the way of Isabella's line of sight, should she get curious. It's a common tactic that we use when we are trying to get information out of a suspect but it's always a line we carefully toe. We can't lead them, or feed them information that they can build on. False confessions have happened that way too many times.

"High school was better. You graduated at least, so that's something. No more fights. No more animal cruelty. But, I'm wondering, did you get bored? Did you need to up your game, move on to something more dangerous?"

"You're cute," she taunts, turning her attention to Eric. "I could definitely move on to you."

"We know you attacked Miss James, Isabella," Dax continues while Eric ignores her. "Those scratches on your neck will tell us so- DNA evidence will give you away. Did you think about that?" He pauses long enough to see if she reacts to this. When he's met by silence, he continues. "There was an ATM across from the ally where she was attacked, so we also have you on CCTV leaving the scene of the crime. That's probably cause enough to get a sample of your DNA—"

I perk up at this revelation. That was news to me; the FBI must have enhanced the video enough for facial recognition some time after my suspension. Drake's favor must have really paid off.

"—We have all the evidence we need to arrest

you for suspicion of the murder of five women and a police officer, more than enough to toss you in for assaulting a police officer and definitely all we need to put you away for the attempted murder of Adelaide James. Eight separate charges and, honestly, us cops don't take too kindly to the stunt you pulled at the hospital earlier today. You're going to look over your shoulder a long time, Miss Turner, unless you can tell us why you went after these women."

They were met by silence.

"Were they just practice for who you really wanted?" Dax spits out.

"Why would I need to practice?" She smiles and continues, showing all her teeth. "Where's Torryn? Is she dead?"

I stiffen at the questions, not liking where this is leading.

"Lucky for you, she's very much alive."

"Good, I want to talk to her."

I watch as Dax turns to Eric, who shakes his head so minutely that I can hardly tell there was movement.

"Out of the question," Dax replies, his tone firm.

Isabella shrugs and sits back in her chair, one leg crossed over the other and her hands in her lap, a small smile playing at the corners of her lips. When it becomes evident that she isn't going to say anything further, Dax turns off the recorder. He and Eric exit the room.

"This isn't good," I say when the walk through the door and approach me.

"You can't interrogate the suspect," Eric says,

"you know her personally and you're suspended."

"So everyone keeps reminding me," I mutter.

"You shouldn't even really be in here."

"I know," I reply, inwardly groaning at how much this is all messed up now.

"What if she's just in the room? Doesn't ask any questions? If I—"

"We don't negotiate with criminals," Eric interrupts.

"No, we don't negotiate with terrorists," I implore, "We negotiate with criminals all the time and right now we need something!"

Drake's voice carries to us as he stands from the chair he was sitting in not moments before. I was so focused on Isabella I didn't hear him enter the room.

"She isn't going to talk unless Torryn is there and we really need this case to go the way we want. We need to be in control here. Right now, she has too much power and she knows it."

Dax nods in confirmation.

Drake continues on, "I don't like it because it could blow up in our faces, but right now? It's the best shot you've got at getting her to confess. Without a confession, if she manages to some how get a good lawyer, she'll only serve two years, maybe five, for assault and battery on a public servant and attempted murder."

"But she murdered Officer Gage before she came into the room, so isn't that—"

"No evidence other than the syringe, no witnesses, no DNA, no cameras. He wasn't stabbed and even if the ME finds a puncture wound my guess is TOX screen will be negative. So we need her to confess to that crime—"

"And I was off duty so even though she knew I was a cop, I was acting as a civilian when she attached me so that felony charge could be reduced to a misdemeanor with less jail time," I groan, running my hands through my hair and looking around the room. Dax's hardened gaze at Isabella, the tick in his jaw, and Drake's arms across his chest and rigid posture tell me that they're just as pissed as I am.

Dax, after a moment, turns his attention to Eric. "If I ask all the questions and we allow Isabella to direct her answers to Torryn would that mess us up in court?"

Eric thinks this over a moment before answering. "I don't know. Maybe not. Go run it by Harris."

Dax nods and glances at me before leaving the room. Eric and I stand side by side, and Drake sits back in his chair, his fingers tapping a staccato against the arm, the only sound in the otherwise quiet room, as we all watch Isabella, waiting for Dax's return.

She looks calm, as though she is relaxing on the beach rather than sitting in a cold interrogation room. Her eyes keep shifting, landing on the mirror that separates us every so often and her gaze holds each time, her lips turning into a sly smile, as if she knows exactly where each of us stands. Goosebumps cover my arms as we make eye contact, as if she could clearly see me, as if she knows I'm behind the glass, watching her just as intently as she watches me now.

I whip my head to the sound of the door opening,

the noise startling me into attention. Dax walks in with four cups of coffee and hands us each one.

"We're a go. You're not allowed to talk to her about the case though, only listen, and if she insists that you answer a question, we'll have to play that carefully."

"Fine by me," I say, taking a small sip of coffee before leaving the room.

When we walk in, it's three against one. I take Eric's seat, trying not to wince at the pain in my side, while he stands in the far corner, arms crossed. Dax moves his chair next to mine. The whole set up is designed to cause stress in the suspect, but it doesn't seem to phase Isabella.

This time, Dax doesn't make a show of recording the conversation. It's not really necessary as the room is recorded anyway.

Isabella smirks at me, "Hows the side?"

"Here's how this is going to work Isabella. Detective Michealson is here on your request, but only to listen. I'll be asking you the questions. Got it?"

Silence.

Dax and I share a look and I glance back to Eric, who just nods for us to continue.

"Why'd you kill these women? Did they offend you in some way? Treat you badly?"

"No."

"No, they didn't treat you badly? But you're admitting that you did kill them?"

She smirks, "No. We're talking about AJ."

"Hm, alright. What about AJ, though? She's a friend, isn't she?"

Isabella stiffens, her nostrils curling back in loose disgust. "AJ was the only one I wanted," she whispers, her voice low but hard.

"You only wanted AJ? Why her specifically?"

She doesn't answer right away, her lips closing in a firm line and her body stiffening.

"Because she was famous? And you thought you'd be, too, if you killed her. Fifteen minutes of fame?"

Again we are met by silence.

"You've had very tumultuous relationships your entire life, haven't you?"

Isabella crosses her arms over her chest and diverts her eyes away from Dax, this action telling us both that he's on the right track.

"But, it doesn't make sense why you'd go after Miss James. What is it about her that gets you so riled up?"

When she doesn't answer, I know that Dax is going to resort to offending Isabella.

"Is it because you were never going to have a fulfilling career like her. You barely made it out of high school. Jealousy?"

Isabella's gaze snaps to Dax and she moves closer to lean against the table, her hands folded over each other casually, even though her posture gives her away.

"Hm, that seems to simple. And let's face it, your not the ambitious career type." He pauses for effect, running his hand along his chin, as if he's thinking. "Well, she has a good relationship her son. Remind you of what you could have had? Or of something you never had?"

"Don't you—" Isabella warns, her hands balling into fists in front of her and her face reddening with effort to hold herself back.

Dax talks over her and presses on.

"And you've known her for a while now—"

"—don't know what you're talking about—"

"—haven't you?" You've seem what a good mom she is to Aidan, and a good friend—''

"She was never a friend—"

"—to you. Is it mommy issues, then? Is that why?"

"—I had nothing and she—"

"You never had a loving —"

"That bitch took everything from me!" Isabella yells, slamming her palms against the table, her facade shattering in front of us splendidly. Her smirk is gone, her eyes wild with anger and hatred and heat, her chest heaving with the harsh breaths she's taking, nostrils flared.

"She took the life I deserved! She took my sister from me and I was left with a drunk for a father who loved to make sure I knew when he was angry—"

"So he hit you, doesn't justify murder—"

"My mom just watched. She stood by and let it happen. And Ava? She got to leave, she got to go to the fancy private school with friends all because of AJ. I was left behind to get the shit kicked out of me. AJ took everything from me so why shouldn't I do the same to her!? Why does she get to have a happy ending while I was stuck in hell!"

"So, that's it? You were upset that you had a rough childhood and you thought AJ was to blame. What did you do? How did you think you were going to take everything way from her if you killed her? That doesn't make sense to me. She'd be dead without knowing."

"I started with her father," she states, all too matter of factly for it to be anything other than the truth.

"Her father was killed by a drink driver roughly eleven years ago."

"No, I did it," she says, collected enough now that her color is coming back and she doesn't look manic. "I was fourteen. I saw a drunk guy passed out in his car near my school and that was the route he'd have to take to get to AJ's graduation. I got in the driver's seat and I rammed into his car when I saw him coming. I made it look like the drunk guy did it and I got away with it."

"You killed Robert James?"

No. No, it doesn't make sense. Unless the drunk guy was already in the passenger seat, how could she have moved a full grown man into the passenger seat herself, then moved him back into the driver's seat after crashing into a car with enough force to kill? Someone would have seen it. It was graduation season and in the middle of the day so there was bound to be traffic, even if it wasn't on the best side of town. She wouldn't have been able to walk away like she's claiming. She would have been injured, too, probably enough to not even be able to make it out of the car before police and first responders arrived.

"Yes, I did." She turns and glares at me, "And then I went after Aidan."

Her words pull me out of my thoughts and my

heart stops beating.

"The spring break camping trip," I whisper, recalling the events of the trip, of waking in the middle of the night to Aidan's muffled screams. "You tried to drown him?"

"Of course I did! It would have killed AJ to loose her son. So, I took him to the dock and threw his in the water but he was screaming and then you and little miss perfect came to the rescue. Accidents weren't enough because there was always a chance someone would save her. I needed to get rid of her. So I practiced-"

And there it was, basically a confession in our laps—

"—so I wouldn't mess it up when I got to AJ."

It takes all the control I can muster to not fling at her, to hurt her, to make her regret everything that she ever did to hurt AJ.

"But you did mess up," Dax says to her. "You let her live and now you're here and you won't be able to get to her again."

"If Torryn hadn't been in the room...you can't always protect her," she directs to comment to me, her eyes dancing with something I can't place. "No matter. Even if she does wake up, she'll never be the same. I still win."

Agent Drake opens the door. "Can I speak with you three a moment?"

Isabella laughed as the three of us follow Drake out of the room and into the other.

"We've got a problem," Drake says and I already know by his tone that I don't want to hear whatever it is. It's never good when he gets that pinch between his brows, and I've only known man for about a week. "There's been another murder."

"Isabella has been in custody all day," Dax says promptly, "and she's our prime suspect. She basically just confessed to everything!"

I can feel sweat gather between my shoulder blades and on my brow, the room suddenly getting too hot, scorching my skin with the overwhelming rage. My hands start to shake at my side, something that hasn't happened in years. "So, either she's taking credit for things she didn't do and we've got the wrong person, or she has a partner."

"Which makes sense," Eric responds. "So far she really only confessed to attacking the James family. She skates around questions of the five women."

"She's already confessed to Ms. James's attack so doesn't it seem more likely that she did in the other women, too?" Dax remarks.

I shake my head, recalling the case. "Not with this latest murder it doesn't. Remember though, AJ's attack was similar, but not identical to the others. We chalked up the differences to the attacker being rushed but what if, instead the differences were because she didn't actually do the first five? "

Drake nods. "Two killers with different experience levels account for the drastic difference in the way crimes were carried out."

"What if they were made to look different so the partner would carry on if she got caught? Ava could have easily subdued AJ and killed her before Mrs. Parks went outside." I turn towards the mirror, "that's pride on her face. She knows we can't pin everything on her and she isn't going to say anything else, either."

"You think she's protecting someone?" Eric asks.

"Has to be. Why not take credit for the other five murders but take credit for the drunk driver, which, by the way, has a lot of hole in it, and for trying to drown Aidan? She's solely focused on AJ and her family, so to her, those other five women don't even mean anything."

Drake comes to stand by me, shoulder to shoulder, followed by Dax to my left and Eric behind me. The four of us look at Isabella through the two way mirror. She sits there with the type of calm and collected that comes with the security of having a partner.

"You're right," Drake says, before turning his attention to Dax. "I'll take over the interview so you can head to the crime scene, make sure the whole MO matches."

I stay behind as the three men leave. Dax to process the new crime scene, and Drake and Eric return to Isabella.

"Hmmm, my how you've changed Detective Grieson," Isabella says as she looks at Drake. "You're cuter. I like you already."

"I'm Supervisory Special Agent Caspian Drake with the FBI. We know you didn't kill these women, well, at least you didn't do it alone."

Isabella didn't respond but for the first time, she looked nervous.

Bingo.

"I've been doing this long enough to know that there's something you're not telling us. You're working with someone, the real killer." Drake continues. "With everything we know about you, it's hard to believe you'd actually be able to pull something like this off alone," he scoffs, shaking his head. "You must be so disappointed in yourself."

Isabella visibly seethes with an open contempt for Drake.

"So, who are you protecting? Is it Ava, your sister? We have enough evidence against you to put you away for these murders and you and Ava are really close. You're living with her, aren't you? I bet it was all her idea."

For the first time Isabella reacts, she's clearly upset at the accusation. "Ava isn't a killer."

Drake simply watches her, not speaking, and his face is a perfect picture of impassivity. I watch the exchange, even with so little happening between the two, nervously picking at my thumbnail. It's too long before Isabella speaks again, he words sending a shock through my system.

"I want a deal."

30

Then

AJ should be feeling good, she should be ecstatic and filled with a sense of right. She knew that Torryn loved her, and even though showing that love was a struggle for the brunette, even after years together. She could see it in the way Torryn always asked about her writing, or Aidan; how she would bring a mug of tea to AJ if she was caught up in a manuscript, adding lemons if her throat was sore; or how she would make sure to turn the heat on at night before they went to bed because the apartment always go too cold for AJ, and how she always made sure to tell Aidan to 'sleep tight'.

She could see Torryn's love for her in so many other small ways and it warmed her heart to know that Torryn could feel that much for her. But, if there is anything she had learned over the past three years is that living together as roommates and living together as partners weren't the same.

There were countless sleepless nights, like tonight, that AJ's anxiety ran high. Her nightly routine consisted of watching her ten-year-old sleep from the doorway, trying and failing to focus on research for her manuscript, or controlling the racing thought fueled by the overwhelming fear she had every time Torryn walked out the door in her uniform.

It never used to be this bad; there was always a fear that Torryn would be injured on the job, but it wasn't until a month ago, when she was shot during a routine traffic stop that it actually hit AJ just how dangerous her profession was. Of course she was aware of the possibility of Torryn getting shot, but in this city, it just never seemed like it could happen, that those events happened in other cities where crime rates were staggering. Since then, it was harder for her to accept that Torryn should willingly put herself in those positions. That, when faced with the possibility of dying, Torryn still chose to put on her uniform and badge and leave. Since that night AJ's support of Torryn's career turned into a bitterness that she couldn't rid herself of.

AJ, in a moment of selfishness, had asked Torryn to find another role within the department a while back. Something safer, a desk job, maybe, so that AJ wouldn't be so scared to lose her. AJ sighed, remembering all the harsh words that both of them had said to one another, how she pleaded with Torryn and accused her of trying to prove something to everyone. How Torryn completely refused to give up the job she loved, without even considering how it was affecting their relationship and family, accusing AJ of being to sheltered and pampered to deal with any of it.

It's not as if AJ didn't know what she was getting

into. She held respect for Torryn and the other police officers in their city, but in their world, with so much fear of their particular uniform, with corruption and hatred on both sides, she was terrified. Even though she knew that Torryn could make a difference both inside the force and out in the community, it was all too much to handle from the sidelines. Torryn constantly reminded AJ that she knew, from the beginning, that this is what Torryn was passionate about, and they both knew the risks to Torryn's safety with the job. But, it felt as if neither of them were prepared for the risks to their relationship. AJ wished she had known from the beginning how difficult being involved with a cop would be. AJ, despite arguments made from Torryn, felt as if her partner had chosen to put her career above everything else, including AJ and Aidan. She could see and feel Torryn's growing resentment the more they fought about it.

The alarm clock next to Aidan's bed went off, causing AJ to jump. She hadn't realized the time. *Torryn should be home soon, at lease she better be,* AJ thought. She silently closed the door and crept away from her son's bedroom.

AJ slipped into the kitchen to prepare breakfast. A few minutes later, Aidan walked into the room, rubbing his eyes, wth suffering feet and oversized pajamas.

"Hey, mom," Aidan said, yawning loudly.

"Good morning," AJ said as she handed him a glass of orange juice.

The door to the apartment opened and AJ felt as though she had been holding her breath all night, a large sigh leaving her body and the tension slowly ebbing away enough for her chest to feel lighter. Things were okay for at least one more day.

Torryn walked through the door of their apartment, looking more than haggard and exhausted, with dark circles under her eyes and particular slump to her shoulders that spoke louder than it should have. AJ's heart immediately lurched at the sight of her, wanting to reach out and comfort her; but she stopped herself, knowing that Torryn would just grumble through it and refuse to admit she actually needed it. She smiled, though, when she saw Torryn ruffle Aidan's already disheveled hair, a large smile on her lips when Aidan batted her hand away.

AJ approached Torryn and handed her a mug of coffee. "You look tired," AJ said, kissing her on the cheek.

"Yeah, a long night will do that to you."

"Well, did you at least arrest any bad guys?" AJ questioned, winking in Aidan's direction as his interest peaked.

"A few," Torryn replied as she wrapped AJ up in her arms.

"Hungry?" AJ asked quietly into the embrace, melting into the comfort of being in Torryn's arms.

"Starving."

Together, Torryn and AJ cooked pancakes for Aidan while Torryn still insisted on staying away from as many carbs as possible. It was in moments like these, too, that AJ knew how much they loved each other, and, more specifically, how much AJ loved living with Torryn. Even if the other woman squeezed the toothpaste from the middle instead of the bottom.

There was always a moment where she thought that everything could be fine, that she could live with Torryn's decision to put her life in harms way, that eventually she'd just toughen up and encourage Torryn to go out everyday. In those moments, though, she was always thrown back into her harsh reality; she knew herself well enough to realize things weren't going to get any better. Not any time soon.

It wasn't until all of them were seated at the breakfast table that AJ noticed Aidan staring between her and Torryn. "Something on your mind, kiddo?"

"When am I going to get a baby brother? Or sister? I don't really care which."

Torryn started coughing, having just taken a sip of her coffee and AJ stared at her son, completely dumbfounded.

"My friend, Bobby, from school, just got a new baby brother. I want one, too."

AJ struggled, mouth fishing for something to say, and when nothing came out, she looked to Torryn for necessary assistance. Torryn's eyes widened and she shook her head slightly but AJ insisted, nodding her head towards her son, scrunching lips together.

"Hey. I've got an idea! Why don't I take you to the range this weekend and teach you how to shoot a gun instead?" Torryn offered.

"Cool!" Aidan exclaimed excitedly jumping down from his chair at the table and rushing away.

"Absolutely not," AJ said. "He's only ten."

Torryn leaned towards AJ and quietly replied, "It got his mind off us having a baby."

"You couldn't have offered him a puppy instead?"

"Yes! Can we get a puppy, too?" Aidan yelled from the living room.

"I guess we're getting a puppy too!" Torryn smirked at AJ.

They finished their respective breakfasts, AJ shaking her head and doing her absolute best to hide her bemusement. It wasn't worth getting into a fight over. Silence fell on the two women and when AJ stood to wash the dishes, Aidan came running out of this room, dressed in his uniform.

"Ah, did you brush your teeth?" AJ asked, questioning the speed of his return.

Aidan rolled his eyes. "Yes, mom."

AJ narrowed hers in return and held eye contact with Aidan for a moment before accepting his answer with a sharp nod. "Brushed your hair?"

At this, Aidan raked his fingers through his locks and replied in the affirmative. It was AJ's turn to roll her eyes but if he didn't leave soon, there were going to be late for his first day of fifth grade and she didn't want a repeat of last year.

"Can you take me in your police car?" Aidan asked Torryn, who looked to AJ, then back to Aidan. "Please? Everyone will think it's so cool one of my moms is a cop!"

AJ noticed how brightly Torryn smiled at Aidan's excitement, and, more probably, at the fact that this was the first time he had ever referred to Torryn as his mom. AJ caught Torryn's eyes for a moment and saw something that made her own water. AJ never failed to notice how hard Torryn tried to be the mom that she should have had, but never did growing up.

She nodded her approval and smiled at both of them.

"Let's go then."

Aidan hollered as he ran to the door, Torryn following close behind him, grabbing her keys off the table as she went.

"Bye, mom," shouted Aidan, as he threw open the door.

"Bye, baby, have a good first day at school!"

****

AJ sat in bed, typing away furiously for her latest novel idea that she barely glances up when Torryn made her way into the bedroom and headed straight to the bathroom, slow and zombie-like. AJ heard the shower come on and closed the lid of her laptop shut.

"Want some company?" AJ asked as she entered the bathroom.

Torryn hmm'd from under the spray of the warm water in response. She opened her eyes in time to watch as AJ slowly slipped off her clothes and entered the shower, gently placing a kiss to Torryn's neck.

Lathering up the loofah, AJ washed Torryn's back.

"That feels so good," Torryn sighed sleepily.

"Turn around."

Torryn complied and AJ could see the exhaustion

pulsating from her dark green eyes. AJ rubbed the loofah across Torryn's body and kissed her lightly on the lips.

"If I weren't so damn tired, I'd be really turned on right now," Torryn whispered.

"Well, you can make it up to me later," AJ smiled.

They finished their shower and climbed into bed. AJ wrapped her arms around Torryn as she fell into a deep sleep, only to be awoken six hours later by the ringing of her cell. She quickly answered it so that it wouldn't wake up Torryn and hurried out of the room.

"Hello?" She breathed into her phone, trying to keep her voice just above a whisper, "Yes, this is Miss James."

AJ paced the living room as she listened, asking a few questions every now and then, making "mhmm's" and "of courses" into the phone every so often.

"It sounds like an incredible opportunity," AJ spoke into the phone when the call headed towards a finish, "Yes, I'll think it over and give you call later. Thank you. Have a good day."

AJ disconnected the call, barely able to contain her excitement when she turned and saw Torryn standing behind her. "I'm sorry, did I wake you?"

"No. What was that about?"

"It was a publishing company in London. One of their best selling authors recently passed away before finishing his book and the want to hire me to finish it."

"AJ, that's great!"

"Yeah, it is. There's a catch, though." AJ said

tentatively as she eyed Torryn, who entered the kitchen and started to work on brewing a pot of coffee.

Torryn sat up at a stool at the breakfast bar. "What's that?"

"Well, we'd have to move to London for a while. The advance they'd give me would cover moving expenses for all three of us. You wouldn't have to worry about the pesky overnight shifts anymore."

"Wait, London? As in London, England?"

"Yeah," AJ said with an exhale of breath, nervousness spread throughout her body.

"We can't move to London, AJ. Why can't you write the book here?"

"Well, in order to write a book set in a particular culture, I'd kind of have to immerse myself in that culture. At least that's what the publishing company believes." She shrugged, grabbing two coffee mugs down from the cabinet, and trying not to notice how Torryn's face crumpled in frustration.

"And what am I supposed to do in London? I'm a cop, AJ, so it's not like I can just transfer to the other side of the ocean. You can write from anywhere."

"Maybe," AJ began, fearful of how her next sentence might be received. "Maybe you could take a sabbatical from being a cop for a while, Torryn. Maybe it would be good for you...us...some good. We could do a bit of traveling, see a bit of the world. I wouldn't have to live in constant fear for your life."

The coffee machine beeped its completion and AJ prepared cups of coffee with expertise. When she turned to hand Torryn her mug, the brunette was staring at her, heat and anger in her tired eyes.

"I'm too close to getting everything I've ever wanted, to making detective. I can't give that up," Torryn spat out with more venom than AJ hopped she intended.

"No one said you'd be giving it up, babe," AJ huffed, rolling her eyes.

"If I move out of the country, that's exactly what I'd be doing. They'll give the position to someone else," Torryn emphasized before she took a few sips of her coffee.

"Okay, so let them give it to someone else. There'll be another opening at some point when we get back, right?"

"Seriously? This is literally the one thing I've been working towards—"

AJ threw her hands in the air, exasperated, and cried, "This is the biggest opportunity for me, right now!"

When the hard thunk of the mug hitting the counter echoed in the kitchen, AJ almost regretted starting this conversation.

"Yeah, *right now,* but something bigger could come along that won't force you to move halfway around the world!"

"How do you know that? What if this is my big break?"

AJ watched Torryn's facial expressions as she stood from her position on the barstool. She wished she could tell what Torryn was thinking, that the brunette would stop pacing the floor and picking at her nails, that she would just *talk* to her.

Torryn stopped mid-stride after a few turns and

looked at AJ. "I don't get it. You don't have to live there, you can just stay for a few months then come back. How long is the even supposed to be?"

At least she isn't yelling anymore, thought AJ.

"I don't know, a couple of months, maybe a year." AJ said with a shrug.

"So you're just ready to uproot everyone on a 'maybe'? What about Aidan? You're just going to take him out of his school and make him leave his friends and family behind, too?"

AJ sniffed, and squared her shoulders. "He'll be okay, we've done it before."

"When he was a toddler, AJ. When he couldn't care about it but now it'll actually affect him," Torryn said defiantly, voice elevated once and again hands on her hips in defense.

AJ's eyes narrowed, her hands moving away from her coffee cup to lay flat on the breakfast bar. "Are you trying to tell me how to raise my son?"

"*Our* so- unless, I'm not included in his life anymore?"

"Torryn, no, I didn't-that's—that's not what I meant," AJ tried to explain but the moment Torryn crossed her arms over her chest, she knew it was pointless. Torryn had heard what she wanted to hear and there'd be no convincing her otherwise.

"Well, it sure as hell sounded like it."

AJ was sure that Torryn could take a personal leave and spend a few months in London with her. They could focus on repairing the damage they've both done to their relationship. AJ was about to bring this up when Torryn spoke again.

"We've done long distance before so why is this

any different?"

"Maybe I don't want to be with a cop anymore!" AJ yelled, the sound echoing once in the small space as she threw her hands out to her sides.

She struggled with seeing how deeply that had hurt Torryn, who, before hand had been just as angry, just as loud as AJ, but now looked resigned, her eyes swimming with untold hurt and anguish. AJ wanted to take it all back but it was too late, the words were already spoken.

"So, this is about my job?" Torryn stated, in a quiet tone that spoke volumes to AJ.

Something changed in Torryn, not just her tone but her whole demeanor, that caused the words in AJ's head to come out of her mouth a stumbled mess. "No—Well—I mean, yes, but—"

"You knew what you signed up for and you were fine with it!"

"Until you got shot!" AJ croaked, her anger subsided, replaced by fear and rejection.

Torryn's eyes softened as she took a step closer and AJ could see the struggle in her eyes when she started to lift her hand to reach for AJ and the resolve when she put her hand back to her side. Her facial features turned stoic, unbothered, only her eyes giving away any sign of emotion. "People die everyday, AJ. I could get hit by a bus tomorrow. Are you going to stop using them?"

"That's not the same and you know it," AJ insisted with a trembling lip as she tried to keep her frustration from spilling over again.

"It is the same. Anyone can die anywhere, at any time."

AJ just shook her head, unsure where to go from here.

"Don't use my job as an excuse, AJ, you know damn well nothing has changed except that you got a job offer that you think is going to make if for you."

"What are you saying?"

Torryn's voice remained calm and steady, only a hint of emotion. "I'm saying that you wanted an out and one came up. I'm saying that you probably haven't wanted this for a while and you were just looking for a reason to leave that wouldn't make you feel so guilty."

"No, that's not—"

"It is, AJ, it is." Torryn sighed, "Because for you, I'm the bad guy and I've always been the bad guy. But y'know what, I'm not as bad as you. You're just as career focused as I am but at least I'm not hiding behind excuses. I at least know what the hell I want so get back to me when you do."

AJ watched Torryn walk towards their bedroom and close the door. She glanced at the time and decided not to follow her. Aidan would be home soon and she didn't want to be fighting with Torryn when he came home. She wiped the tears on her cheeks as she poured out her first cup of coffee, poured a second one, and went to sit out on the balcony.

****

AJ was still out on the balcony when Torryn left for work, still bothered by their conversation earlier that day. It was a few minutes more when she could be sure that Torryn had left the lot that she went back into the bedroom and took out her suitcases, laying them on the bed.

She knew this opportunity in London was too good to refuse and would lead to so many more writing jobs, maybe even her own books being published.

AJ tensed as the memories of their fight came back, mocking her and forcing her to relive the anger and frustration from both of them. Torryn made a valid point, that, yes, AJ could write from anywhere and she could probably convince the publishing house to let her visit rather than actually move. AJ wanted to go to London, even if it was only for a short while.

But that wasn't really the point. She wanted to get away from being the partner of a cop, to focus on her writing without the fear of a middle of the night knock on her door that would change her life forever. That's why she wanted Torryn to go with her.

It was almost summer. AJ could go to London now and Torryn could bring Aidan when school was out. She wished that things didn't escalate the way they did, that they could discuss this calmly and rationally. She knew that wouldn't happen; Torryn was so matter of fact about her decision to not go to London.

You just wanted an out...I'm not as bad as you. You're just as career focused as I am but at least I'm not hiding behind excuses. I at least know what the hell I want so get back to me when you do.

The moment Torryn walked out the door, AJ realized that they both decided they would always put their careers ahead of their love for each other. *Maybe Torryn was right,* AJ thought as she began packing her things. Not about wanting an out, but for being the bad guy. She had accused Torryn for doing exactly what she herself decided to do.

AJ was always running when things got emotionally hard, she knew this, but still continued to follow the same patterns. Just after Aidan had fallen asleep she packed as many of their things as she could and loaded it in her car. After allowing him a few hours of sleep, she woke him up and didn't bother answering his groggy question about why they were leaving when it was still dark outside.

AJ hoped that she wasn't making the biggest mistake of her life, that she was doing the right thing for her, for Aidan, and for Torryn.

She left Torryn a note on their bed that simply read, "I'm sorry."

AJ cried silently on the way to her mother's house. She didn't have the strength to tell Aidan what they were doing when he questioned her again. She didn't know what to say so she had just told him that she'd explain later. She needed a chance to process what she was doing. Had she seriously just made the decision to leave Torryn over a job?

It's not that simple, she thought as she absentmindedly tapped her index finger on the steering wheel as she drove. She knew deep down that she would come to regret making this decision out of hurt and anger. She also knew that had she made the decision to stay, she'd regret that too. Was she really this willing to throw away her relationship with Torryn, as if the past seven years meant nothing? There was no good choice to make, either direction she went would eat away at her until there was nothing left.

At least this way she was protecting Torryn, right? This way gave Torryn the chance to be free to chase her dreams without being tied down to a damaged relationship, the chance to move on. That was the right thing to do, wasn't it? For an all too brief moment she felt as though she would turn the car around and unpack her things before Torryn got home and was none the wiser about what she was doing. Stopped at a red light, where she could either go straight or make a U-turn another thought hit her: Maybe, just maybe, love isn't enough.

At her mom's house, Aidan went to sleep in his old bedroom, while AJ sat with her mother in the living room. She cried as she told her mom what happened, what's been happening.

"I can't pass up this opportunity, mom. I don't know why Torryn can't understand that."

"Oh, baby," said a tearful Mrs. James. "Maybe you should go back tomorrow and try to talk this out, again. There has to be a compromise. Can't you go for only a few months so that Aidan can stay in his school and Torryn doesn't have to leave her job behind?"

"I thought of that, but it all depends on how long this project takes. I don't want to be gone longer than a couple of months without Aidan living with me and Torryn refuses to move."

AJ's mother sighed heavily, folding her hands in her lap. "Well, be that as it may, leaving without explanation isn't the honest thing to do, AJ. I raised you better than that and she'll only resent you for it."

"No. She was very clear," declared AJ, wiping her eyes and straightening her posture. "Her career comes first to her. It's almost as if she doesn't even care if I'm successful in mine. This is best for us both in the long run. Besides, I don't think I was cut out to be the partner of a cop—the anxiety of never knowing if she'll return home—I, I can't keep doing it."

Mrs. James nodded her head and stroked AJ's hair, just as she did when AJ was a child.

AJ fell asleep on the couch and was woken up the next morning by a text from Torryn that only read "Me, too."

She felt like she owed Torryn an explanation but didn't really know what to say exactly, so she didn't reply, deciding it was best to just leave things the way they were. AJ took Aidan to school so she could go to the office and get together all the paperwork she'd need to enroll him in school once she arrived in London. She had decided that they'd leave in a week, giving them both the time to say their goodbyes. A week would be long enough to get her affairs in order, long enough to give Torryn the chance to reach out to her if she wanted, and hopefully for Aidan to get used to the idea of leaving.

When the day of their departure to London arrived, AJ allowed her mother to take them to the airport, giving her a sense of deja vu, the scene the same as when she was eighteen, the day after her father's funeral. Her mother driving her to the airport while she sat in the passenger seat crying, a two year old Aidan in the back blissfully unaware of what was going on. This time though, he was old enough to recognize the sadness that surrounded him, while she cried for a different reason, a different loss. As the song 'Look Away' by Eli Lieb and Steve Grand played on the radio, AJ stared at the rain falling down outside her car window, the lyrics washing over her because she was too numb to do much else.

They remained silent on the way to the airport, through security and as they sat in the terminal waiting for their flight to be boarded. Aidan took his mother's hand, a silent attempt to comfort her. She knew they were both going to miss Torryn for a very long time. Once she found herself hoping she wasn't making a mistake.

It wasn't until lift off that Aidan finally spoke. "Will Torryn be living with us in London?" He asked as he looked out the oval window of the plane.

AJ could hear the hesitation in his voice. Her lip wobbled as she replied, her own voice sounding raw from several hours of disuse and emotion. "No, baby, it's just you and me."

31

Now

Having just gotten off the phone with Dax, I start thinking of everything he told me about the final events that led to the capture of Carmen Turner. As it transpired, Isabella's father left Carmen for a younger, blond woman. He mysteriously died a week prior to the first attack. According to Isabella's statement, his death was a trigger that commenced her mother's killing spree. Isabella had given us everything we needed, the killer and the murder weapon, in exchange for immunity against and accessory charges as well as a lighter sentence for the attempted murder of AJ, and dropped charges of assaulting a police officer. In light of Isabella's mental health and her clear psychosis, it was inevitable she would spend the rest of her life at high security facility rather than prison. Carmen Turner on the other hand, would face trial for the murder of six women.

I haven't yet spoken to Ava about any of this. I imagine she would need some time. I can't begin to comprehend how she must be feeling and decide to contact her once the trial is over. She'll be in lawyer hell for a while and I'm sure I'm the last person she wants to hear from.

I sit in my bed with AJ's book in my lap. It's a crime thriller and as I continue to read I start to notice something odd enough to send my nerves into a flutter. The fictitious victims in the book are murdered the same as my real life victims—the red x, the stab wounds. It was too coincidental to be an accident.

What were the chances that Carmen Turner decided to read this book and use it as a guide for her own murders? Something felt off from the moment Dax told me about the condition of Carmen Turner's home when he and a team of officers arrived. I wish I could have been there. From what Dax said, Carmen was passed out drunk. How could someone capable of organizing a killing spree and leaving no evidence at the crime scenes be dumb enough to have the murder weapon sitting on top of their dresser, out in the open for all to see? All the evidence we needed for a conviction was found in her home. I was instructed to leave the case alone but I couldn't stop the nagging feeling that we placed the wrong person in prison. It just didn't feel right.

My phone rings, cutting those thoughts short. It was the number of the hospital.

****

I rush to the hospital, sirens blazing, and my heart hammering wildly in my chest. This was either going to be the best day of my life or it will provide me the closure I need.

I park the car and run through the hospital lobby and up the elevator. I press the call button a million times, aware that it wouldn't change the speed of the car, but it would make me feel like it did.

"Oh come on," I groan aloud, still impatient.

After a brutal two seconds, I decided I can't wait any longer and I take the stairs in the side corridor, skipping two at a time and gritting my teeth against the pain radiating from my abdomen. I don't slow down until I am at the entrance of AJ's room. I ignore the playback in my mind of the incident that happened last time I was here and take a breath, hoping I didn't rip any stitches.

I open the door and see Aidan standing by his mother's bed, holding her hand, with his grandmother behind him, her hands around his shoulders. AJ's head is propped up and turned towards him, away from the door. Niki sits at the edge of the bed.

Aidan looks up and smiles as I slowly enter the room.

I hold my breath as AJ slowly turns her head towards me and for the briefest of moments, I feel like I can't walk. AJ smiles the smallest, barely there smile, but I know she means more. She whispers my name, her eyes half-open and trying to focus. I take the last few steps to her, unaware I had even started walking, and softly take her hand in mine.

"You're a sight for sore eyes," AJ says to me in a whispery, scratchy voice.

I finally breathe. "Hey, you."

Carefully, I brush hair out of her face and tuck it behind her ear.

She grips my hand tighter, as much as she can, and the pressure is a relief to know she hasn't lost motor function.

"I, um...I'm glad to see you," I stamper

"Me, too."

Aidan grins from ear to ear, "Heard what happened. The nurses are all talking about how you kicked ass earlier today."

"Language," AJ says in a harsh rasp.

I look up at the teenage boy, seeing what appeared to be pride on his face. "Yeah, I've got the battle scar to prove it."

"Awesome."

Mrs. James chose that moment to speak up, "Why don't we give these two a moment?"

AJ's mom reaches out to me and tenderly strokes my hand. Then she kisses AJ on her forehead, brushing back her hair, before heading towards the door.

"Yeah, okay." Aidan replies, too happy to argue. "Catchya later, Torn."

I smile at the old nickname.

"Love you, girl," Niki whispers to AJ, squeezing her ankle.

I watch the three of them leave the room. There's a silence that fills the air for a moment and I start to wonder if I should have even come here. I clear my throat, and, horrifyingly ask how AJ is feeling with a hesitance that surely shows how awkward this is for me.

"Like...hell," she croaks jokingly as she looks up at me before moving her eyes towards the water pitcher on the stand. Immediately move to grab it and pour some into a small cup for her, placing the cup in her hand. She doesn't move to take a sip and I hesitate to ask if she wants me to do it for her. Her body has to still be weak from disuse and acute muscular atrophy from lack of activity—

"Your hair's shorter," her voice interrupts my growing concern.

"It is."

"I like it," she wheezes and coughs, the sound horrible to my ears.

I sit down on the edge of the bed, and lean enough for her to hear me when I whisper, "when you're doing better, we should catch up."

She smiles and it was as if her whole world had suddenly flooded with sunshine, "I'd like that."

"You had me worried for a while there. We all were."

"I had myself worried, too."

I smile, looking at AJ with the sudden realization that these last three years could have been avoided for the both of us if maybe we just did things differently. Maybe leaving was the best thing to do at the time and I can't begrudge her that because neither of us were willing to sacrifice what we had worked towards for the other. But, a small part of me wishes, in hindsight, that we could have made it work, somehow. That she would have been willing to to long distance again, or maybe I would have been willing to move to a different department for a while to ease the tension. It hurts to know that we both missed opportunities three years ago to resolve our problems, but I can't change the way it happened. I can only hope that we go forward from here.

AJ squeezes my hand.

"I heard you," she whispers, her voice still horse even after taking a sip of water. "It was strange." She pauses and winces before clearing her throat. "I was aware of what was happening sometimes."

"You should rest," I interrupt her.

"I think I've done enough resting."

I rolls my eyes at her stubbornness. "Then you should stop talking so much."

She smiles at me again. "I just wanted you to know that I heard you and that I'm sorry...for how I —" AJ's voice falters and her face pinches. She tries to clear her throat again, but ends up coughing, wincing as pain erupted.

I'm not sure what to say, so I try to dismiss the subject, giving out platitude after platitude but AJ shakes her head. "No, listen to me—"

"AJ, now isn't the time," I say with finality. "When you're out of here we can talk about it. Right now, Im just glad you're, y'know, not dead." I try to let a bit of humor slip into my voice, to reassure her and to end the discussion.

"I've missed you," AJ concedes before taking another sip of water.

I smile and nod. "Sh, I already know that."

AJ forces out a small laugh, more a huff of air but once she is done with the cup, I put it back on the stand and lace our fingers together again, my other hand coming to caress her cheek.

It was quiet for a moment, both of us just staring at each other, assessing and remembering. It's bittersweet, to still see the parts of AJ that I was familiar with three years ago, but all the subtle changes that I've missed in our time apart. She looks older, her facial structure more matured. The shades of blond slightly darker now and whereas I've cut my hair, it seems she's let hers grow even longer than it was.

It takes me by surprise when AJ speaks again. "I shouldn't have taken him away from you."

I take a moment to reply. There are so many things I want to say, but now isn't the time. "No. You shouldn't have, but I could have made more of an effort." I shrug, doing my best not to let any bitterness into my voice. "But, again, we'll talk later."

"How very big of you," AJ teases and I know she doesn't mean any harm.

I still don't respond, though, and instead we sit in silence that becomes so familiar, it's like coming home.

Epilogue

Derek Williams arrived at Parker Heights Psychiatric Hospital in a fury. When he reached the check-in counter, he signed in and was then promptly directed to the visiting area. He waited patiently at first, but the subtle bouncing of his leg gave away his nerves at the idea of facing her.

It was a few moments before the familiar drawl of Isabella Turner's voice echoed into the room.

"Hello, my love," the woman said as she sat down across from him.

Maybe is was the intangible, wild look in her eyes, or the tautness of her face pulling her skin thinner over her bones and making them stand out more prominently than they had before, but Derek could see that her time in here had not done her well.

They stared at each other in silence for a minute, each assessing the other, one with a cool indifference, the other with something close to apprehensive anger.

"What are you doing here?" The woman asked without preamble, folder her arms in front of her on the table, her head cocked to the side.

Derek ground his teeth together. "This wasn't the plan!" He clenched his fists and threw them onto the table in a fit. "You ruined everything."

"Did I?" She replied, her voice dripping in saccharine. She lifted her shoulders in a subtle shrug, a smirk plastered on her thin lips.

"Why are you in here?"

"I got caught."

"But, how?" He demanded, his knuckles growing whiter. He glanced around them at the other visiting patrons. No one paid them any attention. "Isn't that why you had me frame your mother for those murders? So you *wouldn't* be locked up?"

Isabella chuckled derisively. She leaned to rest her back against the chair, her hands coming to relax in her lap. "Oh my dear naive boy," she began, her words laced with inhibited venom. "We framed my mother because she's weak."

She paused for all of a few seconds before continuing. Her countenance changes in such a way that Derek wasn't sure he was looking at the same woman as before.

"We framed her because she allowed herself to be beaten bloody and the only thing I could do was watch her get up from the kitchen floor and start washing the dishes." Her voice, when she spoke, did not allow room for the man across from her to interrupt, or do anything other than stare. "She looked me in the eyes and said 'Mija, it's not a woman's place to question her husband. Don't ever get involved with an angry white man, mija.' He beat me in front of her and she did nothing, just sat there, in the corner. He was pathetic so I killed him. But she chose him, over and over again, so she deserves to rot in prison."

"What about our deal?" The man asked, brows

drawn tight and lips even tighter. His frame trembled with barely concealed rage.

Isabella laughed, suddenly and boldly, "Well, I'm stuck in here so the terms of our agreement have changed. I won't turn you in as an accomplice and you will run back home and keep your mouth shut. You don't want to go back to prison, do you?"

Derek Williams opened his mouth, then promptly shut it without saying a word.

"Pendejo," she muttered, leaning in closer again as if she was about to start another tangent. She barely opened her mouth to speak when Derek cursed under his breath and swung his hand out in a blurred slash.

The man's eyes gleamed even as he watched the woman's face crumple, her carotid artery now pumping her blood in spurts that grew with each beat of her heart.

The next moment, the guards were on him, throwing him to the ground and placing cuffs around his wrist in a few seconds. He didn't fight them as they hauled him away. He just smiled and a certain giddiness set upon his person as he looked back at the pool of blood soaking the woman's uniform and dripping onto the floor.

The startled screams from the visitors, the gasps and random applause that erupted from some of the patients did not register for Derek Williams. He let out a small huff of air that grew into a poorly disguised laugh. He was shoved through the doors but he was scarcely hiding his satisfaction now even if the desire wasn't quite quenched.

The plan was for Isabella to kill AJ, revenge was

their common goal. But killing Isabella Turner for her failure would have to do for now.

About the Author

Raeleigh Breaux is a Texas based author, who has a Bachelor's degree in Psychology. She enjoys writing and sharing her stories. Her debut novel, Casualty of Fate, is not the end. It is only the beginning of this journey and is glad to have you as a part of it.

Acknowledgments

Writing this story may have been a one person job, but creating the book that you currently hold in your hand took a team. In light of that, I'd like to take a moment to thank everyone who helped make the creation of this book a success.

I want to thank Joey, my wife, my partner, my inspiration, who supported me even when writing this book created moments of tension and isolation. She listened as I talked through my plot holes, beta read the first draft, indulged in my ramblings of author swag and book merch. She created Special Agent Caspian Drake and even named this novel. She was my first beta reader during my first draft and the first one to read the final product and help me to proof read it. Her remarks gave me to confidence to put this book out into the world, because if I can impress her I can impress anyone.

I want to thank my sister, Rayne, who helped me through hours upon hours of edits. Helped me fix my plot holes and helped me to improve the show don't tell parts.

Mostly I want to thank you, the reader. With out you picking up my book and taking the chance on an unknown author none of this would be possible. If you enjoyed this book, even half as much as I enjoyed writing it. I ask that if you enjoyed this book continue to help make it a success by writing a review and telling your friends and family, or even the random stranger at the book store to buy it, share on your social media, or even ask your local library to stock it so that others can also enjoy.

Made in the USA
Middletown, DE
27 August 2022